BROKEN FOREST

DAATH CHRONICLES

ELIZA TILTON

CURIOSITY
QUILLS PRESS

A Division of **Whampa, LLC**
P.O. Box 2160
Reston, VA 20195
Tel/Fax: 800-998-2509
http://curiosityquills.com

© 2013 **Eliza Tilton**
http://elizatilton.com

Cover Art by Eugene Teplitsky
http://eugeneteplitsky.deviantart.com

ISBN 978-1-62007-250-9 (ebook)
ISBN 978-1-62007-251-6 (paperback)
ISBN 978-1-62007-252-3 (hardcover)

~To SM~

CHAPTER ONE

AVIKAR

I slid my feet into the hard leather boots, hating the feel of the rough material and what it stood for—I was a slave, or at least I felt like one. Trapped and overworked. The rooster crowed again, reminding me of the hour, but I didn't care. Staring at the empty cot across from mine, I wondered if things would be different if my brother were still alive.

"Avikar," my father said. "You get your hide outside before that blasted bird croaks again!"

Arguing with "the king of the farm" would only result in extra chores and no supper. I finished lacing my boots and strapped on my belt. The wooden floorboards creaked beneath me, billowing dust into my sisters' room. I grabbed the small ladder and climbed out of my loft. In the common room, Mother kneaded dough while Calli ate at the table. After washing my hands in the bin, I slumped into the chair next to Calli and grabbed a bowl of rue.

"Where did Father go?" I said. Two empty seats surrounded the table. One for Father and one for Jimri.

"Poppa's outside," Calli replied in between bites. "You're late, again." She swung her legs back and forth underneath the table.

Mother poured me a cup of fresh milk. "You all right, honey?"

"Just tired," I said, and dunked a piece of fanna into the clay bowl. The dense bread absorbed the onion-flavored liquid, and I shoved it in my mouth.

Disbelief filled my mother's eyes. She always seemed to know when I was lying, but she nodded and left me alone.

Jeslyn walked in carrying two wicker baskets. She pouted at Calli. "Calli, you're not dressed yet?" She fidgeted with her dress. "There's too much to do today. I wanted to be gone already."

Calli stuffed the rest of her food into her mouth and jumped off the chair.

"Don't run while you're eating!" Mother yelled after her, but Calli was already halfway to her room.

Jeslyn looked my way, her brows narrowing. For the fifth time, she said, "Don't forget, Avi, keep Derrick busy until supper. He doesn't know about tonight."

She and my best friend were courting.

I guzzled my milk and watched Mother scurry around the table, wiping off crumbs. "Did you ask Father if I could quit early?" My father believed in a full day's work. Anything less was unacceptable.

Mother collected the empty bowls. "Yes, you can leave after the stalls are clean."

Only my perfect sister could get me out of chores. Poppa's little girl. I left the remainder of my bland food and hustled out the backdoor.

Jumper, my father's right hand man, exited the outhouse. The old fellow wore a hat too big for his thin leathered face. "Morning," I said.

"Morning, Avikar, Mr. Kingston will be here in an hour. We need that mare in the corral now."

I pushed open the large barn door; stuffy heat slapped my cheeks. Twenty hungry horses filled those stalls, all of them waiting for me to feed them. One of the other farm hands had already taken the palomino mare out. I grabbed her reins and led her outside.

The horse would fetch Father a high price. Her silky mane glistened like liquid ivory, matching the stripe down her nose. Standing at nearly seventeen hands—and a solid eleven hundred stones—she was a beauty and one of our best.

The horse neighed, and I rubbed her side. "Pretty soon you'll be making some folks a lot of coin."

She snorted in reply.

"I know. Running in a race isn't the same as running free."

Father and Jumper stood on the outside of the corral. I guided the mare through the gate and closed the latch behind her. She trotted around the enclosed circle, and I stepped onto the bottom rung of the wooden fence to get a better view.

A sharp whistle caught my attention. Father, wearing his usual scowl, pointed at the stables.

"Yeah, I'm going." As I contemplated letting the pigs out in Mother's garden, I thought about one thing.

One day, I'd leave and never look back.

The suns blazed, engulfing me in heat. I threw the rake on the ground, wiped the sweat off my brow, and pushed the hair off of my face. My hair always bothered me while I worked, and on the really hot days, I thought of cutting it all off. I'd never do that, though. The village girls had a thing for my auburn hair. They said the color made my pale-green eyes stand out, giving them a haunting effect.

In front of me lay rows of round flat heat-dried dung. I'd become so used to the biting smell it only partially stung my nose. A haze from the cakes hovered above the ground. At this time of day, the suns were directly overhead. Watching. The two giant eyes of The Creator.

Stretching, I flexed my sore muscles, examining the definition in my arms. I'd gotten bigger in the past year. The one good thing about working on the farm.

I wanted to see if Mr. Kingston bought that mare, but stopping to ask would only aggravate Father, and I was already on his bad side. He said I had a lazy attitude. I didn't. I just never pictured living out my days raking manure. This isn't what I wanted, but what I wanted had died with Jimri.

With my chores finally finished, I headed down the dirt road that would take me into the village. Scattered clouds dotted the sky, and a cool wind passed through the trees. I whistled while I walked, enjoying the fresh air. The village was almost half a day's journey from home, but on days like this, I didn't mind the long walk.

Flanking the road were tall oak trees, budding with leaves. Their limbs reaching high into the sky. I gazed up at them. Lakewood was known for its green hues and ancient oaks. Even though we lived inland, streams from the Great River passed through here and intertwined with Middle Lake, the largest lake in Tarrtainya. I wondered what the other eleven lands looked like and if they were all full of Lakewood's richness.

It was late-afternoon when I arrived in the village. Without the shade of the trees, the suns heated the air. We were a small community, but close. Thatched cottages wove in between storehouses, the wooden church, and small school house. Far in the distance, I could see the grey stones of Lord Tyre's castle. We were lucky to have a lord as kind as he. Again I told myself I ought to be thankful for where I was, but I couldn't. Not any longer.

I reached the Blacksmith's shop and peered into the shop's soot-filled windows, but only saw Derrick's father speaking with a customer. Strolling around back, I found Derrick banging a piece of metal.

"You ready to go fishing?" I said. The thought of going to the river, standing knee high in cool water, was just what I needed.

Derrick slammed his hammer three more times before leaning it against the bench. "No fishing."

"No fishing? Why?"

Derrick turned around, smirking. I knew that look. He was up to something.

"I've got other plans," he said.

As long as I kept him busy until supper, it didn't matter what we did. "All right, let's go."

Derrick had me so preoccupied with his story of Marsha Long getting caught in her parents' barn with Philip Baker that I didn't pay attention to where we were walking. Grazing cows nibbled at grass next to a winding freshwater stream. Large hay bales dotted the open land. In the distance, a silo towered over the surrounding trees. We were by the Wilke's farm—and just beyond that, the lake—the last place I'd seen my baby brother.

CHAPTER TWO

AVIKAR

Derrick would never get me to the lake. I'd avoided it for the past two years, but this was close, very close. "What are we doing here?"

"We're entering the match during the festival," Derrick replied.

I shook my head. I'd sworn off fighting. "No."

Derrick folded his arms. "You can't keep sulking around forever. It's been two years."

I glared at him. "I know how long it's been."

Derrick's body shifted into a fighting stance.

"Forget it. I told you. I'm done fighting." And it was true. Fighting was the reason I hadn't been watching Jimri.

Before I could push my way past his stocky frame, he punched me in the chest. The shock of the hit dazed me, and he followed with a left jab. He grinned at me as if this were a friendly spar, like it was old times. But it wasn't, and I couldn't pretend.

He fired three more light jabs, hitting me in the chest and shoulder.

"I'm not fighting!" I pushed him away.

He smiled and slapped my right cheek. I took a deep breath. Adrenaline pumped through my body. "Don't push me, Derrick."

He winked and smacked my other cheek. It took every drop of self-control not to wallop him in the face.

I balled my fists. "You know I won't."

"Then I guess you'll be my punching bag for the day." He jabbed me once more and then came at me with a right hook.

I dodged the throw. "Why are you doing this?"

"Because I have to." He charged into my stomach.

Once we were on the grass, he spun around my side, wrapping me in a headlock. I slipped my palm underneath his arm, trying to break his hold.

"I don't think so," Derrick said, forcing me closer to the ground.

Dirt covered my mouth, and I spit it out. Using two fingers, I found a pressure point in his arm and dug in. It took a few agonizing seconds before he released me. Once free, I twisted his arm back, locking him in a move my father taught me. Derrick's head butted me in the face, and I stumbled back. He jumped to his feet and waited.

This time I was ready.

Blood trickled from my nose. I wiped it away with the sleeve of my shirt. My gaze locked onto Derrick. Only one thought entered my mind—*hit him hard*. My arms pumped forward in quick thrusts to his chest. Each hit I scored released more tension. A mixture of sweat and blood stung my lips. Waves of emotion rolled through my body. I knocked Derrick in the face leaving a large welt. He dodged my next punch and wrapped me in a bear hug. I uttered something guttural and stomped on his foot, trying to dislodge him.

Derrick's grip tightened. "It's not your fault."

Everything paused.

My body slacked as the memory of Jimri flashed in my mind. "Yes, it is … I should have been paying more attention. He was my little brother …"

Derrick dropped his arms and slowly backed away. My knees buckled, and I dropped to the ground. Pulling at the grass, I thought of every stupid mistake that led me to this point, and I wished I could do it all over.

Derrick knelt beside me and put a hand on my shoulder. "I was there too. It was an accident."

I closed my eyes, imagining Jimri's dimpled smile. I could hear his laugh whistle with the trees. Two years later and the pain still echoed through everything. Would it ever go away?

I picked myself off the ground, walked to the stream and dunked my head into the water. Every year since we were five, and even though we were too young to enter, Derrick and I had practiced for the annual tournament. I'd stopped fighting the day Jimri died, but I couldn't ignore the life it sparked in my soul. I missed the rush.

Shaking the water off my head, I glanced at Derrick. "Nice shiner."

He smiled. "I let you get that one in."

I laced my fingers behind my head and looked up at the sky. "Thanks."

"I'm here for you. Anytime you want to get beat up."

"You do know you can't beat me in a real fight?"

Derrick laughed and punched my shoulder. "Say you'll enter."

Jimri had loved watching us train. He used to pick up branches, pretending they were swords.

"Maybe," I said, and then noticed the suns' position. *No!* We were going to be late, and Jeslyn would torture me to death for ruining her precious plans.

"Come on," I said, getting up. "We need to get back."

CHAPTER THREE

JESLYN

We had more than enough berries. Derrick would be thrilled I made him his favorite triple-berry pie. I placed the baskets on the grass and studied my stained hands. It would take quite a bit of scrubbing to remove this mess.

Drops of water sprinkled my face. I turned to see Calli trying to catch a drifting leaf in the stream. While her attention stayed on the frail object, I cupped a handful of water and splashed her. She squealed and splashed me back until the front of my dress was soaked and I cried out, "Truce!"

Calli giggled and shook out her wet curls. I loved the way her springy locks bounced around her chubby cheeks. It made me wish I had curls. Although, Mother said my chestnut hair was like fine silk, and I shouldn't complain.

Between the blades of grass, I spotted a lone dandelion. I plucked the little flower—or weed, as Mother would say—and twirled it, admiring the small petals.

"Want to see something special?" I said.

Calli bobbed her head up and down. I motioned her to come closer. I grabbed her arm and held the flower just an inch or two above it.

"Once upon a time there was a family, and they all drank too much cider. Poppa ran outside, Momma ran outside, the annoying brother ran outside, big sister ran outside, but poor little baby couldn't and peed *all over.*" I rubbed the dandelion down Calli's arm, leaving a faded stain.

Calli frowned and wiped the flower dust. "Now my arm is yellow."

I gasped and dropped the dandelion, my hands clutching my chest. "Oh, no, how did that happen?"

Calli tilted her head at me. I stuck my tongue out at her.

Calli's eyebrows straightened, giving me her mad face. "You did that on purpose!"

I puffed out my cheeks and crossed my eyes. She giggled, and I jumped to my feet and ran, taunting her to chase me. I could hear her high-pitched laughter catching up to me, and I turned around. There, creeping towards her, were three unfamiliar men.

Three men that should not have been this deep in the forest, so far from the local routes.

"Calli, come here, now," I said in a stern voice, trying to hide my fear. A worried look crossed her face, and she hurried to me. I grabbed her as soon as she was close and wrapped my arms around her. No one was touching my sister.

These men were not from our land. Each one wore, what resembled, rags, but I knew what expensive fabric looked like. Every time I went to the market, I touched clothes I'd never have. These men appeared to be Roamers, but I knew better. Roamers couldn't afford embroidered tunics.

"What do you want?" My grip tightened on Calli as they approached us.

"Can't you guess, my lady?" the largest of the three said.

I leaned down and whispered into Calli's ear.

14

"Tsk, tsk," said a man with a garish scar across his right cheek. "No secrets between friends." He took out a small dagger and, with his shirt, wiped off the blood on it.

"Go!" I yelled.

Calli and I dashed forward, kicking the closest two men in the groin as hard as we could. They both yelped and doubled over. We ran past them, heading towards the woods. I knew we were too far from home to make it, but we had to try. If anything, we could hide.

The third one ran after us. He was too fast.

"Run, Calli!" She was by my side. I grabbed her hand, half-pulling, half-running with her. I could hear the heavy steps behind us. We weren't going to make it.

Fingers grabbed my hair, yanking me away from Calli. I screamed and twisted underneath the brute's arm and stomped on his foot. He lifted a sword to my throat.

A voice rasped into my ear, "One wrong move and I'll slit your neck."

Calli stopped and stared at me in horror.

"Go, Calli!" I could see she was terrified, but instead of running away, she ran towards me. "No, Calli!"

Her little fists pounded my attacker's side as hard as they could. When that didn't work, she bit his arm.

"Will you two get up and get this one!" my captor said, swatting at Calli. She fell back, taking a piece of his sleeve with her.

The other two men groaned, stood with a slight limp, and closed in on my sister.

"Calli, please, run. Go get Poppa!"

At the mention of our father's name, her teary eyes widened, and then she sprinted into the woods, the two men stumbling after her.

CHAPTER FOUR

AVIKAR

We'd just arrived home when Derrick pointed to the woods adjacent to the stables. "Is that Calli?"

"Yes," I said, recognizing the running figure.

I ran to her. Her cheeks were flushed and stained with tears. She nearly collapsed in my arms when I reached her.

"Calli, what's wrong?"

Her eyes shut.

"Calli?" I lifted her and carried her inside. Her face had a slight bruise, and she breathed heavily.

"Mother!" I called, bringing Calli into her room, where I carefully laid her on the bed.

My mother walked in, wiping her hands off on her apron. "Calli!" She rushed to my sister's side, feeling her forehead. "Get some water Avikar. Quickly."

I bolted outside and filled a pail with water, then flew back in. Calli moaned and my heart lurched. "What's wrong?"

"Go ask Jeslyn what happened."

Derrick and I both looked at each other. "Jeslyn wasn't with her,"

Derrick said.

My mother swirled around, her eyes wide. "Where's Jeslyn?"

Neither of us had any idea, and my mother's frantic expression chilled me. "I haven't seen her since this morning," I said.

"Calli, where's your sister?" My mother patted Calli's head with the wet cloth.

"Gone, Momma. She's gone."

"What do you mean she's gone?" I said, stepping closer to the bed. "Gone where?"

Calli sobbed and reached for our mother.

"Avikar, go get your father."

I couldn't move.

"Avikar!"

My mother stared at me. Her eyes filling with water. It was a bad dream. It had to be.

Derrick ran outside to get my father, and when they walked back in, I was still trying to convince myself this wasn't happening.

My father knelt by Calli's side, calmly asking her questions.

She sniffled. "They came out of nowhere, Poppa. I was so scared."

The vein in Father's neck bulged, but his voice stayed steady and smooth. "Tell me what they looked like. Think of anything out of the ordinary."

Calli's petite shoulders rose and sunk. "One had an ugly scar on his face, and the other two dressed real sloppy."

Father sighed. "Anything else?"

She shook her head.

"Okay." He kissed her on the forehead and stood.

"What are we going to do?" my mother cried. Her tone tore me to pieces.

"I'll go," I said.

"No," Mother replied. "We'll gather men and send out a search party." Tears wound down her face. "If we can get word to Lord Tyre, maybe he can help."

"There's no time," I argued. "If we don't leave this instant we could lose the trail!"

Father stormed past us. His big bushy brows narrowed in an angry line. I followed him. He ripped his massive battle-axe from its mantle. The only remnant from his war days.

"Father, no!" I protested.

Derrick stood by me. I saw the resolution in his eyes. He would go with me, and together, we could rescue her.

"Boy, now is not the time to test me!" Father pushed past me and grabbed a satchel from the kitchen cupboard, which I snatched away. His gigantic hand grabbed me by the shirt, lifting my toes off the ground. I could feel the growl coming off him. If we were wild animals, I'd be cowering on my back.

"Let me go. You can't ride with that leg. You'll only slow us down," I urged, "I can track whoever took her."

"I'm going with him." Derrick dared to look my father in the eye. "It's only three men. We can protect ourselves and take care of them."

"Garn," Mother said softly, touching Father's arm.

He ignored her and gripped my shirt tighter. "You're just boys. What do you know about killing?"

Nothing, but that wouldn't stop me from going. "Father, you taught me how to hunt, how to track. I will find her." I breathed in deep. "I know you both blame me for Jimri's death, and I will never let myself forget that."

Mentioning Jimri caused Father's jaw to clench.

"I won't fail you this time," I finished.

Father released his hold. I didn't want to wait for an answer, or listen to all the reasons why I couldn't go. I motioned for Derrick to follow me.

We swarmed through the house without speaking, grabbing supplies and leaving as quickly as possible. I tried to think of everything we might need: fanna, my bow, enough arrows to keep my quiver full, and coin.

"Is that all of it?" Derrick asked, throwing one of the packs over his shoulder.

"Yes. We just need the horses, and then we can head to the shop to grab weapons."

Derrick gave me that you're-going-to-get-us-in-serious-trouble look. "Do you think your father is going to let us walk out of here with two of his horses? He wasn't exactly…"

"He's not stopping me."

"Then lead the way," Derrick said.

We marched past Calli's room. Mother held Calli in her arms, rocking back and forth and humming. I stopped, walked in and kissed her on the head. She continued rocking.

Calli wiggled out of her arms and reached for me. I lifted her up, hugging her as hard as I could. "You take care of Momma for me."

She kissed my cheek. "Be careful, Avi, and hurry. I know you'll find Jess."

My eyes watered. No matter what I did, Calli always believed in me.

Calli ran over to Derrick and threw her arms around his thick waist. He placed a hand on her head and rubbed it.

"Don't worry, kid," Derrick said. "Jeslyn will be back before you know it."

She stiffened. "I almost forgot!" She ran into her room, searching the floor and bed for something. "Here!" She ran over to me, her tiny hand holding out a piece of green fabric.

I took it. "What's this?"

"That's from the man who took Jess. I ripped it off," she said. "And he had a snake right here." She pointed to her forearm. "I saw it when I ripped his shirt."

I smiled and shoved it in my pocket. "Good thinking, Calli."

We headed outside where my father stood on the porch staring into the distance. I breathed deep, mustering whatever courage I could to face him. This wasn't going to be easy. I stood straighter, waiting for him to scold me, possibly lock me in the stables, or worse. Instead, he turned around, holding a black sheath in his right hand.

Holy heifer.

Time slowed as he handed the object over to me. I clasped the hard leather, my mouth going dry, my heart spinning. Father was a man of few words, and I didn't need to hear any to understand what the gesture meant—he was giving me permission to go. He patted my shoulder and shuffled back into the house.

Derrick crept closer. "Is that what I think it is?"

"It's my father's dagger," I croaked.

I slid the gleaming blade out of its case. Laying it across my palm, I touched the fine metal. Iron. All our weapons were made from bronze. The iron mines were by the king's land and the metal too expensive to buy. The dagger had a jeweled hilt with two brilliant rubies worth more than our whole farm. Three circular runes were etched on the hilt, between the two gems.

We both gawked at the weapon. When I was younger, my father told me about the family dagger. For generations, it had passed down the Desdar line to the eldest son. After Jimri's death, I never expected to receive it. I didn't deserve such an honor. I had assumed Father would wait until he had another son, but he didn't. He gave it to me.

I put the dagger back in its sheath and belted the sheath around my ankle.

Derrick stepped off the porch. "You ready?"

I didn't think anyone could be ready for what we were going to do, but I was close enough.

CHAPTER FIVE

LUCINO

The clear liquid inside the bowl rippled, revealing an image of four exquisite creatures. Their delicate and sensual features accentuated their beauty.

"Good morning my pets," I said.

They sat around giggling about nonsense and stroking one another's hair. I found it interesting how excitable they became before my visit. Ah, and how beautiful they all were. However, not perfect. The voluptuous brunette had a nose with a slight bump, and the redheaded vixen had a forehead too wide. If I could combine the full lips from the petite one, and take the hazel almond eyes from the shy one . . .

"Spying on your dolls again, hmm?"

With a flick of my hand I brushed the image away. "I'd hardly call it spying."

Romulus bobbed his square head as he waddled over to a table stacked with various beakers and caged animals. He opened a cage and pulled out a large lizard which snapped irritably at his hand.

"You spend too much time on these females," said Romulus. "I wonder what the King would say of this, hmm?"

Romulus only got away with such brazen talk because he was my advisor. Anyone else and I would have cut out their tongue. "It's research. I must understand their ways if I am to blend in."

He scrunched his large nose and grumbled. "Obsession, not research. I do your research."

Insolent fiend. I willed myself to calm, ignoring his brash comment.

"Have you collected the specimens I discovered? I think you will be pleased with what arrives."

"Yes." Lucy had left weeks ago to start the hunt. With the firemares pulling the wagons, they should arrive back in Daath shortly. I trusted Romulus that one of these humans would be the one I had been searching for.

"Good," said Romulus. "I think it's time we discussed your Awakening, hmm?"

My Awakening. A topic of extreme interest. Romulus had been my teacher since I was old enough to kill a wyvern, the smaller dragons of our home world. On my upcoming birthday, the dormant power in me would release. No one knew the extent of my abilities, but Romulus had an idea. I would lead our people into a new era, and it would begin on Tarrtainya.

Romulus dropped an orange liquid onto the lizard, and it screamed. "I have calculated this planet's gravitational pull on the day of your Awakening. You must perform the ritual at the exact moment of the eclipse."

"Yes, Romulus. We've gone over this already."

He grumbled and picked up the decaying lizard with a pair of scissors. "You need to have a pure vessel. This world is different from ours. The pure females emit a specific aura that is critical, hmm. You must capture this during your Awakening. The aura will amplify your magic."

"How strong will I be?"

He laughed a wheezy, gurgling sound. "Stronger than any of us."

"Is The Council aware of your research?"

Romulus shook his head. "No, they have yet to discover the connection we have with the human females, but in time they will learn."

But not before my plan had come to fruition. "Well done, Romulus."

I stood. "I'll see you when I return from the tunnels in a few days."

He ignored me, already lost in his strange dissection.

CHAPTER SIX

AVIKAR

My stomach churned as I studied the red stains splattered across the ground. I knelt and swiped a finger across the sticky substance and sniffed. Berries. I should have known it wasn't blood—the consistency didn't match— but I had to be sure. My heart thumped and I was sure the kidnappers could hear it, but they were nowhere near us. It was just nerves.

Three deep breaths later, I continued tracking, recalling Calli's every detail. I examined the footprints smeared on the grass. The large heavy prints of the captors and the faint small prints of my sisters, both crisscrossing each other in a rugged path.

"Find anything?" Derrick said.

"Not yet."

"Time's running out."

I glanced at the sky. The suns were descending. Soon it would be night. My chest tightened, and I had to control my breathing again, pushing aside the fear of losing Jeslyn.

Wild strawberries spread in all directions. By the stream lay two wicker baskets smashed into splinters.

"Do you think she's still ..." Derrick gripped the wooden emblem he always wore—a symbol of The Creator, three wavy lines, representing water, enclosed with a circle.

"I don't know."

I traced each step, imagining how the attack unfolded. I pictured the three men Calli described—how did she escape when Jeslyn couldn't? I studied the dance at my feet—two had fallen, and then they'd stood. I spun to the left, following the vicious display. In one direction were Calli's footsteps and two of the kidnappers while Jeslyn's tracks led to where the woods began.

There, on a tree, swayed a red ribbon. I walked over and grabbed it from the branch.

"I gave that to her yesterday," Derrick said and I handed him the ribbon.

He tied the cloth around his wrist. His jaw clenched.

The dead forest stood in front of us. I squinted past the long line of black and grey trees. "This way," I said, and slowly we led the horses into the blackened woods.

Cherrywood, a once vivacious forest, had been torched last summer by a lighting storm. Some of the vegetation had started growing back, but not the trees. Beautiful oaks now resembled twisted iron. I stared at the tall black pillars, and my heart sank.

Wind passed through the forest, causing the broken trees to creak and groan. Crows screeched from overhead. A trio of ravens pecked a dead rabbit. Every sound made my pulse beat faster. Derrick pointed out a piece of cream fabric stuck on a briar bush. I inspected it, remembering the dress Jeslyn wore at breakfast. Pain and anger swallowed my fear, pushing me deeper into the woods, towards her.

CHAPTER SEVEN

JESLYN

I don't remember fainting, but I must have, as I awoke in a sea of black. Was I still unconscious? No. The ground moved beneath me. My eyes were still adjusting to the dark, and I couldn't see if I was alone.

It smelled awful, urine mixed with body odor. I covered my mouth with one hand and searched the area with the other. *Is this hay?* My fingers touched the thin, tough object. Yes, most certainly hay. I heard a rustle in the dark.

"Hello? Is anyone there?" On my knees, I inched my way towards the noise, my eyesight getting sharper. Fear pricked my skin, making me hot and cold at the same time. Where was my family? Where was Calli? What if Calli hadn't made it home? What if she was dead?

Don't think such things, I thought. *Everything will be all right. I just need to find my way out of here.* I could hear men talking outside and thought I might be in a wagon.

Searching the rough floor, I grazed cold skin and jerked my hand away.

A hand snatched my arm.

"Get off me!" I yelped.

"Don't scream," said a young girl with haunting eyes, her face barely visible in the dark. Her hand tightened around my arm. I pushed against her.

"Let go of me," I said.

"Shh," she hissed. "Please, you must be quiet."

"Why?"

The sound of metal grinding echoed around me.

The girl's eyes swelled with fear. "They're coming," she whispered, and slid away, deeper into the darkness.

Light poured in from the open door and I shielded my eyes. A man stood in the sunlight, his face and body silhouetted.

"Quiet in here," he said, voice thunderous.

"Who are you?" I said. "Where are you taking me?"

"I said, *quiet!*"

My voice lost itself, and I cowered against the wall.

"Any noise and I'll see that you're silenced."

He didn't wait for my response. The door closed, taking with it all the light. The girl with me said nothing, making the dark even more unbearable.

Pulling my knees against my chest, I closed my eyes and said the prayer for protection. Mother always said The Creator would protect us. I held onto her words, letting them comfort me. I was brave and only a few things terrified me, but my biggest fear of all was the dark.

Panic pricked my chest. I forced myself into distraction thinking of Derrick, pulling happy memories of him from my mind and letting them shield me from the blackness.

If I could pretend I was somewhere else, I would survive this.

The girl across from me coughed.

I followed the sound, scooting closer to her. "Do you know where they're taking us?" I whispered.

"No, and you must be silent. Please."

"I will, just a few more questions. I promise he won't hear us."

When she didn't respond, I continued. "Where are you from?"

"Urima," she said.

"Urima? How? That's on the other side of The Valley of the Kings."

"I don't know …"

Urima was on the western shores of Tarrtainya and, due to the long valley, there were only a few passage-ways to it. It would take a normal caravan weeks, possibly months, to make the journey.

"Do you know why they took us?"

"No, but I heard one of the guards say they only had a few more girls to collect."

"Collect? For what?"

An object banged against the side of the wagon, scaring me so that I lost my breath. The girl placed a hand over my mouth. I could just make out her fear-stricken face.

I nodded, but it was already too late.

The wagon door flung open.

"I thought I said no talking, girl."

His dark hand reached for me, and I screamed, louder than I ever had before.

CHAPTER EIGHT

AVIKAR

Silence surrounded us. No chirps, no big bellied frogs, nothing, not even the wind. Doubt taunted me. All my life I'd wanted to adventure outside of Lakewood. To go on a grand quest and become a heroic ranger. I'd pestered my father to teach me everything he knew about herbs, hunting and tracking. It seems luck has a sense of irony.

The trail we followed from the woods led to one of the main trade routes. Derrick guzzled water out of a canister while I assessed the road. Grooved into the dirt were big wagon tracks continuing north. Jeslyn's footsteps disappeared next to one of them. I counted four wagons next to six horses. Calli described the men as ragged looking. I assumed they were Roamers, nomads passing through. I should have known they would be with a larger group. Roamers always travelled in packs.

"What is it?" Derrick's husky voice cut through the eeriness.

"There are more than three kidnappers." I pushed my flap of hair out of my eyes and sighed.

"What do you mean 'more'?"

"The tracks we've been following end with these wagons. She must be in one of them."

Derrick rubbed his forehead. "How many men?"

"Maybe ten, maybe twelve. I can't be certain."

Derrick's face scrunched in horror. "Twelve men? We can't handle that many."

I refused to believe that. "We'll surprise them. Set traps if we have to. We're both skilled fighters, and I can take down at least three with my bow before they suspect a thing. We can do this."

Derrick began pacing. The claymore strapped to his back bobbed with each step. "This is different, Avi. We should go back to the village and get help."

I shook my head. "No, it will take too long. By the time we return here, it'll be almost two days. And what if it rains? These tracks will vanish." I turned away from him and petted my horse, Brushfire, before climbing back onto the saddle.

Derrick's shoulders slouched. "I hope you're right."

We rode hard and swift, pushing the horses to their limits and only taking brief moments of rest. By sunset on the second day, we had to stop.

"How could they be so far ahead of us?" Derrick said. "They're in wagons!" He tied the horses to a large tree and we searched for water.

"I don't know," I said, rubbing my scalp. "We should have caught up to them by now." Every dung I had checked was old, none of it made sense. We were moving fast. Wagons couldn't move faster than us.

A wolf howled in the distance. I shivered. A fog had rolled in with the setting suns, covering the bottom of the forest. I surveyed the tall pine trees and tried to pinpoint our location. We headed straight, north on the eastern trade route, which would bring us to—Raswood Forest.

"Derrick," I said, pulling my long sword out.

Derrick arched a brow at me, then folded his arms and grinned. "Scared of a wolf are you?"

"We're in Raswood Forest," I whispered.

Derrick's face paled, and in one swift movement, his claymore was out and pointed at a tree. "You could've warned me."

Raswood Forest, one of the wild territories Father taught me about. Full of wild predators, including winter wolves—large white nightmares that hunted in packs and killed anything in their path. I'd rather face a group of Roamers than have to fight one of those beasts.

It was too dark to hunt, but we had to find food. The fanna we packed would only sustain us for so long. I thought we would've found Jeslyn and been back already. Where were they taking her?

We made camp by a large stream. Silver specks darted around the rushing water.

"Glimmer fish!" For once, things were going our way. Glimmer fish were easy to catch because of their shiny scales and big schools.

Derrick and I made a bet that whoever caught the smallest fish would have first watch. I was the better hunter. It would be an easy win.

I watched Derrick take a net out of the pack. By the time he had that mass of string untangled, I'd have caught five fish already. I traded my sword for my bow and lined up a shot. For the past five years, I'd won every archery contest at the Puring Festival, and I never missed.

Ready, set ...

"I got one!" Derrick shouted.

I jumped at Derrick's girly shrill, my left foot slipping on the mossy stone. I flailed my arms, trying to catch myself, but failed and fell backwards into the water. The splash scared away all the fish except the measly one my arrow managed to pierce. I punched the water, getting wetter by the moment. I heard another howl, grabbed the shaft of my arrow and sulked back to camp.

Derrick smirked as he turned the fish over on the fire. I sat across from him, scowling and picking at a fish too pathetic to eat.

Derrick stifled a chuckle.

"Stop it." I threw the fish into the fire and watched it turn to ash. My stomach grumbled and Derrick handed me one of his roasting sticks. Normally, I'd decline out of pure stubbornness, but the fresh scent of cooked glimmer was too tempting. I grabbed the stick and bit into the meat, burning the bottom of my lip.

"It was your fault I slipped," I said in between bites. "You screamed like a little girl and distracted me. You never would've won if you played fair."

"You're one to talk," Derrick said with a full mouth. "You're the biggest cheater I know."

I would've argued, but he wasn't completely incorrect. Three summers ago, we were almost thrown in the river when I got caught cheating at knucklebones.

We sat by the fire, staring into the flames. Clouds covered the stars, surrounding us in a dreary black. Wind wheezed through the old pines, causing them to creak. I held my cape closer to my body, warming myself.

"How did this happen?" Derrick buried his head in his hands.

I perched my elbows on top of my thighs. I didn't want to think about Jeslyn. We bickered non-stop. I'd spent a good portion of my day figuring out new pranks to play on her. Now it seemed such a waste of time. Losing Jimri was hard, but at least he knew I loved him. Jeslyn could die assuming I thought she was a royal pain. I couldn't bear the thought of her in danger.

"I don't know," I said. "Things have been peaceful in the lands, especially with The Puring Festival only weeks away."

There were five annual festivals in Tarrtainya, but the Puring was the most celebrated. It was the only festival when our family ate beef. Cows were needed more for their milk and cheese, and beef was a luxury only the rich could afford, but during the festival Lord Tyre had his own cows killed. Two browns. Father called the Puring a day of remembrance. A reminder of the Dark Wars and how The Order saved us all from the dark mages. Seemed like just another excuse to drink lots of ale and eat loads of meat.

I wanted to tell Derrick we'd find her and that she was all right, but I lost my voice. My thoughts drifted to Jimri then to Jeslyn. Childhood memories flooded my mind. I pushed the images away. Thinking about them only made it worse.

Derrick said goodnight, and I watched him fall asleep. I could never fully relax. Most nights I passed out from exhaustion. Raking manure all day under the suns not only tanned my skin but drained my every emotion. By nighttime, I'd fall onto my feathered cot and into a deep sleep. But sleep brought the nightmares. Visions of drowning. Screams of terror. And everything I deserved.

I rubbed the sides of my head, hoping the pain would dissolve and I could think clearly. It wasn't working. How was I going to scout full of anxiety? Only one thing would help me focus. I slipped out the old leather book I had snuck in while packing. Inside the pages of this journal were laid the anguish and fear of the past two years. No one knew about it, and I'd die before anyone read it. Avikar the Poet is not the title I wanted.

Words flowed out, scripting all the guilt and sorrow I kept inside. The thin piece of red clay I used was shrinking. Once gone, it would be awhile before I could find more. Writing utensils were rare in my village and asking Mother to buy one wasn't an option. With my head a bit clearer, I snuck the journal back in its hiding place.

The fire had trickled to a low pulsating glow. Warmth emanated from it, touching my cheeks and spreading across my body. I listened to the pops of the dying wood. The melodic symphony relaxed me, and I rubbed my eyes. I rolled out my shoulders and cracked my neck. Derrick lay flat on his back, mouth slightly open, snoring nasally. I decided I'd better start my rounds before the wolves decided to brave the fire.

The horses whinnied. A twig snapped in the distance.

Reaching for my bow, I slowly stood. To my left and right were yellow eyes and low growls.

"Derrick."

The massive creatures stalked towards me. I strung my bow, raised it, and pointed it at the closest wolf. "Derrick!"

Derrick groaned. I hoped he was getting up, because in a few seconds we'd be surrounded.

The first wolf stepped forward. Two more wolves appeared on either side. The one in the center growled, revealing rows of pointy teeth. Winter wolves were bigger than the small brown bears that lived near our home. Their ears pointed straight up like a jack rabbit and their eyes glowed a sickly yellow. In a white flash, the center wolf sprang forward. I released the arrow and it sunk into furry flesh, but still the wolf came and fast. It pounced and I stumbled back, trying to switch to my sword. Before the beast's teeth closed, Derrick's claymore sliced into its side.

"Aren't you supposed to have first watch?" he said, turning to face the other wolves.

"I was getting bored," I shouted. "We need to drive them away from the horses."

Derrick yelled out a war cry before charging ahead. Letting out my own war cry, hardly as menacing, I ran at the snowy white creature. I sidestepped to the left, sweeping my sword, hitting one in the chest. The wolf whimpered, then fell.

Derrick yelled again and I spun in his direction. The distraction almost cost me my arm. Claws raked against me as a wolf jumped, trying to knock me down. I backtracked to the fire and, using my sword as a poker, pulled out a flaming timber.

"Ya, ya!" I waved the torch back and forth, pushing the remaining animals away. When the last set of glowing eyes retreated into the dark, I exhaled. "That was close." I expected Derrick to make another snide remark, but he didn't. I turned around and saw him running straight for me with his sword drawn and eyes wild.

"Behind you!" he screamed.

I whirled with my sword out, thinking a ball of fur would be the last thing I'd ever see; instead, it was a man, about two hundred stones heavier than I.

With the flat of my blade, I barely managed to block the descending axe. Both arms shook as I tried to push the razor edge of his axe away from my face. Sweat dripped off the giant, splashing me and the blade. His foul breath showered over me and I kicked the brute in the kneecap while angling my blade to allow the weapon to harmlessly pass. The move did little to slow him, but it gave me enough time to regain my wits.

It was then I noticed Derrick fighting with another man. He'd have to make do as the man in front of me was more than I could handle. The axe swept in low. The brute had stayed in a crouch while swinging a backslash at my knees. A mistake. His back was open to a desperate counter, one that meant leaving my sword on the ground.

The same lighting reflexes that saved me before won again.

Driving the tip of my sword into the ground to parry the incoming attack, I spun along his massive weapon arm, leaving my blade in the dirt. Even though he was big, he couldn't match my speed. As he tried to stand, I was on him. I jumped on his back, sliding my thumb and wrist across his throat and locking him in a deep choke hold. It would take all my strength to subdue someone of this size.

The behemoth wriggled and used his fat fingers to pry at mine. When tugging at me didn't work, he slammed me against a tree. I don't know how I held on, but I did. I squeezed again, harder, trying to take his last breaths. Bark rubbed against my back, shredding it. I clenched my jaw, holding in a scream. The man dropped to his knees, gasping and clawing. Then silence.

Jerking away from the body, every part of me trembled. My heart raced so fast, I thought I would die.

It dawned on me the fight wasn't over.

Derrick.

I rushed to my feet. Derrick hunched over, his back facing me.

"Derrick!"

I ran over, thinking the worst. Closer, I could see he was only catching his breath. At his feet lay a man with a jagged scar on his face, surrounded by blood.

"Are you all right?" I grabbed Derrick's shoulder, and he nodded.

He glanced back and his eyes widened. "You took that down by yourself?"

"I'm sure it was luck."

"Impressive." Derrick straightened and wiped his claymore on the grass.

I knelt next to the corpse, examining the body. Sweat slid down my neck and back. "Do you see it?"

"I do."

We both looked at the scar on the man's face. It had to be the one Calli described. But where was Jeslyn? Hadn't Calli said there were three kidnappers?

I grabbed my head, breathing rapidly. I needed water and air, cool air. I stood. *Too fast.* Everything spun. My mouth tasted like metal.

"Avikar?"

Words were lost to me; instead, I responded with a stream of vomit.

CHAPTER NINE

JESLYN

How much time had passed? Was it night or day? I couldn't tell. Dark fabric blocked the small window above the door, and I didn't dare try and peek through it. I learned why the girl was terrified of the guards. When I'd screamed for help and they threatened me to be quiet, I chose poorly. They gave me a tainted drink, and for longer than I can remember, I couldn't move. That was the last time I screamed for anything.

They never let us out. We had to urinate in the wagon. The smell permeated everything. When they opened the door to feed us, I noticed four other wagons. The same guards by each one. We resembled Roamers. No Tarrtainian would think twice about the caravan.

There must be a way to escape.

The wagon stopped, and I heard a loud commotion, a woman yelling. While trying to navigate the dark space, I listened as best I could. If fortune smiled upon me this day, I'd learn a detail about where we were, or where we were headed.

"What do you mean they haven't returned? They have two of the firemares and one of them is an enforcer. This should have been a simple task."

"They were due back this morning."

I recognized the second voice. It belonged to the dark man who'd given me the paralyzing drink.

The woman grunted. "Lucino will be furious if we don't stay on schedule. Pick up the next girl. I'll make sure we are not being followed. Since your men are incapable of doing anything useful."

Another girl? How many were there?

CHAPTER TEN

LUCINO

I lunged, stabbing the sword forward until the tip met soft flesh. The guard recoiled into himself and fell over, clutching at his bleeding stomach. I growled and catapulted the sword into the far wall. "Find me someone who will not die within the first few minutes of my training!"

The standing guard removed the dead body from my sight. Training with humans was an utter waste of time.

Lucino.

You better have good cause for bothering me. You should be collecting my shipment.

My sister's mental intrusions always happened at the most inconvenient times. Our races' bloodline communication trait tended to be more of a nuisance. I had already ordered Romulus to discover a way to block her, but so far I had only learned how to break the connection once she entered.

We ran into a situation.

Go on. I shook my head and walked toward the bubbling salt pool that reminded me of home, then threw off the remainder of my clothing and stepped down into the hot water.

During one of our pickups, we were spotted and the two men I sent back have not returned. I think we should call off the rest of the mission and return to Daath.

Are you giving me orders? I stretched against the hard stone.

No, brother. It is a suggestion.

Finish your task and handle the mess you've made. I broke the connection before she could respond. Hearing my sister babble about minor complications irritated me. I needed quiet, especially after a visit with my pets. Today they had been extremely talkative and touchy; they always wanted to poke or caress me. I spent quite a bit of time trying to learn why. This world varied from ours, in strange ways. I wondered if our people could survive among these humans.

Steam rising from the pool blocked my vision, but I sensed someone approach. "Speak."

A young servant stumbled forward. "Your grace, there is an urgent message from Lord Thebas."

The boy placed a scroll onto the table.

"You may go." I waved the boy away and closed my eyes. *Urgent, everything with that obese fool is urgent.* I regretted revealing my presence to him, but it was a necessary move. We had control of only three of the thirteen lands (not including Daath—I alone held that treasure). I could've slipped one of our own in his place and disposed of the man, but humans were very fanatical, and I found his undying devotion pleasant. My following had bred in his large village, spreading and infecting the surrounding areas. By the time we began the invasion, I'd have thousands of hungry followers, and The Order would easily be replaced.

Yes, The Council made a grave mistake putting me in charge, but one from which I would greatly benefit. They assumed they would take control. Fools.

CHAPTER ELEVEN

AVIKAR

Derrick paced back and forth across the camp, mumbling to himself. I rubbed my head, releasing the building pressure. The two corpses lay in front of me. Dead eyes staring.

"Finished?" Derrick said.

Standing, I nodded.

"We need to get rid of the bodies and get out of these cursed woods," he said. "I still think we need help, even if we hire a merc."

"There's no time," I said, walking over to the corpse with the scar. I lifted one of the lifeless limbs and searched for the tattoo. *Nothing.* I moved on to the other dead man. *Nothing.*

"What if we're killed and Jeslyn disappears? I can't live with that." Derrick continued ranting and pacing around the camp.

"We can't stop," I said in a hushed voice. "We'll lose her."

"You don't know that."

"It's up to us." Mixed emotions swirled through me. Nothing settled. I rubbed my temples, trying to rid myself of the intense pounding.

Derrick dropped to one knee. He clasped his emblem and prayed. I used to wear one, too, but that was before Jimri died.

"You're wasting your time," I said.

Derrick shut his eyes. "We need a miracle."

"The Creator doesn't care about us," I grumbled.

Derrick ignored me, and I thought on how to dispose of the bodies.

After a very long debate, we came to a decision. We dragged the two dead men from camp and hid them beneath the brush. Then we scurried around the area, gathering twigs and branches to cover the rest of the remains. Afterwards, I wiped our footprints and removed any signs of our passing.

We rode in silence. The sky stayed dry, and we continued following the tracks. Luck smiled on us. The hooves of the horses had a distinct shape, different from most I've seen. They were easy to follow.

We arrived at the town marker around noon. An old sign read Bogtown. We were in Lord Belfur's territory. Out of the twelve territories in Tarrtainya, only three were considered unsafe. This was one of them.

I still had a dull ache in my head. I needed to unwind or I'd get sick, again.

"First one to Bogtown is in charge of dinner," I said. "Deal?"

Derrick grinned. "Deal."

He kicked his horse into a running start.

"You're supposed to wait and count to three!"

Derrick grinned and sped down the road.

"Hee-ya!" I slapped the reins and galloped after him. The wind on my face energized me. My family bred racehorses, fierce and dangerously quick. Brushfire wasn't from that stock, but she could run just as fast.

"Show them what you can do, girl."

She galloped around the curve of the road, catching up to them. I urged her to pass Derrick. He glanced my way, and I winked. I slapped the reins again, pushing Brushfire into the town.

"Whoa." I pulled back on the reins as we entered, Brushfire slowed, and I waited for Derrick before going any further.

Dirt covered the town in a beige blanket. Most of the housing resembled wooden shacks. Haggard citizens dressed in rags passed by us, never making eye contact. The desolate atmosphere reminded me that we needed to watch ourselves.

The local tavern was the only building teeming with activity. "I'll go inside and see if I can find anything out about the wagons we're following. Tie up the horses, then meet me inside." I dismounted and patted Brushfire before leaving her with Derrick.

I'd only been in a tavern once, and I doubted the one in our small village was anything like this. I slid my hand into my pocket, searching for the pouch of marbles I always kept in there. I found it and grabbed one of the smooth stones, rolling it back and forth in my palm. *I am the son of Garn Desdar, a warrior,* I thought, *just like his father before him.* I breathed in, stood straighter, and walked inside.

The second I entered through the swinging doors, I knew I didn't belong. The stench of sweat and smoke assaulted my nose. Old wooden tables haphazardly filled the room, surrounded by empty steins and loud scoundrels. An old chandelier hung from the center of the ceiling, arrayed with melted candles. With my chin held high, I walked across the sticky floor to the long bar.

I sat on a stool. A busty woman in an unfitting dress stood across from me, filling a mug with golden liquid. "What'll it be, hun?"

"A cup of ale." I left a coin on the bar.

She returned with a glass of milk and pushed the coin back to me. I frowned. "I believe I asked for ale."

The barmaid smiled and leaned over. "And I believe you to be a bit too young to be drinking any ale."

"I'm nearly eighteen!"

She pursed her lips. "That may be true, but you won't be getting any ale from me. You can drink your milk and stay, or leave. It don't make a difference to me." She left to help another customer.

I sighed and grabbed the mug.

In the back of the tavern, two men argued, one stout, the other about half his age and weight.

"It's your fault," said the stout man. "I tell you, your fault. I know you're up to no good."

"I didn't do anything. Why would I?"

The two men eyed each other and the stout man erupted.

"I don't believe you! My daughter just don't go off frolicking in the woods, and she don't go off before her chores are done. What did you do with her?"

"I said, I didn't do noth…" A mouth full of knuckles cut off the reply. A small brawl broke out.

Putting my two fingers together, I gave a sharp whistle, drawing the attention of everyone in the room.

"I don't mean to interrupt," I said. "But we may be in the same predicament."

The father of the missing girl stomped over to me, large nostrils flaring.

Okay, bad idea.

"I don't believe I've seen you here before. State your name, boy."

Stepping back, I tried to put some distance between us while searching for Derrick. I spotted his cropped dark hair near the front entrance. He nodded at me, hand on his claymore, ready to fight, but by the time he reached me I'd explained all I knew about Jeslyn's kidnapping to the man towering over me.

The father rubbed his shaggy red beard, grumbled, and stuck out his hand. "The name's Rudy."

"Well—met, Rudy. I'm Avikar." I shook his hand, wincing at the strength of his grip.

"I got a feeling my Charlotte is with your sister. A group of Roamers passed through here a few hours ago. Me and my boys will be coming with you."

Rudy introduced us to six men. Henry, a wily man with an

extremely long mustache and black suspenders. Rudy's younger brother, Steven, a chubby and cheerful fellow. A young man named Lucas, who was in love with Rudy's daughter and the recipient of Rudy's right hook. Twins, named Nathaniel and Davin, who seemed very quiet and secretive, and Reaper.

Reaper's black oily hair fell to his face and his albino skin appeared translucent. Rudy explained Reaper got his nickname from working the graveyard shift. Reaper smiled at us, revealing more than one missing tooth.

Rudy sent the twins out to gather supplies while the rest of us waited in the tavern.

Derrick sat next to Lucas, probably talking about their lost loves, not a conversation I wanted to be a part of. The bar went back to its loud, rowdy state and I tried to distract myself with the strange black bug crawling down the side of the bar.

The tiny bug, which turned out to be a plain old cockroach, landed on the floor and skidded towards the entrance. A girl in a tight-waisted crimson dress stood there, eyeing the tavern. Men glanced her way, but only briefly. I'd overheard some of the stable hands talk about ladies at taverns who traded favors for coin. I'd never seen one in person. Her black hair hung past her shoulders offsetting her ivory skin. She glided over to the bar, sat and ordered a drink.

One patron went over and whispered in her ear. I could tell he was irritating her. I walked over, deciding that, whoever she was, she didn't need to be pestered by a drunk.

"There you are. I've been looking all over for you! Excuse me sir." I pushed the guy aside. "I hope you weren't waiting very long."

Her thin lips curved into a smile. "Not very long."

The drunk stumbled off to the side, and I sat on the stool next to her, instantly hypnotized by her brilliant blue eyes.

"Thank you," she said. "He was a bit too rude for my liking."

"You're welcome. The name's Avikar." I dipped my head in a slight bow.

She held out a delicate hand and I reached for it. "Lucy. A pleasure to meet you."

I kissed the top of her soft hand, which smelled like roses. "The pleasure is mine."

Lucy shifted on the stool. One of her slender legs slipped through the slit of her dress. "How about you order us a drink?" she said.

Holy heifer, those are nice legs. I tried not to stare at her smooth skin, or voluptuous body, but it was right there. I left another coin on the bar, never taking my eyes off hers. The server came over. "A drink for the lady and water for me." After the server left, I inched a bit closer. "What brings you to Bogtown? This doesn't seem like your kind of place."

"What do you mean?"

I noticed her decorative bodice. "You're dressed for castle life. Are you a noble?"

She smirked. "I'm no one of importance."

"And you came all the way to this filthy town for...?"

Lucy's hand grazed my forearm. The sensation filled me with hundreds of inappropriate ideas. This wasn't the time for flirtatious fun, but I couldn't pull away, even though I knew I should.

"Enough about me. I'm much more interested in you. Are you travelling alone?" Her delicate fingers trailed up my arm.

I watched them, praying she'd never take them off. "No," I said, glancing over at Derrick who stood between Rudy and Steven as they argued.

Her gaze followed mine. "Quite a bunch you're with." She gently tugged on the tawny cloth of my shirt. "Where are you headed?"

"I'm on a quest."

Her face brightened, and I regretted blurting it out.

What's the matter with me? I should be focused on Jeslyn.

"Really, sounds exciting. What kind of quest? I find them exhilarating, especially when such a handsome man is involved."

Her floral scent surrounded me and I couldn't help myself. I leaned in and whispered, "I don't know if I can tell you."

"You can trust me."

I never wanted to kiss anyone as bad as I wanted to kiss her. The desire overpowered every other thought in my mind, but before I could act, Derrick appeared at my side.

"We're ready to head out," he said.

Lucy pressed her hand against my chest. "So soon? I hoped we could get more acquainted." She swept away a lonely strand of hair covering my right eye and stared at me with an intense hunger.

In any other instance, I would have said yes. "I wish I could, but I can't. It was nice meeting you, Lucy."

"Wait," she said, and stood. "For your kindness, allow me to thank you with a song before you go. It will be a blessing for your journey."

"I'd be honored."

Lucy smiled and waltzed into the center of the room.

Derrick grabbed my arm as I headed to a table. "What are you doing?" he hissed.

I nudged him away. "She wants to sing us a song."

"We don't have time for this."

"Maybe it will bring us luck," I said, sitting. "We could use it."

Derrick sat across from me and folded his arms. "Fine. One song."

The tavern was disorderly, but when Lucy opened her mouth, everyone quieted. Her hips swayed and the glow of candlelight highlighted her curves. Words from a strange language poured out of her petite lips, sounding like a hundred birds harmonizing at once.

Her body moved, slow and seductive. Each graceful step matched the tempo of the song. The corners of her mouth curled up as she circled the room, her attention on me. She glided to me and sat on my lap, never once missing a beat.

Sweat slid down the back of my neck, and a wave of exhaustion hit me. I blinked twice, my vision blurred for a brief second. I grabbed Lucy's arm, trying to keep myself awake. Her soft hand caressed my cheek, and the last thing I saw was her wicked smile.

Cold water slammed my face, waking me. Davin stood next to the table holding a bucket. I lifted my head from the table and pressed my palm against my forehead. Moving shot pain into my head.

"What happened?" I asked, noticing we were all still in the tavern.

Davin dropped the bucket and wiped his hands against his pants. "You've been out all day."

Derrick and I jumped to our feet.

"We've been trying to wake you guys," Nathaniel added. "I thought you'd be sleeping forever. That's the fifth bucket we dumped on you."

"It was that woman," Rudy replied. "She's some sort of enchantress. Put us under a spell by that singing of hers. Knocked everyone in the tavern out cold!"

Derrick kicked the table. "They could be days ahead of us!" He glared at me with that fiery death stare.

"I didn't know she would put us under a spell!" I said. "Only The Order can use magic!"

Derrick stepped around the fallen table, his eyes wide with fury. "For all we know Jeslyn could be dead. All because you had to listen to some wench sing."

His words were daggers, slicing into my soul. I pushed him back. "Shut up!"

Derrick charged at me, pummeling into my chest. We crashed into a nearby table, knocking it over. I twisted out of his grip before he could get a lock on me.

"Fighting isn't going to get anyone, anywhere," Rudy said as he pulled us apart. I tried to break free, but age had given that man a bearlike strength. "Let's be on our way. No more fighting, unless it's with the enemy."

He released us and we both grunted in agreement.

"And you." Rudy pointed a stubby finger at me. "Don't ever trust a woman that beautiful, especially if she's taken an interest in you."

Derrick picked up his pack and shoved past me. I watched him leave the tavern. I'd always gotten us into trouble, either with a stupid prank or a crazy idea, but this was different. For the first time, I realized how much he was right.

CHAPTER TWELVE

JESLYN

The world inside this wagon became the only reality I knew. Bread and water twice a day and nothing more. I longed for the suns and a bath and for home. The girl in the wagon spoke very little. I don't think she was well at all. Her wheezing gave me shivers.

We stopped. I prayed we were finally at our destination. I didn't care where we were going as long as I could leave the horrible stench of this prison. Anything would be better than sitting in here.

The dark material covering the wagon window flapped with the wind. A breeze blew in and I inhaled the sweet fresh air. I could hear the sound of rushing water, loud and powerful, like thunder. I desperately wanted to see outside, to see anything.

My hands trailed the wall until I grasped the small bars. I squeezed my hand through, and pushed the fabric to the side. A dark face scowled at me.

I stifled a scream and jumped back.

The door unlocked, and the captain stood before me. "Come," he said. "And don't try to escape or we'll slit your throats."

I was too stunned to obey.

"I said, git." He grabbed my leg and dragged me out. The girl with me screamed as the next guard pulled her out as well.

It took a moment to readjust to the bright sunlight. I shielded my eyes.

"Over here." A man dragged me to a huddled group of girls. He pushed me onto the grass.

"They smell like dogs," said one of the guards, covering his nose while another brought over a bucket of water.

The captain was as tall as my father and just as frightening. "You three," he said. "Start cleaning out the wagons. We can't be bringing them in with that stench."

Outside, the sound of water thundered. I tried to pinpoint our location. The Great River ran through the center of Tarrtainya. We could be in ten different territories, ranging from the royal lands of King Corban to the low marshlands of Hasideon. The options were too many and entering in the wrong territory would be deathly. With no weapon, I'd be a walking meal for some horrible beast.

One by one, the guards dumped cold water on us, seeming annoyed by the task. Four girls cried from the cold while others screamed. I covered my ears, shivering and dreaming of home. A cold body huddled next to me. She wheezed. I recognized the sound and allowed her to lean into me.

Even covered in grime, she was pretty. In fact, all the girls were beautiful. I counted nine altogether. I shuddered at the thought of what was to become of us. Who would kidnap girls? And in this number? I recited the prayer for protection—and repeated it over and over until the warmth of the suns dried my skin.

CHAPTER THIRTEEN

AVIKAR

We rode hard, only stopping to let the horses rest. The twins were ahead, scouting the area. The caravan led us towards the Great River. Few bridges would be big enough for them to cross. On horseback, we saved a day and a half of riding by taking a smaller path. We would cut them off at the east bridge.

I kept thinking about Lucy. I had never met a mage before. Anyone showing magical abilities was sent to The Order. There they would be tested and trained. You only had two options as a magic user: work for The Order or join the king's army. I'd rather be in the king's army. King Corban had kept Tarrtainya peaceful for the past thirty years. He ruled the various lords justly, and the drifters across the seas hadn't returned in generations.

No one really understood The Order. My father said they protected us from secret threats in our own borders. I didn't believe him. The Order had as much power as the king, and they enforced it.

But how did Lucy escape them? Were there other mages outside of The Order? And why would she be attacking us?

The twins returned with a full layout of the enemy's camp, which consisted of thirty men. I watched Nathaniel draw a map of the terrain. I reached into my pocket, searching for the familiar pouch. I loosened the knot and grabbed one of the marbles.

Davin explained our route in, but I could focus on nothing beyond the smooth stone in my hand. I wasn't ready for this. They talked about battle, a real battle. What did I know about war? Only the stories Father told me. How did a trio of Roamers turn into an army? I glanced around at the other men, every expression stoic except Derrick's. His brow creased, his gaze glued to the map.

In order for us to succeed, each of us had to take down four men. Four men! The ache in my head returned. My family counted on me. I swore I would bring Jeslyn back, but what if I failed? I'd be responsible for two siblings' deaths. I couldn't bear that much guilt.

A strong hand gripped my shoulder. Rudy stood between Derrick and me with a knowing look. "I think you two boys better come with me," he said. We both followed him away from the group.

"This here be your first battle?" he asked, his large arms resting on his belly.

"Well ..." I was embarrassed by my inexperience.

"I thought so. Well, there be a few things you two ought to know. Sit down."

Rudy spent the next hour explaining battle tactics, the importance of watching one another's back, and how to fight multiple opponents. He called Reaper, Henry and Steven to help us practice. Overall, Derrick and I handled ourselves well. Sparring together had trained us to fight side by side. We were used to each other's movements. It was just a matter of knowing how to navigate.

Night had fallen, and it was time to get some much-needed rest before the attack. Rudy took first watch. The past week's journey had exhausted my body and mind. I picked a spot near the campfire and lay on the ground.

One of the men hummed a dark melody. I repositioned my pack

under my head, trying to get comfortable. A memory of Jeslyn and I feeding one of the colts entered my mind. Every detail about that afternoon seemed alive. It was one of the last times we laughed together. Water stung my eyes and I closed them, hoping I would get to her soon.

A strange high-pitched cry woke me. I opened my eyes but saw nothing unusual. Derrick lay across from me, snoring. *What is that?* I tried to sit up, but couldn't. *Am I dreaming?* A heavy fog pressed in around me. My eyes flickered open and shut. It was the only part of my body that responded.

The wailing grew louder and closer. The hair on my arms stood. A bright mass of swirling light caught the corner of my eye. The mass resembled a hundred moonbeams vigorously twisting and turning. I attempted to roll on my side.

What's wrong with my legs? And my arms? Why can't I move?

The haunting mass spiraled closer. Soon, it was right above me. I gaped in horror as it transformed into the face of the giant I'd killed. Vacant sockets bore into me, seeking revenge. Paralyzing fear overwhelmed me. Every muscle ignored my desperate plea to move. I tried to scream with every breath I had but could only choke. Derrick lay only a few feet away.

The creature hissed, crushing my chest. The face distorted and changed into Jimri's. I blinked twice, trying to drive the image away.

It's not real. It's not real.

Every time I blinked that white face still hovered above me, invisible hands pushing me into the ground. A weight pressed upon my chest. I struggled to breathe. I'd never encountered a spirit before. I never imagined all the stupid fairytales could be true.

It's trying to kill me.

A surge of adrenaline pulsed through my veins. I bolted upright, screaming and flaying my arms like a wild beast.

Derrick woke, rubbing his eyes with one hand while grabbing his sword with the other. "Are we under attack?"

"No," I said in between breaths. I scanned the area. Whatever it was had vanished.

Rudy came charging over, battle-axe drawn. "What's wrong?"

I rubbed my arms, erasing the chill that lingered. "Did you hear screaming?"

"Besides yours?" Rudy squinted at me. "Are you all right? You're white as alabaster."

I nodded, even though I was far from all right. "I must have had a bad dream. Go rest. I don't think I'll be going back to sleep."

Rudy propped his weapon against his shoulder. I picked up my bow and began pacing around the camp. I couldn't explain what just happened. I'd had nightmares before, but this was different. I felt that thing on top of me.

The bow shook in my hands. *Breathe.*

Behind me, a rustle in the bush. I steadied the bow and crept forward. One slow step at a time. Tiny beads of sweat soaked the back of my shirt. Every step I took felt like walking straight into death itself. Silence filled the night, except for the loud pounding of my heart. Leaves crunched under my boots. I strung the bow and aimed at the intruder hiding behind the shrubbery.

Out scurried a small brown rabbit.

Stupid bunny. I spit at the rodent, just missing its back. The nightmares were enough to make me crazy, but being frightened by bunnies? I was losing it.

CHAPTER FOURTEEN

AVIKAR

The suns peeked over the distant horizon. Their rays slowly rose, awakening the day with dawn. Rudy told Derrick and me to stay behind the rest of the pack. My job was to shoot as many enemies as I could while Derrick guarded me. We trotted our horses to the perimeter of the enemy camp, spread out and awaited the signal. Last night's fog lingered over the sleeping grounds. Guards that should have been patrolling lay against tree trunks, clueless to our approach. One dark figure emerged from a tent at the far end. He stretched and wandered off into the woods, probably to urinate.

The wagons surrounded the site in a semi-circle. Sweat pooled in my palms. I had to take out the guards closest to that entrance. If I failed, so did the mission.

Get a grip.

I clenched the arrow in my right hand. Brushfire shifted nervously, sensing my fear. I rubbed her neck. I felt safer with her. She'd been with me since Jimri's death. At night when the nightmares taunted me, I'd sneak out, riding until dawn forced us home. I'd rescued her from the burning woods, she'd rescued me from despair—today, I prayed both of us would make it out alive.

Rudy raised his arm high. My sign to attack.

Balancing myself, I let go of the reins and began firing arrow after arrow, taking out the first guards. When they were down, we moved in.

Brushfire maneuvered through the opening, following Derrick's steed. Two guards aimed bows at me, but I shot both before they had a chance. My quick speed was my one good quality. Very few people could match my pace.

I notched another arrow and shot a swordsman attacking Derrick. Derrick kicked him in the chest, shoving the arrow clean through. One of the kidnappers banged a pot and screamed, alerting everyone else. Brushfire galloped into the circle. A nearby guard ran towards me. He was too close for the bow. I swung my sword, barely blocking the incoming attack.

The clash knocked me off Brushfire. Pain shot up my back. My vision blurred. The guard raised his sword, ready to split me in two. I rolled at the last second. The sword gashed my left arm. I screamed. The guard growled and again lifted his weapon. I stared up in horror, realizing this was the end. The guard's head fell off and landed between my legs. Blood shot like a red geyser from the body. Derrick emerged from behind the man and held out his arm. I grabbed it and climbed onto the back of his mount.

Grimacing, I ripped off a piece of my shirt and tied it around the wound. Metal clanged against metal, creating an eerie sonnet that played for the suns as they rose. Screams and war cries arose from the camp. I could smell death. My heart lurched when I watched Steven fall under the blade of a grinning solider. As Steven's dying action, he took his killer down with a final blow to the chest, ripping it open. There wasn't time for me to go to him. Steven would slip alone into the abyss.

Derrick's horse jumped over a burnt out fire pit and headlong into a group of charging men. Before we touched down, I sent two arrows flying over Derrick's shoulder. One man grabbed at the arrow protruding from his eye socket as he dropped to his knees. The other never had a chance to react. The feathered shaft stuck out from his neck as he toppled to the ground.

Derrick, beast that he was, clutched the reins in his left hand while his right wielded the claymore, which he swung into the closest standing man, decapitating him.

Does he ever hold back during our spars? I thought. How else could I have so many victories over him?

Out of the corner of my eye, I spotted the twins, cornered by six guards. I nudged Derrick. "Stop here."

Derrick halted the horse. We slipped off and ran. Nathaniel saw us approaching and taunted the attackers, grabbing their attention. The ruse worked. I shot one guard before any of them turned. Derrick sent his sword straight through another's chest.

The twins were a blur of spark and metal, circling each other in perfect unison, an image of white fury.

"We need to find Jeslyn." I panted. My lungs were on fire and it was getting harder to breathe, but I pushed past the pain and charged towards a nearby guard. I blocked him with my sword, dipped down quick and slashed his ankles with my dagger. The man howled and fell over. I jumped over him and plunged my knife into the back of another.

One of the wagons creaked and rolled away from the circle.

"Derrick!" I threw my sword into its sheath and strung my bow. I pulled back, lining up the shot. Once I locked on, I sent the arrow flying into the unsuspecting target.

Derrick pushed his way towards me, knocking out a man in the process. He glanced back, seeing my arrow land perfectly in the man's chest.

"Nice shot!" Derrick cried. He rested his hands on his thighs, catching his breath. "What's the plan?"

I pointed to the wagons north of us. "You check those. I'll check the ones on the other side."

He nodded and ran off.

My arms ached with fatigue, and the wound stung. I wanted to stop and rest, just for a minute, but I couldn't. I ran in the direction of the other wagons where I was stopped by a stocky man with a goatee. He didn't count on my quick reflexes. I dodged him. When our swords clashed, I noticed the rip in his shirt and a snake tattoo. Calli's description rang back in my mind and my head exploded with anger. Standing before me was the man who'd stolen Jeslyn.

I growled and kicked his knee. Jeslyn's kidnapper stumbled for a second and that was all I needed. I shifted my hands up the hilt and slammed the metal edge against his head. Blood trickled from the spot. I jabbed the hilt again and the wound gaped. Anger clouded my vision in a haze of red. I threw the sword, wanting to strangle the man with my hands. He glared at me with one good eye and smirked. I ducked as his blade swished above me, slicing air. I belted him in the gut. The punch rocked him back a step. Grabbing his wrist, I squeezed a pressure point, forcing the weapon to drop. I now had full control of the fight. I stepped around him, twisting the arm I held. The kidnapper grunted and tried to dislodge me by elbowing my stomach, but I was too quick. I avoided the elbow and brought the man to his knees.

I pulled the dagger from its sheath and held it to his throat. It seemed fitting to finish him off with my family's weapon. I pushed the dagger into his skin and he started praying. That only angered me more.

Rudy came up behind me. "Leave that one alive!" Rudy's brows narrowed. I must have looked like a wild beast. "We'll need to be asking him questions. Everyone else is either dead or has run away."

"This is the man who kidnapped my sister, and you want me to keep him alive?"

Rudy furrowed his brow. "Aye."

Shaking my head, I pressed the blade deeper, drawing a thin line of blood. "No."

Rudy propped his axe on his shoulder. "Kill him after he talks."

"What do we need him for? The fight is over!"

"We need to know who these men be working for."

I stood over the man, debating his death.

I should kill him. Father would want it.

I waited for Jeslyn's kidnapper to beg, but he didn't. Slowly, my anger faded. Nauseous guilt crept in. I couldn't do it. I couldn't kill a defenseless man. And Rudy was right. These men had to be reporting to someone—and that was the person I needed to kill.

CHAPTER FIFTEEN

JESLYN

Shouts and slamming hooves boomed outside. **Were we** being rescued? If not, I figured I could use the distraction to escape. The guards would be too busy to notice me. I hoped.

I slid my shaking hand between the bars of the wagon door, trying to reach the lock. The tip of my fingers touched the top. It was too low. I pulled at the fabric covering the window. After numerous tries, it ripped from above, hurling me back.

Carnage covered every inch of the ground. Bile rose in my throat and I held it back. I watched a giant sword impale through a man's chest. I screamed when the attacker looked up.

"Derrick!" I waved my hand, hoping he could see or hear me.

He did.

He slashed his way towards me, chopping down anyone in his path. He screamed my name and tears slid down my cheeks. I was safe.

He stepped onto the wheel, taking my hand and kissing it feverishly. "You're alive."

"Get me *out* of here," I cried.

"Don't worry. Everything's going to be fine. Are you hurt?"

I shook my head. "I'm scared, Derrick."

"Nothing is going to happen to you. Okay?"

"Where's Calli?" I said, praying she had made it home to our father.

"Safe."

Derrick would protect me. This nightmare would finally end.

"I love you," I said.

"I love you too." He winked and jumped down. "I might be able to break the lock with my sword. Stand back."

I scooted away from the door and waited. I heard a loud thump, then silence. "Derrick?" When he didn't answer, I panicked. "Derrick!"

The door opened, and the captain stood there, grinning.

"You! What have you done?"

"Lord Lucino will be very unhappy if I come back empty handed. But you, pretty thing, might compensate for our losses."

I kicked and screamed. The girl with me clawed at him. He punched her in the face and she slumped to the floor.

"I'll do the same to you if you don't shut up. We can do this the nice way, or the hard way."

I spit in his face.

"Okay, guess it's the hard way." He drew back. I tried to avoid the incoming blow, but there was no escape.

CHAPTER SIXTEEN

AVIKAR

Jess!" **Derrick opened his eyes and tried to sit up. I** grabbed his shoulder, steadying him.

"Careful," I said. "You were hit pretty hard."

"Where's Jess? Is she okay?"

I helped him to his feet. "She's not here. I searched everywhere."

Derrick's eyes widened. He spun around, grabbing the lock on the nearby wagon. "What happened? She was in here!" Derrick examined the metal contraption, his shoulders slumping. "This was locked." The words were barely a whisper.

A girl with blonde hair and a dangerous bruise on her cheek walked over to us. "Excuse me," she said. "I think the girl you're looking for may have been in the wagon with me." The girl looked around at the other girls who were now out of the wagons. "I don't see her here."

Derrick grabbed the girl by the shoulders. "Did she have long brown hair and blue eyes?"

The girl nodded.

"How long ago?" Derrick asked.

"I don't know. The man hit me, and I didn't see anything." She shook her head and sniffled. Derrick let go of her.

I grunted and punched the wagon. Pain shot through my arm. How could this happen?

"We have to go, Derrick," I said. "Now."

He nodded, and I whistled for Brushfire.

"Whoa, now hold on you two." Rudy stepped behind us. "You can't just be running off. You're both too weary, and that wound needs to be cauterized." He pointed to the gash on my arm that seeped with blood.

Ignoring him, I whistled again. My stomach clenched in anguish as I saw Brushfire limp towards me, an arrow stuck in her backside. "Come here, girl," I said softly, reaching for her.

She whinnied. I rubbed her muzzle.

"It's okay." Looking at her, I knew she needed rest, even if I didn't. I pressed my head against hers.

Derrick stood behind her, his face solemn. "Hold her," he said.

I grabbed her reins.

"Hold still, girl." I held her firmly, staring at her big eyes, keeping her calm. I nodded to Derrick. He put one hand on her back and grabbed the shaft with the other.

"One, two…" He yanked the arrow free. Brushfire neighed and kicked her back legs.

"Whoa, girl, whoa." I held onto her, pulling the reins down. "Easy girl."

"Rudy's right," Derrick said, tossing the arrow into the brush.

I couldn't believe he agreed with Rudy. Staring at Derrick with disbelief, I furrowed my brow. "How can you say that? We need to go now! They can't be that far ahead of us." If Derrick was stupid enough to listen to that old man, I'd leave him here. "I'm going."

"And what happens when you lose so much blood you pass out? You can't fight and your horse can't hold you."

Jeslyn was out there, probably terrified, and now with a man who could do a thousand horrible things to her. I couldn't stomach the idea of just sitting here.

"You know I don't want to stay either," he added. "But we have no choice. We'll leave as soon as you're able."

Maybe Derrick was right, but how could I stay? How could he stay? I patted Brushfire, still debating. I pulled my quiver off and counted the arrows. I sighed and looked around. Before I did anything, I'd better re-stock.

Blood covered the ground. A stark reminder of the battle. Retrieving arrows was a gruesome task, but I was running low. Each time I pulled one out of a corpse, nausea spread through me. The adrenaline that fueled me during battle disappeared, leaving me weak and disgusted. Is this what my life had become, a series of complete failures? I'd thought, I'd really thought, this time would be different. I should've known better. It was never going to change. Why, why, did I always screw up? I just wanted, for once in this miserable life to do something meaningful. I didn't want to face my father and tell him, for the second time, that a family member was dead.

An empty wagon held our only prisoner. His head was wrapped in linen and his hands were tied behind his back. I wanted him dead, and yet here I stood, playing nice. If he gave me the information I needed, not chopping his head off would be worth it.

I paced back and forth in front of the wagon. "You're alone," I said. "No one is coming for you. You have two choices. Your first choice, and the one I recommend, is that you tell me what I need to know, and I might let you live. Your second option is to keep quiet and I'll bring you to Crain Village prison. If you know nothing about them, know their judicial system is a bit skewed, and you'll most likely face the gallows for mere entertainment, but only after you've been tortured for weeks."

The fear in his grey eyes became apparent. I didn't know if Crain Village was as bad as the few stories I'd heard, but it sounded good.

"You have until nightfall to decide."

In the middle of camp, Derrick and the others sat by a large fire. They cooked game they'd managed to catch. A few of the girls helped to clean the injured men. We were lucky to have only one causality. I sat near the fire and pulled out my dagger. It gleamed under the firelight. Using the sleeve of my shirt, I wiped off the blood. I loved fighting, but killing was different. I hadn't expected to feel so sick. Blood didn't bother me, but splattered all over a man I just killed? That made my stomach spin. Every life I took seemed to chip away at my own.

Rudy stood in front of me with Reaper. "You ready to clean that up?"

Reaper stuck a sword into the fire, and I watched the metal glow.

"It's not that bad," I said.

Rudy huffed and lifted away the makeshift bandage I had put on. He rinsed the cut with water. I winced. "Here, bite on this." He shoved a leather belt at me.

You'd think after a vicious battle, I could handle a simple cauterizing. Sweat dripped down my neck and my heart pounded so fast it made me dizzy.

Reaper walked over, holding that poker of death in his hand, and I swear he was smiling. Having him close the wound made me even more panicky.

"Hey, Derrick!"

Derrick looked over, and I waved at him. He saw Reaper, and his eyes widened.

"Hold my right arm," I said. "I don't want to accidentally punch Reaper when he burns it."

Derrick smirked. "Sure."

I took a deep breath; put the belt in my mouth.

HOLY-BEARDED-MOTHER!

CHAPTER SEVENTEEN

AVIKAR

L oud shouting woke me. The cut on my arm throbbed, and I winced while stretching to see who was yelling. A small crowd had gathered around the wagon holding the prisoner. I scrambled to my feet and headed over. There, shivering and lying in a pool of vomit, was our only prisoner.

Derrick and Henry began pulling the man out, until Derrick noticed the snake tattoo. He yelled, stepped back and unsheathed his sword. I moved in front of him and grabbed his arm.

"Don't," I said.

Derrick glared at me and lifted his claymore. "Get out of my way."

"I know how you feel, but we need him alive."

He cringed. "This man kidnapped Jeslyn. He's the reason for all of this and you're protecting him!"

"No. I want him dead too, but we don't know where to find her. He does. Once we rescue her, we'll deal with him. I promise."

Derrick growled and lowered his sword. "You better be right about this, or you'll be my next victim." He stormed off into the woods.

"Give the boy some time. He's angry. He didn't mean it." Rudy helped Henry bring the prisoner to the fire.

A young girl touched the prisoner's forehead. She ripped a piece of her dress and patted the sweat off his face. I ran my fingers through my hair, watching the scene in a daze.

"He burns with a heavy fever," she said. "I'll need water."

At least we saved them. With all the chaos, I'd forgotten we rescued nine other girls.

I bent down and untied the man's hands. The fever burned through his skin.

"He was fine before," I said. "I don't understand."

The prisoner heaved, and the girl rolled him over on his side. "He's been poisoned," she said.

One of the twins brought over a pale of water. The young girl dipped the cloth into the bucket and washed the prisoner's face. This man could be our only link to finding Jeslyn. "Can you get rid of it?" I hoped she'd say yes.

She shook her head. "If I knew what it was, maybe, but this? Look at his veins." She showed me his arm laced with greenish lines.

I searched his body for anything unusual and found a tiny dart lodged in the back of his neck. Slowly, I pulled it out. "What is this?" I turned it over, looking at the tiny runes on it.

"Let me see that, boy." Reaper held out his hand and I gave him the dart. He held it between his two fingers. "This is odd. I don't recognize the metal."

"What does that mean?" I asked.

Reaper ran his bony fingers through his oily hair. "This dart is not from our lands. Could be from one of his own men."

I reached for my sword, expecting a dart to come flying at me.

"Find Nathaniel and Davin," Rudy said to Reaper. "Tell them to do a perimeter check and have everyone else on guard."

The prisoner wheezed and blood trickled out the side of his mouth.

"Where's a priest when you need one?" I mumbled.

A small plump girl stepped forward. Her red curly hair resembled fire and matched the shade of her freckles. "I can help," she said.

"Thank you," I said, trying not to be rude. "But what we need is a priest."

"My name is Manna, and I am a priestess."

Did she say a priestess?

"Welcome," I said and dipped my head in a bow. Priestesses were rare, very rare and their healing abilities were powerful.

Manna prayed over the prisoner. Then she sang, raising her hands high in the air, reaching to the stars. Her voice was a deep baritone with a hint of femininity and power. The campfire backlit her with a golden halo. Her voice echoed off the trees.

It reminded me of a day, long time ago, when I'd gone to temple with Mother. I watched two people standing in the front, singing a hymn. I hadn't understood what they were saying, but I'd felt it. And just like then, Manna's song pierced every barrier around my heart. The air tingled with a foreign sensation both uplifting and terrifying. No one moved. No one spoke.

Her voice reached a crescendo, and she bent over the prisoner. She placed her hands on his chest, leaned down and whispered in his ear.

"Sleep now, but when you arise, know that by grace you have been saved. Right your wrongs." Manna slowly rose and lifted her hands. "Praise be to The Creator!"

She touched my shoulder, smiled and disappeared amongst the rescued girls.

I wanted to run after her and tell her she was amazing. Instead, I watched the sickly green leave the prisoner's body, and wondered why my cheek was wet.

Chapter Eighteen

Avikar

Morning arrived and everyone prepared to leave for Crain Village. We decided it was the closest place and we could escort the missing girls to the temple there. The men circled Derrick. They were pointing to a map. I started to walk towards them when I noticed Manna talking to the prisoner who was awake and untied. He sat on a log with his head buried in his hands.

I gripped the hilt of my sword and marched over.

Manna stood and intercepted me. "Be still," she said softly, placing a hand on my chest.

Is she crazy?

"Listen to his tale. Your heart will tell you the rest."

I grunted and pushed past her. Priestess or not, she had no right to untie him. The prisoner looked up, then back down. I folded my arms and glared at him, focusing on talking and not walloping him.

"Tell me everything," I said. "And I mean everything. You can start with your name."

The man swallowed and cleared his throat before talking. "My name is Jericho."

"Where were you taking the girls?"

"Back to Daath."

That can't be right. "Daath?"

He nodded.

He had guts to lie. I took a deep breath and tried to calm myself. "Daath is a myth."

"It's real."

I pulled out my sword and pointed it at his lying face. "The thirteenth land is an old fable. Don't lie to me! If you don't tell me where my sister is, I swear I'll kill you."

He held up his hands in defense. "I swear. It's the truth. Lord Lucino gave us specific orders on where to take the girls. We had only a few more stops before returning back home."

"You were specifically told to take my sister?" I paced back and forth, hands trembling. "First, you tell me Daath exists. Then you tell me some lord is kidnapping girls from everywhere. Am I supposed to believe that?" In a rage, I kicked the log next to him. His eyes widened.

"Lord Lucino is searching for a bride, and he is very particular when it comes to women."

"Why should I believe you?" I gauged his expression, trying to figure him out.

"Because I have no reason to lie."

He looked right at me when he said it. I was pretty good at reading people and I almost believed him. "Let's pretend I think you're telling the truth. Where is Daath?"

"If I tell you now, you'll kill me, and you need me alive in order to pass through the barrier."

Barrier? What is he talking about? My head ached, and I needed to think. It would be a risk trusting him, but what other choice did we have? I could try and locate the kidnapper's trail, like I did before, but if this man was telling the truth about a barrier…

"Fine," I said. "You'll take us to Daath and help me get my sister back."

"Lord Lucino is very powerful."

"I don't care how strong he is. He kidnapped my sister, and for that, he pays."

"I understand, but trying to go after Lord Lucino is impossible."

In a flash, I had my sword tip pressed against his throat. "Because of you, my sister is gone. By all rights I should kill you." I pressed the blade in, nicking his skin. "Do you have family in Daath?"

"Yes," he whispered.

"Any children?"

"Yes."

"Any happen to be a girl?"

He glanced down.

"What would you do if Lucino took your daughter?"

"Same as you."

"Then we understand each other. I can't abandon her, no matter what the odds are."

Jericho nodded slightly. "I'll escort you to Daath and help you find your sister."

I pondered his so called oath. I lowered the sword and stepped back. "Remember, if you turn on us …"

Jericho bowed his head. "You have my word."

Satisfied with his answer, I led Jericho to Derrick. Men grumbled and glared at Jericho. Derrick straightened.

"I know where Jeslyn has been taken," I said. "Daath"

"That man be telling lies!" Rudy yelled. "Everyone knows Daath's an old wives tale. They've been talking about that hidden land for centuries!"

Out of the corner of my eye, I saw Derrick grip his sword. "I thought so too, but I believe him," I said, even though I wasn't really sure myself.

"You gonna tell me next that legendary guardian is real too?" Rudy scoffed.

"May I say something?" Every man glared at Jericho, as if he'd suggested executing our King.

"You don't hear about Daath because no one but the guard is allowed to leave, and the entrance is concealed. And yes, the guardian is real, but as long as you bear the seal, you're safe." Jericho lifted his sleeve revealing the snake tattoo on his right arm.

"I can't ask any of you to risk your lives for me," I said, turning to the men. "You've done enough. Derrick and I will go to Crain Village with you; after that, we'll be on our way."

Lucas approached me, holding Rudy's daughter's hand. "If it wasn't for you, I never would have found Charlotte." He glanced at her and squeezed her hand. "I'm indebted to you, and I'm going with you to Daath."

"Now, now, don't you be making promises." Rudy scrunched his bushy face at Lucas. "You'll be taking my Charlotte back home."

"But—"

Rudy raised a hand. "No butts. I need someone I can trust. I'll follow these lads."

"Don't forget about us," the twins said in unison, grinning at me.

Days ago, we were strangers. Now they're willing to risk their lives for me.

Deep down, I knew we needed the help, but what if one of them died? More blood and more death. I couldn't allow them to do that.

"Thank you," Derrick said, before I could convince them not to come.

I was ready to argue with Derrick when he grabbed my arm and pulled me to the side. "I know what you're thinking." He held up a finger. "We need them. This is too big for us, and I'd feel a lot better if we weren't alone with that guy."

I knew he referred to Jericho, and Derrick was right: we couldn't trust him, at least not yet. I had to remind myself who this man was—Jeslyn's kidnapper.

CHAPTER NINETEEN

LUCINO

I wanted to thrust my sword into Gerard's pitiful face. "I hope you have a very good explanation as to why my entire caravan is missing!"

He knelt. "We were attacked just before dawn. Lady Lucy informed us she had taken care of our pursuers. We were unprepared."

I walked down the red carpet and thought about slicing off his head. "Do not blame Lucy for your incompetence. You are the captain." I glared down in disgust. The males of this race served little purpose, and they smelled like a mule. "Where are the rest of your men?"

Gerard clenched his fist. "Most of them were killed during the attack. I assume the rest fled. They caught one of the guards, but I made sure he would not be able to speak. Daath's location is safe."

"What else do you have to say for your failure?"

"When I realized the battle was lost, I escaped with one of the girls. She—"

Before the words had left his lips, my foot snapped out, nearly breaking the ribs of his frail weasel-like chest. "Coward! You think a girl would redeem you?" I drew my sword. Enough of this.

He buckled, gasping for air. "She is the most beautiful woman I have ever seen. She would make the perfect bride."

Now, that was interesting. "All right, Gerard. Let's see this little treasure you've brought me. If she is what you say she is, you get to live." Slowly, I slid the sword back into its gold sheath, accentuating the sound of its keening blade; a melody that reminded Gerard his folly would not be tolerated. "Take me to her."

CHAPTER TWENTY

JESLYN

A slow drip echoed off the stone walls. I curled into a ball on the hard wooden cot, trying to convince myself it was all a long dream, one from which I couldn't wake. They'd put me in a horrid room, covered in dark stone with only a wash pan and a small round window well out of reach. When the suns disappeared, I lay in darkness, listening to the murmurs and cries of other prisoners and waiting for the rays of dawn.

The guards refused to answer any of my questions, and I still didn't know why I was taken. I wanted Mother and Father, but most of all, I wanted Derrick and wished he would come crashing through the door, rescuing me.

Questions circled my mind. What had happened to Derrick? And my brother? For where one is, so is the other.

Footsteps sounded outside the door, followed by the twist of a key. I rolled over and faced the wall. The guards enjoyed staring, and I refused to give them any attention.

The door creaked open.

"Hello, my lady," a refined voice said.

This wasn't one of the guards. Curious, I turned to acknowledge my visitor. I didn't expect a handsome boy. He stared at me with deep sapphire eyes. His shoulder length hair color reminded me of the pale yellow honeysuckles back home. His chiseled features resembled a stone statue, perfectly carved. My gaze drifted to his long velvet robe decorated with intricate gold symbols. Beneath the brocade vest, he wore a silk shirt and from his neck hung a gold medallion of a snake eating its tail.

He glided towards me like a swan on water. I combed my fingers through my hair, smoothing out the wild strands. He sat down on the cot. I was surrounded by the scent of cold winter air.

"What's your name?" he asked.

I should have replied, but fear closed my throat.

He smiled and held out his hand. "My name is Lucino."

"Jeslyn." I placed my hand in his, anxious and uncertain.

He gently kissed my hand. I shivered. No man had ever looked at me with such desire—not even Derrick—and it frightened me.

"Hello, Jeslyn." His smooth voice rang with power.

My hands trembled, and I dug them into my tattered dress.

"Are you feeling well?"

It angered me that he acted so frivolous. I wanted to scream and cry. Did he not realize I was a prisoner?

"I know you're frightened. I'm not going to harm you." He peered at my arm. "That's quite the cut. May I?"

He didn't wait for an answer and gently lifted my arm, examining the deep scratch running across it. I thought back to my blinded journey, and the trembling fear came flooding back.

"Who did this to you?"

"A man blacker than night. He was in charge of the men who stole me."

Lucino's brows slanted down. "Did he do anything else to you?"

I nodded, remembering the last time I saw Derrick, back at the wagon. A single tear slid down my cheek.

"He hit me."

Lucino wiped my tear. More followed. "Jeslyn, please—be calm. You have nothing to fear from me."

His pupils dilated, and in their center swirled something like a hurricane. I leaned forward, not trusting my own eyes.

"You are safe," he said.

Suddenly the fear subsided, the storm from his eyes gone. My stomach grumbled. It had been awhile since I'd last eaten.

He stood, offering his arm. "Come with me. You can eat and bathe. This is no place for a beauty like you. There's much we need to discuss."

I agreed, eager to leave this room, eager to bathe. Once I left this prison, I could think of a way to escape.

Outside the enormous wooden structure in which I'd been housed, a black carriage waited, led by two magnificent white horses. I spotted the captain standing next to it and huddled closer to Lucino, seemingly far saner than the dark beast who'd dragged me here.

"Please, wait inside, my lady." Lucino hoisted me into the carriage, and I climbed in. He closed the door, and I peered through the window. He gestured the captain away.

"Kneel!" Lucino ordered.

The captain knelt and bowed his head. Lucino took out his sword and slashed it across the captain's face. It happened so quickly, I almost missed it.

"That is so you remember how to properly treat a lady." Lucino kicked him in the chin, sending him backward.

My heart hammered as I watched Lucino defend my honor, but why would he be so angry with his own man? Did he not order him to take me?

Lucino motioned for the two nearest soldiers and whispered to them. Their expressions turned to shock.

"Yes, Master," they said, picking up their comrade while Lucino walked back to me.

Upon entering the carriage, Lucino snapped his fingers. The driver whipped the reins, and the horses trotted up the winding road.

I peered at the passing scenery with wide eyes. "Where are we?" I asked.

"Daath."

All my life I've dreamed of it being real. Mother had told me the old stories. Daath is the birthplace of our world, a magical paradise. No one else believed Mother's old tales, not even Calli and especially not Avikar, but I did.

Lush vegetation, greener than a shining emerald, surrounded us. Exotic birds chirped from the brush. Prancing unafraid alongside the carriage was a creature that resembled a deer but smaller and snow white. Delicate flowers larger than a melon weaved with the grass. In the trees lurked black crescent-browed monkey creatures. I pressed against the glass. My breath fogged my view, and I rubbed it away.

I could feel Lucino's eyes observing me in silence. I shifted in the seat.

"I'm sorry if I stare," he said. "I have never seen anyone quite as exquisite as you. You are extremely beautiful."

"Th ... thank you."

"You must have some questions you'd like to ask?"

I slid back and folded my hands in my lap. "Why am I here?"

He sighed and glanced out the window. "It was not supposed to be like this, but my Council is desperate for me to have a wife. You see, I'm reaching that age when a boy becomes a man and I need to be married. Sadly, I haven't found the perfect girl, and I ceased searching. At the age of twenty-one, I must be wed. It is tradition. Unfortunately, my birthday is in a few weeks. My Council was running out of options and acted hastily. Many girls were taken from their homes." He looked at me, genuine concern on his face, and leaned forward. "I am sorry you were kidnapped. If I had known what was happening, I never would have allowed it. They figured if they found girls outside of Daath, one of them might pique my interest."

I debated the truth of his words.

"The girls were going to be presented to me at the upcoming ball, and I'd have to choose one. I overheard the men talk about you and knew I had to release you from that prison." He leaned closer and grabbed both my hands.

I wanted to pull them away, but was afraid to anger him. I'd play along, for now.

"All this, anything you seek, could be yours if you marry me, my lady. I don't need to see any other girls. I know you're the one."

With no food in my stomach—and the constant fear and anxiety, I felt dizzy and lightheaded. My mind could not take in a lord's proposal.

Our destination came into view: a four story white-stoned mansion with spiraled pillars and arched windows. The narrow driveway was set against a perfectly manicured lawn broken with grey statues and geometric bushes. Gardeners tended potted flowers and multi-colored rose arches decorating a myriad of walkways. The workers bowed their heads as we rolled by.

"Welcome to my home," he said, sweeping his arm out towards the scenery.

When we stopped, the driver opened Lucino's door. Lucino exited and stretched out his hand to me. I grabbed it and swayed. Bright sunlight beamed down at me, and the heat made my stomach roll. Lucino asked a question, his voice muffled. Brown spots clouded my vision. I gripped Lucino's hand harder. He said my name, and then I fell.

CHAPTER TWENTY-ONE

LUCINO

My Lady!" I caught Jeslyn in my arms as she fainted. Her icy blue eyes fluttered open. "Jeslyn," I whispered with the litheness of a harp. I activated my captivation spell, watching the storm in my eyes reflected in hers, pulling her conscience in, knowing she could not escape. I drew closer, washing my cool breath over her face.

"Sleep, my beauty," I said. "Sleep, and when you awake, all will be well."

Her eyes closed, and the serenity of sleep filled her face.

Willis appeared by my side. One of the few competent servants I had; although, his human form did not suit his lanky Reptilian body well. I handed Jeslyn to him. "Take her upstairs to the red room."

He bowed his head and carried Jeslyn inside. I wiped my hands with the handkerchief under my lapel. Lucy stepped out of the massive doorway and down the stone steps. Passing Willis, she examined Jeslyn and smirked.

"What a delicate face," said Lucy. "Is she your newest doll?"

I laughed. "Ahh, my dear Lucy, that is my future bride!" Lucy raised an eyebrow and I offered her my arm. "Shall we?"

We strolled down the curved walkway leading to the gardens. "Tell me, dear sister. When were you planning on informing me that my entire shipment of females had been intercepted?"

"That's why I came outside."

I placed my hand over her arm and squeezed. "Lucy, Lucy, you knew how important this assignment was. And one I expected you to see through."

"Why can't you choose one of your many dolls to wed? I have more important things to attend to."

I stopped and tightened my grip. She winced as I dug my fingers into her skin.

"Securing your rule outside of Daath is the main goal. You know this!" She struggled to pull away but I held her in place.

"I will not be questioned," I said. "You are under my authority. Do not forget that."

"And I am your sister. Your fate is the same as mine."

That was true. The females of our race were only as powerful as the ruling males and we were royal blood. "Then you will listen to my orders. Do we have an understanding?"

"Yes."

A butterfly flew past. I swatted the insect, killing it instantly. "I cannot stand these bugs. I'll never fathom the obsession humans have with them. They are vile things. Where was I? Oh, yes." We passed the marble fountain and continued walking.

"In order to appease The Council, I must be married, this you know. The dolls are my private collection. The finest specimens from all of Tarrtainya, and sadly, I cannot tolerate any of them, None of them have the aura I seek. All you had to do was take the girls Romulus instructed and bring them here. Yet, somehow, you managed to fail at such a simple task. If it weren't for Gerard's quick thinking, we would be having a different conversation.

During our last meeting, you said you took care of the problem. What happened?"

"The spell broke sooner than I planned."

I disengaged from her. "Only Gerard survived. Do you know what happened to the rest?"

"Not yet, but I have sent out one of my personal scouts. He should report back within a week."

"The Council is not going to be pleased."

Lucy cleared her throat. "Eldesar has called a meeting."

I backhanded her across the face. "I want these boys dead!"

This was turning into a disaster. Eldesar had already warned me once about sending men out of Daath for what he deemed unnecessary assignments.

"I will see to it personally."

"No."

"Lucino, I will—"

"Enough! You will stay here and be Jeslyn's caretaker."

"You want me to babysit?"

"Yes, a job you are more suited for." Lucy glowered. I knew it would agonize her, such a menial task. I placed a hand on her shoulder. "She will be awake soon. Go and introduce yourself, and do make sure she's properly dressed for dinner."

Lucy bowed and walked away, her frustration clearly visible in her loud steps.

CHAPTER TWENTY-TWO

JESLYN

Hours ago, I'd been a prisoner. Now I sat in a room of royalty, richly decorated with a speckled granite fireplace and an oversized white bear rug. Ruby silk draped the mahogany four post bed. Garnet and maroon pillows covered the bed, matching the delicate rose petals on the butter-cream wallpaper. My mind was hazy when I first woke, and it took a while to get my bearings straight, but after soaking in lavender bubbles, I felt like myself again.

I brushed my knotted hair with a silver comb I found on the table. The hot bath had washed away the past weeks' grime leaving my skin soft and smooth. It was the nicest bath I'd ever taken.

The brush passed through my hair methodically. I sat on a velvet seat in front of a large oval mirror that hung above a vanity table, arrayed with perfumes and powders my family could never afford. I loved my home, but my heart had always desired finer things. I wasn't meant to live on a farm pulling weeds and milking cows.

I wanted to believe in this fairytale setting, but my heart refused to be steady. I recited the prayer for protection. When I spoke the final words, an intense urge to flee swept over me. Even though this was all very wonderful, I couldn't trust it. I had to leave.

I threw the brush and ran to the door. I grabbed the knob and the door opened.

"Going somewhere?"

In the doorway stood a catlike girl with black hair. She wore a full-length gown, laced in a tight bodice, revealing too much skin. Around her neck hung a giant sparkling ruby—the biggest gem I'd ever seen.

She circled, inspecting me. "Hmm, such a pretty girl shouldn't be dressed in such dreadful attire. I'm sure there's something in here you can wear."

The girl walked to the armoire and flung open the wooden doors. Hanging inside were a myriad of gowns. She took a honey brown dress off the rack.

"This will do." She threw the dress at me. "Get dressed. I'll return for you in a few moments." She opened the door and looked back at me before leaving. "The name is Lucy."

The door slammed shut, confirming no escape.

Chapter Twenty-Three

L U C I N O

I sat at the head of the table waiting for Jeslyn. Bowls of fresh cabbage dressed in a lemon-garlic sauce and honey breads surrounded the duck in the middle of the table. She entered the room, escorted by Willis. He pulled out the chair for her.

From here, I could see the golden hue of her aura. Romulus had been correct in his choosing. Not only was she a pure vessel, but the purest human I had come across.

"Thank you," she said, and sat at the opposite end of the table.

I raised my goblet. "Good evening. How do you find your room?"

"Very well, thank you," she replied.

Watching her, I sipped the deep bodied wine.

She is ravishing. Her chestnut hair hung around her shoulders, her skin like a warm peach. I stared at her, examining each freckle lightly sprinkled around her petite nose and the loose tendrils of hair caressing her high cheekbones. I had spent decades in this world collecting women of exceptional beauty, and she was unique. Delicate features, almost perfect. Other men might not notice her left eyebrow was slightly higher than her right, but I considered the female anatomy the humans' greatest form of art and studied it intently.

Jeslyn shifted in her seat, picking at her meal. Perhaps the kidnapping still bothered her—a minor detail.

"Does the duck not meet your satisfaction?" I asked, knowing very well it was not the taste that disturbed her but me. I relished in this and enjoyed her silence. Very few women disliked me.

"It does," she replied. "It's very good." She continued in her silence.

Her lack of conversation did not bother me. I found human females tended to talk often and without good cause.

I put the goblet down and clapped my hands. Four minstrels, strumming violins, entered the dining room. I walked to Jeslyn and bowed. "May I have this dance?"

She slipped her hand into mine, and I placed a hand around her thin waist. In one swift movement, I twirled her up and around. The momentum swept her off her feet and the tiniest gasp slipped out of her. I glided around the room. Each step matched the slow melody flowing from the strings.

She gazed at me, intrigued.

"You will be happy here. There is no other place like Daath," I whispered. "You will be loved by everyone." I let the words sink into her mind, watching her face light with wonder.

I danced her outside and into the gardens. We stopped and sat down on a bench underneath a rose-covered archway in front of my favorite fountain. A marble statue of a serpent encircled the stone woman standing in the center, water spurting from her mouth. This symbol represented conquest of the humans.

Jeslyn stared at the beds of sunny yellow and cadmium roses. No one could deny the beauty and magic of this land.

I grabbed her hand and she flinched. "Have you made your decision about my proposal?" I wanted her to think she had an option.

She sat in silence.

"Do you find me attractive?"

She looked away, her cheeks tinted pink.

"There is nothing to be embarrassed about," I said.

"It's not proper for a lady to reveal those types of things," she said softly.

I chuckled. "By the color of those perfect cheeks, I will take that as a yes."

She continued in her silence, not once looking at me.

"Any woman in your position would not hesitate at such an offer."

"Am I free to go?"

"Go?"

She pulled her hand away. "You said you knew nothing about the kidnappings. My family will be looking for me. I cannot stay here."

"I understand. I have a proposition for you."

She stared at me with cautious eyes.

"The ball is in a few weeks' time. You can write a letter to your family, explaining the misunderstanding and I'll have it sent immediately. We can invite them here."

"Mother wouldn't believe me if I told her where I was," Jeslyn said, looking around. "She's always talked about Daath."

"Then you must stay and bring her here. It's the least I can do for the horrible way you were treated. If, by the ball, you still do not accept my proposal, I will not force you to stay."

"It's very kind of you, but …"

"Will you not give me a chance?"

Her fingers tapped against her thighs. I held my composure, playing the dashing lord.

"You are most gracious, but this is not my home."

"I understand, and again, I apologize for the kidnapping. If you can wait until after the ball, I will personally escort you home, if that is what you truly desire."

She glanced at the fountain, then at the roses sprouting from the nearby bushes. "How soon can we send word to my family?"

"You can script a letter to them tonight and at dawn I will send my fastest courier. He would arrive faster than we could travel."

She breathed in, then faced me. "Very well. I will stay for the ball, but I cannot promise you anything more."

I smiled, knowing she would give me so much more.

CHAPTER TWENTY-FOUR

LUCINO

The twelve members of The Council sat around a black table debating our next move. The Eldest of the order, Eldesar, spoke.

"It is time," he said, "for you to retreat from Daath and return to Mirth."

"Retreat?" I said. "I have invested over a century in that place!"

Eldesar raised his hand. "This is not a discussion. We have made our decision. Your carelessness has brought too many wondering eyes. We will not risk all we have accomplished to appease your hobbies."

I folded my hands, trying to contain the fury boiling within me. Teeth clenched, I said, "I was following this Council's orders to find a bride."

"You could have taken a female from Daath," said the elder across from me. "That's what you should have done!"

"Enough," Eldesar said. "You will present this bride to the nobles at the ball. This marriage is for appearance. The nobles would find it odd that a young lord of your age would be unwed. There will be much talk amongst the lands once Daath is revealed. We must tread carefully. You're absence in Daath will be reported as special business. It has been too long since you visited our people. This visit will remind you of your duties."

No one understood the plan better than I. "Eldesar, my awakening is fast approaching. I will leave after my ritual is complete. Preparations have already begun."

Eldesar regarded me from under his hooded cloak. He was an ancient, wise beyond years and older than any of the other members. It was no secret he disliked me, but that hatred traced beyond me, back to when my father was a prince on this Council.

"We have found the humans who attacked your men. They will be disposed of shortly. Complete your ritual and then return home," Eldesar said, arousing unified agreements.

"We will meet again in seven days." Eldesar lifted his dreary hand and flicked a dismissal at the group. "Leave."

I rose and he pointed at me. "Not you."

Holding back my annoyance, I sat down.

"Do you know how we stay in power?" he asked.

"Because we are the superior race," I stated.

"Wrong. Patience."

"Patience?" I said in surprise.

"Yes, our vision takes time."

"Why not now? With our technology and magic we could easily wipe the humans out."

"A war with the humans would cause great destruction on this planet. No, our current plan is the only way. Once our people are in the right places of power, we can begin the transition. The humans will have no choice but to serve or die. This planet is the key to our survival."

He paused and pulled back his hood. Power emanated from his black eyes and dark green scales covered his skin. He spoke in the ancient tongue. "Your fascination with their females is becoming troublesome. I expect you to end your obsession. Be careful of your next actions, very careful, or your reign in Daath will be over." He eased back in his chair. "Leave."

Without hesitation, I stood and walked out the side door. The Council building had been relocated after the discovery of the gate. The gate, though unstable at times, needed to be monitored constantly, and not just by our guard. The Council preferred to have their toys closer.

Outside, the sky bled, looking vicious and deathly, streaks of grey and indigo amongst the clouds. A hovercraft sat nearby, waiting. One of the royal guard stood watch. I did not need a babysitter. I was more than capable of handling any threat, but Father took precautions. Times were dangerous and our people frightened.

From here, I could see the triangular structure. "Take me to the gate," I said as the guard opened the door.

"Yes, my prince."

The hovercraft sped across the dry and barren ground. The Council was right, we had little time left.

CHAPTER TWENTY-FIVE

AVIKAR

Crain Village sat on the eastern trade route, west of Nod Mountains, in Lord Thebas' region. The Village had an unusual taste for hangings, an eerie habit that came about recently. Even the smallest of crimes could end with a noose around the neck.

We walked down the main road, and I spotted a black snake painted on a stone building with strange scratchy writing beside it. The image gave me a chill and I didn't know why.

Three women dressed in purple and crimson robes approached me. Their eyes had a glazed appearance and each one wore a gold snake medallion. An emblem identical to the drawing on the building. I stepped out of their way—none of them noticed they'd almost walked into me. They chanted in a weird language and continued down the road.

Tarrtainya had one main religion with a few minor ones. Most people believed in The Creator or the woodland goddess, Everling. Cults never lasted or spread—The Order saw to that. I'd never been a fanatical follower of anything, but I knew those strange women were fanatical. New cults brought The Order and The Order brought trouble. I hoped they both would stay far from Lakewood.

Derrick suggested we go to the temple. We could leave the rescued girls there and then receive a blessing before we departed. I groaned, but agreed.

The large temple sat at the edge of the village. The suns seemed to shine brighter here. Four-foot-high sunflowers flanked the path heading to the temple doors. I knew each one had a library, one of the few places you could find a book. Maybe in that pile of information I could learn something useful about Daath.

One of the priests showed me to a row of books in a stuffy room beneath the temple. I scanned the dusty tomes for anything mentioning Daath. I was drawn to a worn-out brown cover. I pulled the book off the shelf and dust flew into my nose. I sneezed.

"Doesn't anyone clean down here?" I said.

Using my sleeve, I wiped the cover. It read, *Places of Old*. The name sounded familiar, but I couldn't remember where I'd heard it before. I carried the heavy book to a table and skimmed through its pages. The old paper crinkled as I turned page after page, and then there it was—a picture of a waterfall with a snake coiled underneath it, eating its own tail.

My heart stopped.

That's the same image I saw outside. How can that be?

Daath was written on the bottom of the page, and on the adjacent page, the beginning of the fabled legend. I skimmed over the lengthy tale. It sounded more like a bedtime story my mother would tell. Instead of throwing the book aside, I inspected the ornate drawing accompanying the passage. Underneath the snake were runes and a sentence that read *the hidden visitor*. I continued flipping through the book and stopped when I saw writings on The Puring.

Father had told me a little of the Dark Wars and how they resulted in The Puring. Magic fascinated me. Over three hundred years ago, magic entered our world. No one understood it, and everyone was terrified. The Order had begun hunting mages, afraid they would take control of Tarrtainya. They had discovered blood crystals, a red stone that could disrupt magic, and they used the stones to subdue the mages.

The hunted fought back.

Then, The Order created the Blood Knights, whose sole purpose was to capture or kill mages. The war destroyed the lands on the western shores and it lasted three bloody years. Ever since then, magic had been controlled by The Order. If you had the ability to wield magic, and you were smart, you'd hide. Magic was a curse.

The book didn't have any maps. The old tales about Daath suggested it disappeared into the East Sea after a terrible quake. Many men had died trying to climb Nod Mountains in search of the treasured land, said to have mystical plants and wonders unimaginable. Anyone that had ventured into the East Sea never returned.

I flipped back to the text and carefully re-read the tale. I gagged when I reached a part about a man and a woman and a line about starless nights. I slammed the book shut and banged my head against it. I didn't have time for stupid love stories.

"Have you found what you're looking for?" said a voice.

The priest who escorted me in stood above me. His wooden emblem hung around his neck.

"No. All that's in here are useless stories. I need answers!" My voice echoed around the cramped room.

"Perhaps those answers can be found elsewhere," he said, clearly asking me to leave.

"Perhaps."

Back upstairs, I aimlessly zigzagged through the wooden pews. I passed the confessional and stopped. In order to give an offering at the altar, one had to speak with the priest first. Every temple had a high priest. One that would sit, listen to your confession, then allow you into the altar chamber.

I thought back to all the men I'd killed. I entered the scarlet curtain and plopped down on the hard bench.

"Yes, child?" the priest asked.

I cleared my throat. "I have come to confess."

"What is your sin, my son?"

I wiped my forehead and grabbed one of my marbles. "I killed someone, well, a few people."

When the priest didn't respond, I continued. "I had no choice."

"We are always given a choice. It is up to us to make the right one."

I leaned against the dark wood and thought of banging my head against it. Why had I walked in here? I didn't need a lecture. Trying to convince the priest, and myself, I explained my reasons. "My sister was kidnapped. The only people I've killed are the ones who took her and any that try to stop me from finding her."

"Saving your sister is indeed a noble cause. There will be many obstacles on the way, but how you rise above those obstacles is what separates you from everyone else. Do you think killing everything in your path will make it easier?"

I frowned. I already knew the answer to that. If anything, it made it harder. Killing wasn't as glorious as I had imagined. It made me sick, but I had no choice. Jeslyn's life depended on it.

"Have you prayed to The Creator for guidance?"

The priest couldn't see, but I was rolling my eyes. "I don't believe in The Creator," I muttered.

"That is unfortunate because he believes in you. May The Creator bless you on your quest. You may enter the chamber."

That's it? I sat there feeling awkward and unfulfilled. A part of me expected the priest to say I was forgiven and I only did what was necessary. The air in the wooden booth became hot, and my chest tightened. I pushed back the curtain and stepped out.

Another priest stood in front of the arched door leading to the altar room. He nodded and allowed me to pass.

Sweat tickled my neck. This was a stupid idea.

The altar room was an empty round chamber with a stone shelf and a giant likeness of The Creator against the far wall. There was something intimidating about that giant statue. The face resembled a lion but the body was man with giant arched wings.

On the shelf sat a stone basin filled with water, candles surrounding it. A golden pitcher on the right and left of it. The floor beneath the altar had been covered with tokens: coins, flowers, crafted figurines.

The only thing I had to offer was one of my marbles.

I took out the pouch and opened it, remembering when my mother brought it home from the market. It was the best gift she had ever given me. The marbles were black with swirls of red. I took one and placed it on the pile of tokens.

Next, I was supposed to take a candle and light one of the unlit candles. I grabbed one from the holder. Wax dripped onto my hand and I dropped the candle.

"Ouch."

It landed right on top of a cotton figured token. Lighting it.

"No," I said, and stomped it out before the flame caught something else.

Not only did I stomp on a bunch of The Creator's tokens, but the priest walked in right as I was doing it.

"Sorry," I said. "I dropped the candle."

The priest's mouth hung open as if I had desecrated the entire place.

Time to go. I hurried past the flabbergasted priest and back into the main chamber.

Sunlight filtered through the openings on the temple walls. The arched doorway leading outside seemed farther than I remembered. Long chords flowing from the organ filled the temple. Each note sounded ominous, and I walked faster, trying to escape the judging room.

When I reached a comfortable distance, I took a deep breath and thought about my failed attempt at an offering. I didn't believe The Creator would help us. Could you be cursed for disrupting an altar? I hoped not. I had enough bad luck.

We were out of Crain Village and heading towards Nod Mountains when I realized I'd left my pack. I groaned and turned Brushfire around.

"I forgot my pack in the Temple," I said. "You guys keep going. I'll catch up."

"I'll go with you," Derrick said.

I nodded, and we raced back.

My pack was in the confessional. I could tell Derrick wanted to ask me a bunch of annoying questions. I held up my hand in protest. When we walked outside, Jericho was on his horse, racing up the hill.

We immediately mounted our horses.

"What's wrong? Where are the others?" Derrick said.

"There's been an attack," Jericho said in a grave voice.

My stomach dropped. "What happened?"

"After you left, a group of bandits came; they were looking for you two," Jericho said, his eyes shifting from me to Derrick.

No. "We have to hurry!"

Jericho guided his horse in front of mine. "Rudy told me to get you two out of here. They will hold the bandits off."

"I don't care what he said," I argued, "we can't leave them— Derrick?"

Derrick nodded. "I'm with you. It's our fault they're in danger."

Jericho rode closer to us. "Rudy and the others are risking their lives so you two can escape. Don't let their sacrifice be in vain!"

"And you expect us to trust you?" Derrick glared at him.

"No, but do you think those men would've allowed me to escape?"

No, they wouldn't have.

"Come, there's not much time." Jericho didn't wait for us to respond. He galloped away, and we followed.

We didn't stop riding until the next morning. The horses needed to rest and we needed water. During our ride, I told Jericho about the dart. His face paled. He said it belonged to his captain. A sure sign that his return would bring a lot of questions.

"What happens when we get to Daath? Won't they wonder why you're back? You did say they tried to kill you." Derrick folded his arms, glaring at Jericho.

"I'll take you to my house; it's on the outskirts of town. I have friends in the guard I can trust. I'll speak with them first."

"What do you plan on telling them?" I said.

Jericho dipped his hands into the stream and drank before answering. "That it's time for a rebellion. Lucino has oppressed us for too long. It's time Daath became free."

A rebellion? I just wanted to save my sister, not the whole forsaken town!

"We don't want part in your war," Derrick said. "Jeslyn is the only reason we're going."

Jericho looked at us. "There's something you need to know about Lucino … he's not human."

CHAPTER TWENTY-SIX

JESLYN

Soft light slipped through the arched windows, basking the room in a warm glow. I heard the clink of a serving tray, the opening of the curtains. A petite servant girl with shiny blue eyes said, "Good morning".

Three days had passed since I ate dinner with Lucino, and only once had he visited me. I spent a good portion of the time walking the beautiful grounds. His gardens were massive and intoxicating. I'd no difficulty losing myself in their splendor.

I'd been thinking much, wondering where Avikar and Derrick were. I prayed daily for their safety. I knew they were searching for me, but I had little hope they'd find Daath. If Lucino was kind enough to send word to my family, he might send someone to search for Derrick and Avikar. Yes, I would ask Lucino as soon as I saw him.

The servant politely ushered me out of bed and over to a small table covered with food. I sat on a large cushioned chaise and eyed the assortment of fresh fruits, cheese and roasted figs—a delicacy back home.

Since my arrival, I'd indulged in various delectable treats, foods that melted on my tongue and tasted of a hundred flavors. At home, the only time I experienced anything other than rue and leavened bread was during a festival. I closed my eyes and bit into one of the sweet figs. The soft meaty taste reminded me of pear and apple with a hint of honey.

The servant bustled around the room, making the bed and picking my robe off the floor. I wanted to ask her if Lucino would visit with me, but she moved around the room, cleaning, and avoiding me. Watching the girl work filled me with longing. I dreamt of a life filled with riches, servants and the pleasantries of wealth. Was I wrong to want more than my parents could ever give me? I loved my family, but this place called to my every wish.

Lucy entered the room wearing another low cut dress. The bodice hugged her curvy frame, and I wondered if a gown that size could ever fit me, even though it was very improper.

"I'm assuming a girl your age knows how to ride a horse?" Lucy asked, rummaging through the massive wardrobe.

She speaks to me as if I'm a child and she's a woman. She cannot be that much older than me. I nodded, remembering my manners.

"Good," Lucy said. "Now get undressed."

I slipped out of my chemise and covered myself with my arms while the servant brought a pile of clothing. The girl helped me into a petal pink dress and asked me to turn around. With a sharp tug, the servant laced the back of the bodice.

"Tighter," Lucy said while standing behind me.

The servant pulled again, and I thought my chest would break in two. I gasped as she forced every breath out of me.

"That will do," Lucy said. "We'll need to fix that tangled mess on top of your head."

Lucy pushed me onto a seat and began pinning my hair and dabbing powders and perfumes over my body. When she finished, I stared in the mirror at the reflection of a girl much too pretty to be me.

We walked outside to where Lucino sat on top of a black steed, outfitted in a black and crimson riding outfit. The fitted jacket hugged his muscular frame, flattering every beautiful feature. He looked regal and confident.

The white stallion next to him had delicate flowers threaded through its mane. I remembered what Mother said about the proper way to ride. I wished I'd practiced it more.

The servants hoisted me onto the mount, and I dangled my legs off the one side. I gripped the reins tightly, hoping I could ride in such an uncomfortable position. Before I could think of switching my legs, Lucino's horse took off in a gallop, and my stallion quickly followed.

The further into Daath we rode, the more enchanting it became. Spiraled around great trees were flowers redder than blood, more vibrant than amethyst. Musical birds cawed from high above. Their large calico wings fluttered in rhythm to their song.

I turned my gaze to the opposite side of the path and spotted a large furry creature, half-ferret and half-caterpillar, inching along an enormous branch that dipped to the forest floor. The small animal disappeared into a hole in the bark.

Could anything in Tarrtainya be more magnificent than this? Daath was more breathtaking than a butterfly's first flight. I wished Mother and Calli could see it. I prayed they would accept Lucino's offer, if only to see Daath.

The horses trotted down a winding path until it ended on white sand.

"Is this the sea?" My heart swelled with wonder.

"Yes, have you never seen it before?"

"Never like this," I replied, remembering the busy port at Luna Harbor where my grandfather lived.

Lucino hopped down from his mount and walked over to me. "Would you like a closer look?"

I smiled. "Oh, yes!"

He helped me off the horse and then tied the horses to a nearby tree. He removed his black boots and rolled up the bottom of his pants.

I slipped out of my slipper shoes and dug my toes into the sand, feeling the warmth. I wiggled my toes, enjoying the feel of the soft texture moving across them, and watched the distant waters lapping on the shore. I grabbed my dress, lifted it, and walked to the water's edge. The breeze blew through my hair, and I inhaled the salty scent. Aqua blue stretched before me with no end in sight.

"It's magnificent." With my eyes glued to the shining horizon, I stepped into the cool water. "Where are the waves?" Mother had shared bits of information about the sea, which I'd mostly forgotten, except the waves. I remembered her saying they were tremendous.

Lucino placed a supportive hand on my back. "The barrier reef stops them."

"What's a reef?"

His lip curled, and his blue eyes shined underneath the suns. "I'll show you."

I followed him down the beach to a rocky out cove. Tied to wooden poles were a handful of rowboats. He untied one and pushed it to the shore.

"Get in," he said.

I climbed into the boat and sat on one of the planks. With a few shoves, Lucino had us in the water, and he jumped into the boat. He grabbed two oars from the floor and rowed us out to sea.

With my hands folded in my lap, I watched him. He wasn't like other boys. He exuded nobility and power. He reminded me of Lord Tyre riding through our village. The first time I'd seen Lord and Lady Tyre I'd been overcome with envy. It didn't seem fair that they rode around in fine silks while I dressed in rags.

Lucino stopped, placed the oars on the bottom of the boat and smiled. "Look below us."

I peered over the side and gasped. Orange stone, surrounded by hundreds of bright colored fish, reached out in every direction.

"Where does this come from?"

Lucino explained the natural barrier in great detail. The stone he called coral was a living life form. Face aglow, he spoke about the community of fish, and he gladly answered my many questions.

"How come no one has found Daath? Surely many boats have tried."

"Yes, many do, and die. Past this barrier, the air wavers, and a man's perception, becomes distorted. They go in circles, lost beyond reason, until one of the whirlpools swallows them."

"That's horrid. Have you ever tried leaving?"

His gaze went past me, out into the open water. "I have a ... tool ... that allows me to navigate around the whirlpools and find the shores."

Fish swam under the boat. A turtle floated by, as large as a pig. I'd never imagined the sea could hold so many beautiful creatures. Each animal different than the next. And the colors. Different shades of reds, even purple. Mother never mentioned how colorful the sea was.

The touch of fabric hit my feet. I looked over at Lucino, barechested and beautiful. I knew I should avert my eyes, but besides my brother I'd never seen a man topless. Heat rushed over me in a vicious wave.

"What are you doing?" I asked.

He stood and put a foot on the edge of the boat.

"You're not going in there, are you?"

"Don't worry, my lady. I'll be back shortly. Stay in the boat, and you shall be safe."

Before I could reply, he dove in.

The wind was my only companion. Lucino had been gone too long. I rung my dress in my hands, and my left leg trembled. Instead of making a fuss over nothing, I kept my thoughts focused on the world below. I leaned over the side and dipped my hand into the sea, tracing my fingers across the surface, loving the refreshing feel.

A silver object appeared on the north side of the boat. I squinted, wondering what it might be. With my hand, I splashed the water, searching for the peculiar sight. I looked behind the boat and spotted a shape moving in the water. My eyes widened at the size of the creature as it swam past. I reached out and touched its smooth and slippery skin.

I smiled.

The fish disappeared again. I hoped it would return. I wanted to stroke it once more. I scooted to the opposite side, placing both hands on the ledge and peered into the water. Two similar shapes swam beneath me. I reached into the water attempting to catch the friendly creature.

Something slammed into the boat and I lurched forward. The boat rocked again and I slid away from the sides, my heart hammering louder than the waves. The rocking turned violent. I grabbed the edge for support.

"Lucino!"

The front of the boat popped out of the water, and I was thrown into the sea. Salt water filled my lungs and I swam to the surface, breaching right below the capsized boat. My dress weighed me down, threatening to send me to the sandy floor. One of the fish swam at me and bit the dress, dragging me away. I kicked my heel into its eye and it retreated, taking with it half my dress.

Three more grey shapes darted underneath me and to the side. I was scared of the dark and terrified of snakes, but nothing compared to the growing fear inside me now. I treaded water and tried to keep my head above the surface. The bodice that had desirably shrunk my waist now constricted me.

I didn't want to cry. I was afraid if I let one tear fall, I would panic. *Think of the prayer Mother said to use*, I thought. She said The Creator always protected his own if they called on him. I closed my eyes, forgetting the shiver of death grasping my skin or the monsters below, and whispered the words.

"Creator above, merciful and pure, surround me with your holy aura and protect me from those who would do me harm."

"Are you alright?"

I opened my eyes to see Lucino in front of me. I threw my arms around his neck and squeezed. "Thank The Creator!"

He pulled my arms off. "I need to flip the boat. Swim over there."

"No, I can't!"

He held my face with both hands and stared into my eyes. Again, that strange stormy image swirled inside his pupils. "Swim over there and wait for me. Go now!"

I took a deep breath and plunged back underwater. The salt stung my eyes, but I refused to close them. I glanced down and saw pools of crimson mixing with the sea.

Blood.

I vigorously swam through the water until my head reached the surface. "Help!"

The boat turned over, and Lucino appeared beside it. He swam to me, grabbed my waist and, in one swift movement, he hoisted me up and over. I fell onto the bottom of the boat and hugged my shivering body. Lucino returned with one of the oars and climbed in next to me.

"The blood," I whimpered. "I thought they'd killed you."

He looped my wet hair behind my ears.

"I killed them," he said, without the slightest hint of remorse.

CHAPTER TWENTY-SEVEN

LUCINO

When we arrived at the beach, Jeslyn sighed. I helped her onto the shore. I stepped back, examining her disheveled appearance. Humans never seemed to do well in difficult circumstances. A Reptilian female would never allow herself to look so disarrayed.

"You are an absolute mess," I said.

She looked at her tattered dress. It had been ripped in half, revealing her thin legs. She touched her messy hair and water sprung from her eyes. I wanted to be on our way, crying humans made me uncomfortable.

"Can you ride?" I asked.

She nodded, but her wavering steps proved her instability.

"Such a fragile creature you are." I swooped her into my arms and carried her to the horses. I tied her mount to mine, lifted her onto my horse then climbed into the saddle. She sat behind me and wrapped her arms around my waist. As we galloped back to my home, her small sobs faded into sniffles, then into heavy breathing.

We arrived at the mansion just before night—the hour I

preferred. The day had been strange. I sensed the dolphins' presence but the intelligent beings kept their distance from me. I assumed they'd been trying to take her away from me, not actually harm her. If she had known about the docile beings, she would not have been so terrified.

As she was still in no shape to walk, I carried Jeslyn inside. Willis greeted us at the entrance.

"Willis, take Jeslyn to her room."

"No, please," said Jeslyn, "don't leave me."

I held my irritation in as she clung to my neck. "Very well. I'll take her upstairs. Willis, have the servants prepare her a bath."

"Well, today was interesting." I glanced at her flushed face. Even with puffy rings around her eyes, she was still beautiful.

She buried her head into my chest as we walked up the curving staircase. The sensation invoked in me a strange emotion. I opened her bedroom door and walked inside, then gently placed her on the chaise and went to retrieve a towel from the washroom.

"Here."

I wrapped the towel around her shivering shoulders. One of the servants entered the room and curtsied. Then she began running the bathwater.

"Lucino." Jeslyn looked up at me and reached out her hand.

I knelt beside her, taking her hand in mine. "Yes, my lady?"

"Thank you, for saving me." Her lips parted as if she wanted to say more, but no words followed. She stared at me, cheeks flushing pink.

It seemed our little escapade had a positive effect on her. Interesting.

I could sense her wild emotions, bordering on admiration and passion. Her golden aura shone even brighter than before. I took out the black pearl I'd pulled from the sea floor and placed it in her hand.

"Is this what you dove for?" She rolled the pearl back and forth in her palm, eyes wide with intrigue.

I nodded.

"It's beautiful." She fell into my arms, hugging me. "Thank you."

A current spread across my chest as if the places she touched lit on fire. I placed my hands on her waist, pushing her away. I didn't know what magic she possessed, but I'd soon learn.

Lucino. Lucino?

Yes, Lucy, what is it now?

"The bath is ready, my lord," the servant said.

I helped Jeslyn to her feet. "I will see you at dinner," I said.

She nodded, and I left the room.

I received word from The Council, Lucy continued, *that the hunters they'd sent out were successful. The group who attacked the caravan has been eliminated.*

Very good.

I broke the connection before Lucy could drabble on. My sister tended to abuse our telepathic connection with nonsense, and I didn't have time for her. I needed to see if Romulus had finished the tonic I requested. He was always testing, testing, three trials were never enough and he had been on his fourth last I saw him. He'd better have completed the formula and prepared it for the ball.

CHAPTER TWENTY-EIGHT

AVIKAR

The sound of water rushed from behind the overgrown trees. The dirt path we were on curved and opened before a large lagoon. An enormous waterfall plunged from a hidden ridge high in Nod Mountains, a place where no man dared travel. The dark pool funneled into the adjacent river that continued west. Deep below the surface slept an ancient beast, a deadly creature who could eat Brushfire and I whole.

He isn't human.

My stomach twisted as I replayed those words over and over. Jericho told us the rumors circling around the guard about Lucino. One of them had seen Lucino transform into a monster, a kind of half-man, half-reptile. Soon after, the guard had mysteriously fallen ill and died. The rumor had stayed.

Jericho lead and slowly guided us around the lagoon. I knew it wasn't my best idea, but I had to see. I veered Brushfire closer to the water, trying to peek beneath the surface. I wondered if the beast was as big as Jericho claimed. I got my answer when I spotted its long white shedding on the grass. Suddenly, seeing the big snake didn't seem so important.

An arrow whizzed by my ear, scraping it. Brushfire neighed. I gripped the reins trying to steady her. "We're under attack!"

Derrick pulled out his sword and turned his horse around. We waited for another shot but none came.

"We need to get out of here," Jericho hissed.

I scanned the area, bow ready. If someone was out there, I'd find him. I closed my eyes, breathing in my surroundings, listening to everything.

A twig snapped.

There!

I opened my eyes and let the arrow fly. A scream followed and Derrick charged in the direction of the yell.

"It's one guy!" Derrick shouted as he jumped from his horse. "You got him in the arm!"

I rode up beside Derrick.

"Who are you?" I asked our attacker, my bow aimed at his head.

The man held his bleeding arm. He dressed in all black and tied around his head was a red cloth with strange writing on it.

Jericho shuddered. "That's one of Lucy's men, her personal guard. Tie him, quickly."

Derrick grabbed rope from his pack.

"Did you say Lucy?" I asked.

"Yes, why?"

"Does she have black hair and gorgeous legs?"

Jericho's brow furrowed. "How do you know her?"

I rubbed my forehead. "We met her in Bogtown. She put us under a spell."

"If she's tracking you, we're in great danger. We'll take him with us. He can't be allowed to report back. Once we get into Daath, we'll question him."

Derrick yanked the man to his feet. He tied the guard's hands and looped the rope to the back of the saddle. "We're all set," he said and hopped onto his mount.

Jericho continued to navigate us through the dangerous pass.

Brushfire whinnied, and I patted her mane. "It's okay girl."

She whinnied again. Cold traveled up my back.

The prisoner screamed. I turned around and watched a gigantic snake snap its mouth over him.

Derrick slashed the rope still connected to his horse.

"No!" Jericho screamed. "The seal must be broken! Run!"

I heard him, but I couldn't move. The snake's head had to be the length of Brushfire's body. It was impossible for anything that large to exist! The snake dragged the man under water and disappeared.

"Avikar, *move*!" Derrick yelled. "What are you doing!"

I thought of the grizzly bear I'd seen while hunting with my father, how large I'd thought that was. But this … I'd never seen anything like it. I pulled on the reins, but kept my eyes on the water.

Brushfire halted. I heard Jericho curse. The tail of the snake blocked our path. It thrashed around, making it impossible to cross.

Jericho reversed his mount. "We can't get through."

"Is there another way into Daath?" Derrick asked.

Jericho shook his head. "There's a tunnel system, but with my seal broken, we won't be able to pass through any of the magical barriers—I don't understand how it happened. It can only be removed by magic."

It didn't matter how the seal broke. We only had one option. "We have to kill it."

I knew our chances of living through this would be slim, but we had to try. "Jericho, you're sure there's no other way?"

"None that I know of."

"We have no choice then." My hands shook as I strung the bow. The more I pictured the giant snake, the more they shook.

I thought back to my tenth birthday. Father had promised to take me hunting. I'd stayed awake all night packing and thinking about all the wild animals I'd kill. In the morning, I'd practically run out the door. Father had taken me deep into the woods where the elk lived.

After a few hours, we'd found one. He'd instructed me on how to aim the bow, but I couldn't stop shaking.

As we crouched in the brush, he placed a strong hand on my shoulder. "Take five slow breaths, in and out. When you reach five, shoot."

I imagined my father here with me now, and counted. When I got to five, the shaking stopped.

The snake was nowhere in sight, the forest eerily silent. The horses shifted and bellowed. I scanned the trees.

A large red shape slithered behind Derrick.

I tried to call out a warning, but my voice disappeared. I watched in horror as the snake grabbed my best friend. Derrick screamed and twisted, but it was useless. The beast coiled around his body and began squeezing. I was going to lose everyone I loved. I was going to die, and the last thing I'd see would be Derrick's broken body.

"Now, Avikar. Shoot its eye!"

Glancing back, I saw Jericho stab the snake's tail with his sword.

I released the arrow and watched it drive straight into the snake's eye. A perfect shot. The snake recoiled a little, giving Derrick enough room to pull out his arm, and he slashed the body with his sword.

Snapping out of my daze, I jumped off Brushfire, loaded another arrow and shot. I ran to Derrick. If he could cut the snake a few more times, we might make it. The arrows did little damage. The snake's scales created a tough natural armor.

Large beady eyes focused on me, and a long forked tongue hissed as the snake slithered forward. Its massive head lurched at me, but I dove to the side. Dropping my bow, I pulled out my sword.

Jericho roared from our far right, still hacking away at the monstrous tail. For one split second, the snake turned his attention to Jericho. Derrick's muscles twitched and bulged as he tried to push the coiled body away. I grabbed one side and tried to help, but even with our combined strength, it wasn't enough.

"Move your hands!" I yelled. I raised the sword above my head and slashed through flesh. A loud screech erupted from the snake as it turned its attention back to me.

"Again!" Derrick urged.

I got in three more strikes before the snake lunged at me. I fell backward, and the beast's large mouth opened to reveal two dripping fangs, descending towards me. I thrust the sword into the pink maw. The snake thrashed violently, attempting to dislodge the metal toothpick as it withdrew back into the lagoon.

I can't believe we survived that. I thought we were dead.

I caught my breath and stood, brushing the dirt off my pants. "Everyone all right?"

Jericho splashed into the water.

What's he doing? I looked around and realized someone was missing. Derrick.

I ran to the bank and froze. An image of Jimri's dead body flickered through my mind.

If I'd been in the water with Jimri, he would've been fine. You knew how to swim Jimri. What happened?

"Avikar!" Jericho yelled, "we don't have much time. I'll distract the beast while you free Derrick. Hurry!"

My body moved on its own, racing forward and diving into the water. The water stung my eyes as I searched its greenish hues. The cloudy mixture made it hard to see. I swam deeper until I could make out the large ruby scales.

Small bubbles traveled to the surface, lighting a direct path to Derrick. I followed the trail to where Derrick struggled against the coiled body. I took out my dagger and sawed at the top coil. Whatever distraction Jericho provided, worked. I didn't see that deathly head anywhere. The dagger shred through, splitting the snake open, and Derrick pulled himself out.

I grabbed the back of his shirt and swam upward. My chest burned. I kicked my legs faster, reaching the surface. I gasped.

To my side, Derrick lay unconscious and floating.

NO! I wrapped my arm under him and swam us out of the lagoon, then hauled him out onto dry land.

"Derrick, wake up!" I slapped him across each cheek. His head flopped lazily to the side. I shook his body. "Derrick!"

"Move!" Jericho pushed me aside. He tilted Derrick's head back, opening his mouth. He breathed three slow breaths into Derrick and pumped his palms vigorously against Derrick's chest. He counted to thirty and did it again. Derrick lay still.

Don't die. Don't die. Please, don't die. Oh, Creator, please! I clenched the top of my thighs, and rocked back and forth. *Don't die. You can't die. Please. PLEASE.*

In phlegm-ridden coughs, Derrick spat water. Jericho rolled him on his side and slapped his back, getting it all out. Jericho leaned back on his legs.

Derrick sat up and rubbed his chest. "I hate snakes."

I laughed and wiped my eyes with the back of my hand. "Too bad, I had a nice one all boxed at home for your birthday."

Derrick chuckled, but I knew he was spooked. That was too close.

"Come, before the beast returns." Jericho helped Derrick to his feet. With a sharp whistle, Brushfire returned, followed by the other horses. We continued into the lightless caverns of Nod Mountains. The cavern was narrow, dark and smelled like moss and sulfur. Stalagmites ranging from six to ten feet tall rose from the ground reaching towards a ceiling unseen. The sound of dripping water created a constant drumming. I had never been in a cavern like this. Being surrounded by stone was a strange feeling, not one I liked.

"B-U-R-P."

The belch echoed off the cavern walls. My head whipped back around to Derrick, who rubbed his belly.

He frowned. "I think that snake upset my stomach."

"Cover your heads!" Jericho called out.

Hundreds of bats swarmed down on us. I threw up my hood and pulled out my sword. Bat after bat came at us and the horses.

Holding my sword double-fisted and high above my head, I swung it around in one big circle. The horses panicked, kicking their back legs. I closed my hood tighter and focused my swings on the bats nearest Brushfire. I could already see little nicks of blood where the bats had scratched her.

Stupid rodents!

For every bat I killed, another took its place. I thought our journey would end at the hand of vermin, but after a few minutes of chaos, the bats disappeared back into the shadows.

"Everyone okay?" Jericho asked, brushing off the guano on his arms.

I glanced back at Derrick, who was heaving.

"Fine here," Derrick replied in raspy breaths, "although, I don't think I can take any more near-death experiences."

My stomach rolled with nerves, and then I noticed the large red bite mark on the tip of Derrick's nose, and laughed. Derrick rubbed his nose in aggravation.

"Let's get out of here before those bats decide to come back," Jericho said, taking the lead. "We still have two days travel before we reach Daath, and I don't want to stay in these caverns a moment longer than we need to."

Chapter Twenty-Nine

Jeslyn

I swirled my finger in the fountain, watching the ripples. I never thought I could be bored in such a beautiful place. I decided it was time to do more than stare at the sky all day. Reginald, the guard assigned to watch over me, stiffly followed as I walked through the gardens. He was quite a nuisance. Never speaking, but always watching.

Tall shrubbery blocked my path. Two marble statues of dragons, I think, guarded the entrance. Their dark expressions didn't fit with the enchanted surroundings. I cautiously walked past them, entering the giant maze. Reginald followed.

The green walls of the maze rose to the sky. They were at least triple my height. I turned around with a fabulous idea. "Oh, my, look! What a magnificent creature!" I pointed behind Reginald, who turned.

"Where? I don't see anything?" Reginald said.

I hoisted up my dress and ran. A moment's distraction, but enough for me to get a head start.

"Lady Jeslyn!"

I turned left and then right, giggling as the cries of my watcher decreased. Wind caressed my cheeks with my quick steps. I felt free. I knew I'd most likely be scolded for this, but I didn't care. For the first time in weeks, I was on my own.

The maze twisted and bent. I let it take me wherever it wanted. Dead ends forced me to double back more than once, but I was finally rewarded with a secret cove.

Beautiful.

In the center sat a giant willow tree surrounded by wildflowers. I caught my breath and stepped into the luscious garden.

"Not many people are able to find this place." Lucino sat on a bench nearly hidden within the green surroundings.

"What are you doing here?"

"I come here when I need to think. Walking the maze can be daunting and no one bothers to search for me once I enter." He stood, eyeing me with curiosity. "How did you find your way here?"

I thought back to my run and shrugged. "I'm not sure. I ran in the direction the maze took me."

He grinned.

My heart raced with exertion and bliss as he stepped closer. Since our day at the sea, I hadn't been able to stop thinking about him. How he looked, painted against the stunning waters, and how he rescued me from those vicious animals. I knew these feelings were wrong, and I tried to push the desire away. Yet it stayed, tugging me in every direction.

"Is that why your face is flushed? And I thought it was because of me," he said, stroking the left side of my cheek. "I'm glad you found me. I have something for you."

He handed me a scroll.

I snatched the letter out of his hand and carefully unrolled it. "It's from my mother!"

Dearest daughter,
I cannot tell you how relieved we are you are safe. We have been worried sick

since your disappearance. Lord Lucino's courier explained everything. What a horrible misunderstanding! I pray Lord Lucino disciplines those responsible.

As for your engagement … I always dreamed of my sweet girl marrying a lord and now it's happening. And to think Daath really exists. It's all so wonderful. We are overjoyed and give you our blessing. Due to your father's current work, we will not be able to come see you until after the summer season. I wish we could visit sooner. I miss you terribly.

Stay safe, and enjoy the ball, darling. We love you very much.

"What does she say?" Lucino asked.

My hands clenched the sides of the paper. "She says, she's thankful I'm safe, they miss me terribly and would love to come but can't … she says to enjoy the ball and they give me their blessing …"

"That's wonderful." He followed me to the bench.

I stared at the letter, re-reading Mother's words. What did the courier say? I never agreed to marriage and yet she wrote as if it was a certain thing.

"What's wrong, my lady?"

"I wasn't expecting that. I thought she would want me home. She doesn't even know you."

Gently, he placed his hand over mine. "Every father and mother wants the best for their child, and I can give that to you."

My eyes watered. "She said nothing of my brother. Isn't she concerned for him?" I looked to Lucino, who seemed thrown by the statement.

"Your brother?"

"Yes. When I was kidnapped, he and his friend went looking for me. They were at the attack when your captain took me back here. I didn't mention it in the letter; although, I should have. I need to find him."

Lucino sat very quiet. I watched his face, searching for a response, but his expression was stone, imparting nothing.

"He could be anywhere."

"Please, I need to know he's safe." I squeezed Lucino's hand forcing his attention back to me. "Do this for me, and I will be forever grateful. I don't want anything to happen to him."

"Very well, my lady." Lucino stood. "If you'll excuse me. I must leave you for now, but I will send some men out to look for your brother. I'll have Lucy get the details from you."

"Thank you, my lord," I said, bowing my head and watching him disappear into the maze.

CHAPTER THIRTY

JESLYN

Lucino had been pre-occupied the past two days, but I could wait no longer.

"Reginald, I need to speak with Lucino, immediately."

"As you wish my lady. I believe he's training."

"I don't care. Now, Reginald."

"As you wish, my lady." Reginald walked down the corridor. I followed.

Even after spending time here, I still couldn't navigate the twisty mansion. A secret stairway here. A locked door there. I had gotten lost once and never tried again. Although, I couldn't place the fear, the mansion frightened me. A strange darkness hovered over everything, including the silent servants.

We walked down a stone curved stairwell leading deep into the mansion. The sounds of fighting echoed up towards us. Reginald opened the oak door and we entered into a sparring match.

Lucino fought another man. His bare skin glistened with sweat and he shouted as he thrust his sword forward. There was no doubting his beauty, and my own heart betrayed me by beating faster. I shouldn't stare at such a sight. A proper lady would avert her eyes.

"Jeslyn?" Lucino stopped once he saw me, flicking his partner away. Willis handed him a towel, and Lucino wiped his face.

"Sorry to interrupt, but may we speak?" I kept my eyes away from his bare chest.

"Of course." Lucino waved the other servants and guards away, including Reginald.

I clasped my hands together and waited while Lucino drank from a nearby mug.

"Do you have news of my brother?"

Lucino stood, wiping his mouth with the back of his hands. His look chilled me.

"I meant to see you later," he said softly.

"What is it? What do you know?"

He stepped closer. "I'm sorry, Jeslyn. There was an attack on one of the villages. Your brother and his friend are dead."

No.

"You lie!" My legs crumbled.

Lucino's hands caught me before I reached the ground. "I'm sorry. We arrived too late. There was nothing we could do."

My brother … the boy who teased me and put a frog in my bed was gone. I'd never hear his loud boisterous laugh or his constant grumbling. Another brother lost.

Tears filled my eyes. "No, this can't be. It's a mistake!"

"Let me escort you back to your room." Lucino guided me, and I walked in a daze.

"I am sorry for your loss," he said, his arm holding me up. "If there's anything I can do."

"I want to go home."

"Of course, my lady."

CHAPTER THIRTY-ONE

AVIKAR

Well, boys, welcome to paradise."

The sight of the painted landscape made me forget about everything. Scarlet and cerulean hues covered the rolling hills. I slid off Brushfire, bent down and picked a sunset-colored flower out of the flowing grass. I lifted it to my nose and inhaled. It smelled like honey. My hand grazed the silky wildflowers covering almost every inch of the area. Closing my eyes, I breathed in the dewy scent of fresh rain. The tranquility of the terrain pulsed around me. Every thought vanished as I let Daath pull me into her essence. I belonged here. I didn't know why, but I felt it in my bones.

"We need to move," Jericho said.

I picked another flower, inhaling its honey scent. I twirled it around, examining the bright red petals. In the valley, every flower, blade of grass and small tree became alive. I watched the landscape breathe. In and out. In and out. An invisible weight pressed against my chest and warmth spread through me. I needed to lie down for a minute. I spread out my arms as I lay on the grass, watching Derrick stretch and grin.

Jericho grabbed me by the shirt, pulling me away from my nice, soft bed and forced me onto Brushfire.

What's gotten in to him?

He snatched the flower out my hand, threw it away and dashed over to Derrick.

"Hey!" I reached for my falling flower. "Why did you do that?"

"Because those are deadly," he said while struggling to get Derrick on his horse. "It's one of Daath's natural defenses. If you fall asleep here, you'll never wake up." He slapped Brushfire's backside, and we took off, leaving the beautiful valley far behind.

We approached a two-story cottage with a thatched roof. A petite woman worked in the garden on the side of the house. She looked up when we were close.

She dropped her spade, dusted off her hands and ran towards us. "Jericho!"

Jericho jumped off his horse, and she threw her arms around him.

"Hello, Anna." He hugged and kissed her.

"I was worried when you didn't come back. No one knew what happened. Where have you been?"

"It's a long story, but first, I'd like you to meet Derrick and Avikar."

She turned to us and smiled. "Hello boys."

"Hello," we both said.

"I ran into them on the road," Jericho said. "They saved my life. They wanted to see Daath. I thought it was a fair trade and invited them to stay with us."

Anna's smile faded. "Jericho, you know visitors are forbidden. What if someone notices? You'll be executed!"

"Everyone will be busy with the summer festival. You forget how big Daath is, dear. If anyone asks, I'll say they're from the shores."

Anna cringed. "Those people are savages, but they do keep their distance." She sighed. "Very well, you boys come inside and I'll fix you something to eat."

Anna served pork that had been smoked and glazed with apple. It was the most amazing thing I'd ever tasted. Derrick ate a good portion of the pork and half of the almond bread. Back home, we ate rue, lots and lots of rue. There were other things, like beans, potatoes, fanna, but never anything as delicious as this.

After we ate, Jericho showed us to a room upstairs where we could sleep. Derrick threw himself onto one of the cots. "It feels like forever since I slept in a bed," he said. "We'll sleep well tonight."

I sat across from him, untying my weathered boots. "Not me," I muttered.

Derrick laced his arms behind his head. "Still having nightmares?"

I leaned against the wall, thinking about the drowning dreams and the spirit that attacked me before battle. "Yes."

"Want to talk about it?"

I crossed my arms. "Not really."

"We've been friends since we were kids. I know how hard Jimri's death was for you, but talking about it would help. It's okay to cry. Here rest your head, little one." He rolled his shoulder in my direction.

Is he kidding me?

"Don't give me that look. We can talk about our feelings and cry our eyes out until morning. Oh, it will be splendid!" Derrick's voice ended in a girlish pitch, and he cradled his hands to his chest.

I threw a pillow at his head, but he ducked and it just missed him.

"You've been hanging around my sister too much," I said.

"Probably," he huffed. "I still can't believe we're staying with her kidnapper."

"The man saved your life!"

"This has to be the stupidest thing we've ever done."

I smirked, remembering all the trouble we used to cause. "What about the time we sneaked in on Susan Beatrice?"

Derrick grinned. "That was only stupid because we got caught."

And, boy, did we get caught. "I know working with Jericho feels wrong, but what choice do we have, and after what he did today, well, he's okay."

"I don't care that he saved me. It doesn't excuse what he did." Derrick stared at the ceiling. "We have to find her."

"We will. We were lucky. I don't know how we would've found Daath on our own."

"I know," Derrick murmured. "I'm going to sleep. Try and get some yourself." Derrick pulled the blanket over his head and rolled onto his stomach.

Leaning against the wall, I thought about Jeslyn—my annoying, good girl sister who I loved to prank. We used to be closer when we were younger, but after Jimri's death, and Derrick courting her … we grew apart. Unimaginably, I actually missed her nagging.

Sitting in Jericho's house, my head spun. I wanted to hate him, but he saved Derrick. If Jericho wasn't there, I would've been responsible for another death.

"Ugh, what is that smell?" I covered my nose and bolted towards the window.

Derrick chuckled.

"Derrick, what did you eat?"

"Not sure. I ate a lot. Uh-oh, hold your breath."

I poked my head out the window. "No more pork for you, or you're sleeping in the barn."

"I'm nice and relaxed." Derrick yawned.

I fanned the putrid air outside, wishing I was sleeping in another room.

CHAPTER THIRTY-TWO

AVIKAR

Jericho took us into town. He planned to talk to one of the other guards, who he swore was a loyal friend. He had wanted us to stay at his house, hiding, while he investigated. Derrick nearly cleaved off his head after that suggestion, and Jericho agreed to bring us with him. He gave us a quick overview of the surrounding area and told us not to bring any attention to ourselves.

Derrick and I headed towards the crowded market. The air smelled of fresh bread, reminding me of home. Houses made of green and orange mosaics with curved archways and round windows loomed on each side of the cobblestone street. Roofs resembling dragon scales created a unique architecture.

While we walked, I rolled one of my marbles in my hand. I didn't trust anyone and this place seemed otherworldly. Every townsfolk seemed either strong and tall, or lithe and beautiful. Women dressed in bright colors filled the street. I'd never seen so much color in one place. I caught the sight of a girl with mesmerizing green eyes. Derrick said something, but I was locked in her hypnotic gaze and voluptuous chest.

I bumped into a hard structure.

Stupid. I grinned at the girl, pretending I did it on purpose—I don't think she believed it. When I looked at the obtrusive object, a large snake head stared back. I grabbed my sword and jumped away from it.

"That's from that snake cult," Derrick said.

"What cult?" I stepped around the statue.

Derrick scrunched his brow. "My father got a shipment of weapons from Crain Village. A lot of it had that emblem. Father said a serpent cult was spreading, very big in Lord Belfur and Lord Thebas' regions."

A serpent cult? I remembered the strange girls from Crain Village, chanting, and the symbol drawn on the wall and in the book. The symbol I saw in Crain Village bore a striking resemblance to this statue, but how could that be? No one else in Tarrtainya knew Daath existed. It had to be a coincidence.

I tightened the hood on my cape. "Let's keep looking around."

We veered off the main street and headed down a cobbled alley. The town was designed as one big maze with the market as the center. The side streets were narrow and twisted into dead ends.

I heard yelling and held out my arm to stop Derrick. I pointed ahead and we crept forward. Around the bend, two men cornered a slender girl and a big shaggy dog. The dog growled, but the girl seemed calm.

"Don't be afraid little lady, we won't bite."

The girl glared back. "But I do. *Now* Bruno!" The dog bolted at the nearest man, grabbed his leg and shook his head back and forth.

"Ahh, get him off me, he's biting!" His friend ignored the plea and met the girl head on.

She charged, and when she was in range, kicked out her right leg, sweeping the thug off his feet. The fall knocked the wind out of him, and before he could get up, she planted her black boot on his throat.

I stepped into view. "Nicely handled. I'm impressed. I thought we were going to have to save you."

Her doe like eyes peered curiously at me. "As you can see, I can take care of myself," she replied. "Down Bruno."

Bruno let go of the man's leg and she took her foot off the other. The two men ran shamefully down the alleyway. Bruno trotted back to her and she rubbed his floppy ear.

"You two don't look familiar. Where are you from?"

I glanced back at Derrick who suddenly looked vexed. "My name is Avikar and this is Derrick. We don't often come to this part of town."

Her face scrunched. "I'm pretty good with faces, and I know almost everyone my age."

"We came from the shores," Derrick said.

That seemed to pique her interest. "The Shores? We never get visitors from there. My name's Raven. Nice to meet you." She smiled.

A smile like that could change a man's heart.

She had smoky brown eyes with big curled lashes and long straight hair. Just my type, and she was the first girl I'd met who didn't wear a dress. I never thought a girl could look cute in a pair of tight-fitted breeches.

"And this," she said, patting the dog's shaggy head, "is Bruno."

Bruno barked.

Derrick leaned over to me and whispered, "Whip out that charm of yours and learn what you can about Lucino. I'll meet you at Jericho's later."

Easy.

"What brings you to town?" Raven said. "I thought the shore people never left their homes?"

I slipped my hands into my pockets and took a step towards her. "We grew curious. Derrick and I were venturing here when we ran into a local who offered us a place to stay."

She folded her arms and eyed me suspiciously. "Who?"

I ran my hand through the front of my hair. "You probably don't know him."

Her lips pursed. Apparently, some fast talking was called for.

"Jericho, didn't catch his last name," I said.

Her button nose crinkled. "Jericho? He's back?"

She knows him? What are the chances of that? Keep calm.

"Is something wrong?" I asked.

Raven bit her bottom lip which made me realize she had very nice lips. "I don't understand. I thought he was dead?" she murmured.

"Dead, why would you think that?"

Her eyes darted left then right. "We can't talk here, follow me."

Raven led me out of the town and into the nearby woods. I kept my hand on my sword just in case she tried to attack.

The woods opened. In its midst was a giant lake.

Raven breathed in and stretched out her arms. "I love this place. It's peaceful. We can talk safely here."

My eyes fixated on the immense lake in horror. Tall drooping trees surrounded the dark water; a sight too familiar. There could be no peace in a place this monstrous. I imagined Jimri running around laughing ... then his still body floating on the water.

"Avi, you promised we'd go swimming," Jimri had moaned.

"Go play, Jimri," I said while circling Derrick.

"But, Avi ..."

I groaned. "Jimri, the tournament is next week. We need to practice. It won't take long. Now, go away or I'm never bringing you with us again."

Jimri frowned and wandered off.

"Don't go far!" I yelled.

Derrick watched Jimri walk away. "We should let the little guy join in. Teach him a few tricks."

"I should have just left him home," I grumbled. "Let's get a few rounds in before he annoys me again."

I closed my eyes. I didn't want to remember. But no matter how hard I tried, the facts stayed the same: my little brother died because I didn't care enough to play with him.

Invisible daggers ripped at my stomach in a repeating crescendo. I wasn't ready to face this, especially around some girl I was supposed to be questioning.

A gentle hand touched my arm. "Are you okay?"

My hand clenched my belly as a sharp pain dug into my side. "I'm fine." I don't think she believed me, but I couldn't tell her the truth. I scanned the area. "Mind if we sit over there?" I pointed to an old weeping willow.

"Sure."

Bruno ran off and jumped in the water while we sat beneath the tree. Raven plopped down and leaned against the trunk.

"I come here when I want to be alone. It's serene, plus Bruno likes the water." A duck squawked and Bruno swam after it.

I rubbed a knuckle against my chest, hoping the tight pain would go away. I sat with my back facing the lake. If I couldn't see it, it wasn't there. I played with the dipping leaves hanging off a nearby branch which did nothing to steady my erratic pulse.

Raven sighed. In feathered waves, long strands of her hair blew with the wind.

Focus on her, forget where you are.

A lone dandelion stood out of the grass. Raven plucked it from the ground and twirled it between her slender fingers. "I overheard the guards talking the other day."

"What did you hear?"

She bit her bottom lip. "They said the supply caravan was attacked and they lost all the men, except the captain who narrowly escaped. Jericho was one of those proclaimed dead. The guards were waiting to tell the families until after a full investigation. It doesn't make sense. Why would they lie?"

I ripped in two the leaf I pulled from the tree. "That's pretty strange. Whatever they were talking about, I wouldn't dwell on it.

He's home now. That's all that matters, right?"

"You're right." A small smile formed on her lips. "Tell me how you met Jericho. It's rare we see anyone from the shores. You're not what I expected."

"What do you know about the shores?"

She shrugged. "Not much, just that you're wild savages who live by the sea far up north. Anyone who has tried to venture that way, never returns."

"We tend to stay to ourselves, but as you can see, I'm no savage."

She grabbed her hair and twisted it in her hands. "The shores are nowhere near Jericho's home. What was he doing that far North?"

Leaning over, I motioned her closer with my finger. She moved until there was only a small space between us. The wind blew her hair into my face. She quickly snatched it back, leaving behind a scent of honey and oatmeal in the air.

I stared into her doe eyes, my lip curling into a grin. "It's a secret, and I can't share that kind of information with just anyone. We should get to know each other better, first."

She crossed her arms. "Playing hard to get?"

I gave her a big smile. "Always."

She uncrossed her arms and laughed. "You're good. I have to admit. Charming and cute are a deadly combination, fatal to almost any girl. Except me, of course."

"Of course."

Bruno finished swimming, ran over to us and shook off all the water on his coat. I covered my face, chuckling, while Raven yelped and scolded Bruno for being a dumb wet dog. Upset, his ears drooped. A butterfly flew past and he forgot all about Raven and chased after it.

"Nice dog." I watched Bruno run around.

"He's my best friend. We go everywhere together." Her eyes met mine then she turned away. "It's going to be dark soon. I'll take you to Jericho's." She stood and whistled for Bruno.

I faked a smile. How did she know where Jericho lived?

CHAPTER THIRTY-THREE

AVIKAR

Raven!" Jericho swept her up in a big hug. "How've you been? I hope you've stayed out of trouble. You know I can't bail you out of prison if I'm not here." He put her down and playfully tussled her hair.

I cocked any eyebrow at her. "Prison?"

She winked and found an empty seat at the table.

Derrick sat at the table, eating. He stopped once he saw us, eyeing Raven.

I shrugged. I had no idea how she knew Jericho either.

"How do you guys know each other?" I asked.

"She's my cousin."

"Cousin?" I looked at her.

"You never asked."

"Sit, sit, dinner's ready," Anna said.

I sat across from Raven, watching her pile food on her plate. For a petite girl, she could eat. I grabbed a passing bowl of creamed kale and spooned the vegetable onto my plate. My stomach growled at the buttery-garlic smell.

"How did you and Raven meet?" Anna asked while handing me a chunk of fanna.

"We found her beating some guys in an alley," Derrick said, before shoveling a piece of fanna into his mouth.

Jericho laughed. "That's my Raven, always getting herself into trouble."

"It seems I'm not the only one." Raven frowned. "I overheard the guards in town talking about you."

"Oh? What did they say?"

"They said you were dead."

"What?" Anna gasped. "What do you mean? Why would they say that, Jericho?"

"Now, Anna, be calm," Jericho said. "There's no reason to be upset. I didn't say anything because I didn't want you to worry, dear, but I suppose I owe you both an explanation. Our wagon broke an axel and we had to stop. We were attacked and I was left for dead."

Anna's eyes glistened and she cupped her hand to her face.

"I had to find another way into Daath," Jericho continued, "and ran into Avikar and Derrick who were coming from up North. I was wounded and they offered to escort me home. In return, I offered them a place to stay."

I fell back in my seat, exhaling a long-held breath.

"How about some of that date cake I smelled?" Jericho said.

Anna bustled into the kitchen.

After we finished eating, Raven asked if anyone wanted to join her on a walk. Derrick excused himself to bed; I think he ate too much date cake. Anna was giving her daughter a bath and Jericho was napping.

With nothing else to do, I followed Raven out into the cool night. We walked in silence. She twirled the ends of her hair between her fingers, and I played with the marbles in my pocket. Normally, I never ran out of things to talk about, but I went blank. I had too many thoughts running around in my head, and chit-chatting with a girl wasn't one of them.

Frogs croaked and hundreds of crickets rubbed their violin legs. It was cool for this time of year. I wondered if the climate in Daath matched the rest of Tarrtainya. I glanced to my left and saw Raven rub her bare arms. I slipped off my cloak and placed it around her shoulders.

She smiled, moonlight touching her cheeks. "Thank you."

I scratched the back of my neck. "You're welcome." We went back to the boring silence, and I wondered why I had even followed her outside.

"Look, a firefly!" Raven knelt and pointed at the lonesome bug sitting on the edge of a wild fern.

I stopped beside her. "Do you know why they glow?"

She shook her head.

I shifted my body, closing the gap between us. "For each firefly there is only one perfect mate. The males spend their nights creating a unique glow pattern in search of a female. When one comes along and repeats the pattern, they know they've found their soul mate. The two are mated for life."

Raven's eyes gleamed. "Is that really true?"

"My mother told me that when I was little. She had a gift for turning everything into a fairytale." I rubbed my head and chuckled. "Sometimes I wonder how much of what my mother says is made up."

Raven frowned at the firefly.

"Does your mother tell stories like that?"

Her lip quivered.

"Did I say something wrong?"

She shook her head. "No, it's all right. My parents died in a fire last year. That's why I live with Jericho."

Losing Jimri was hard, but losing both my parents? I didn't think I could live through that.

"I'm sorry," I said. I wanted to know more, but noticed the way she bit her bottom lip, her eyes swelling with water.

"What are the shores like? I've always wanted to go, but they're forbidden."

"Why?"

She shrugged. "No one knows, Lucino's orders."

She watched me, waiting to hear some grand details, but I didn't know two licks about the shores, except ...

"The sea is different from the woods," I said. "I bet you'd like it. Most of our food comes from the water, and the beasts are monstrous." I silently thanked my mother for all those bedtime stories about her home village on the southern coast. "The tide can be dangerous, and if you're not careful, it'll sweep you away."

"Have you finished your schooling? Do they even teach out there?"

"Last summer. Now, I take care of the horses on our farm. We're one of the few families that breeds them."

"I love horses!" Her face brightened with her smile. "What kind?" She sat cross legged, staring at me.

"Mostly thoroughbreds, and a few mustangs."

Raven's smile grew wider and she jumped.

"What is it?"

"I want to show you something."

She grabbed my arm and pulled me up. A shock ran through me, as soon as her fingers touched my arm. Raven's eyes popped and she quickly let go.

"Sorry," she said.

"No apology needed."

Raven led me to Jericho's barn. Inside, she skipped to the last two stalls. The first stall she stopped at held a big black mustang. The horse neighed and nuzzled her face as she patted his muzzle.

"This is Onyx," she said.

I slowly approached the horse, letting him get a good sniff, and then reached to his side and scratched. "Hello boy."

Onyx snorted.

"He's beautiful. Is he yours?"

"I've had him a long time. We've been through a lot." She kissed the side of Onyx's face before moving to the last stall. "And this is Ghost. We found her recently; must've been separated from the herd."

Another mustang, black and white but Ghost had a wild spirit in her eyes.

"Want to go for a run? You can ride Ghost."

I looked at the stall across from us. "I wouldn't want my girl to get jealous." I walked over and rubbed Brushfire's mane. "Want to get out of here, girl?" She brushed her foot against the ground. I smiled and unhooked the latch, opening the stall for her.

We saddled the horses and galloped out of the barn and into the surrounding fields, running side by side. The silver moon lit the night, and the hooves of the horses created a comforting tempo. Occasionally, Raven would glimpse my way, her expression pure bliss, black hair flying around her in whipping waves. At times, she and Onyx blended into one dark shadow zipping across the grass.

Raven stopped on top of a large hill, overlooking the town which shone from all the flickers of candlelight.

I whistled. "Now *that* is a view."

Raven smiled. "This would be my second favorite place."

I leaned back in the saddle, enjoying the sight and the crisp air. Onyx and Brushfire moved closer to one another and nuzzled. Causally, I glanced Raven's way and found her already looking at me.

Embarrassed, she stammered, "I ... I was just noticing your eyes. The color is very unique."

"I am one of a kind." I leaned in her direction, giving her that smoldering gaze I do so well. "Want a closer look?"

She nodded and moved forward, mouth slightly parted, eyes wide. I don't think she realized how hard she stared or the fact she'd been doing it now for a few minutes.

"Boo," I whispered and playfully blew into her face.

She gasped, snapping out of her daze.

"Done staring at me?"

She pointed a finger at me.

"You're the one with the staring problem," she huffed.

"Hmm." I eyed her, grinning. "I'll try my best not to stare at you anymore."

"Thank you," she said, turning her head from me.

I don't know how long we stayed on that hill, but it had to have been for a while. She rambled on about Daath and all the wonderful things I couldn't care less about; not even one fact about Lucino and his shapeshifter form.

I watched her expressions change when she spoke. Those full pink lips became my favorite trait of hers, and when in deep thought she would bite her bottom lip, it drove me crazy. I wondered if she was emotional like Jeslyn, or carefree like Calli. I wondered what kind of friends she had or if she was a loner.

But I shouldn't have been thinking these things, no matter how cute she was.

CHAPTER THIRTY-FOUR

JESLYN

I sat by the window, staring out. Emptiness shrouded me, and I couldn't feel anything other than heartache.

Avikar and Derrick ... both of them ... dead. Cold crept into my dress, and I hugged myself trying to remove the chill. *How could this happen? They were there because of me, and now they're dead.* Tears streamed down my face. I should have sent word to Mother and Poppa but I couldn't. The loss would kill them both. Another son gone.

And Derrick, sweet, charming Derrick. The only boy who flustered when I whispered in his ear, and the only boy to ever kiss me. He may not have been a dashing lord or one of the king's knights, but he had protected me since we were little. Our friendship grew and one day, maybe, we would have married. Derrick would have been a kind husband and a loving father. Instead, Avikar and he would rot away in the ground, leaving nothing but dust and bones.

I looked to the door as Lucino entered the room, then returned to staring out the window.

"How are you feeling?" he asked. He'd moved so quickly, I was shocked to see him at my side.

There were no words to describe how I felt, only tears.

"I am sorry, Jeslyn. Would you like to see more of Daath?"

I sniffled and wiped my eyes. "Can you take me where there's no pain?" My words came out raspy and hoarse.

"That I can do," he said, taking my hand.

We were far in Daath's woods. Lucino allowed me to ride with him. I didn't have the strength to ride a horse. We rode past a few awkwardly bent trees covered in green moss. I hugged Lucino's waist tighter, waiting for the scenery to change, and it did.

Massive white-flowered willows arched above us, a canopy of sleeping leaves. Bushes filled with red and violet specks of color surrounded the ancient trees, leaving me breathless with their beauty. The air grew hazier the deeper we went. A low rhythmic humming replaced the silence. I searched for the noise, wondering what natural thing could be creating such a beautiful harmony of harmonic sound.

Hummingbirds dotted around bushes, almost invisible. Their gossamer wings flapped rapidly, carrying their delicate green bodies from bush to bush. The sight both wowed and pained me because it made me think of Calli and how much she loved hummingbirds.

The horse trotted down a slight incline into an enclosed garden.

"We're here," Lucino said, and stopped the horse.

We were in a secret place hidden in the middle of the forest. A small waterfall fell from a high ridge, pouring into a clear pool. A tree with gnarled roots reached into the pool, almost like steps, and a thin mist hovered over everything.

Lucino dismounted and then helped me off.

"What is this place?" I asked, entranced by the magnetic beauty. I could feel the sorrow lighten as I breathed in the fresh air.

Lucino took my hand as we walked. "A sacred grotto. These waters hold power."

"Power?" I found a spot on the mossy floor, right by the edge of the hypnotizing pool, and sat.

"Healing power."

Could it be possible? I dipped my hand into the water, expecting to feel a sense of magic but only felt the cool liquid.

"You look disappointed." Lucino leaned against the tree, arms folded.

I patted the ground next to me. He raised an eyebrow. I patted again.

"Very well," he said, a little begrudgingly.

I smiled at the annoyance on his face as he tried to clear a space free of dirt. "Afraid to get those regal clothes of yours stained?"

His mouth hung open for a moment as if he had an excellent response, but he said nothing. Instead, he muttered a word I didn't quite catch.

Satisfied he was a bit more relaxed, I went back to admiring the enchanted pool. "To think water could hold such a quality," I said and dipped my hand back in, letting it wash over my nails and fingers. "Think of all the people it could help."

Past the pool, where the beginning of a grotto jutted out, I saw a flash of blue. Vibrant blue. Then another. Then three more. A mass of blue, more brilliant than the blue jays back home, swirled toward me.

The closer the mass came, the better I could see. Butterflies. A single swarm of them. Lucino scoffed as the butterflies flew around me.

"Disgusting things," he said and went to flick one.

"Don't!" I grabbed his hand. My eyes widened as the butterflies flew in a singular motion and landed on my arms. Suddenly, a warm sensation fluttered in my body and joy burst through my chest. I didn't dare move, afraid to scare the magical creatures away. Whatever they were doing to me, I didn't want it to stop.

"That's strange," Lucino said. "They've never touched anyone before." Lucino's forehead scrunched together as he glanced at the creatures decorating me.

Then as fast as they came, they left. I watched them fly away, taking with them a sense of longing. "They're beautiful." I turned to Lucino, who still looked a bit perplexed. "What do you know about them?"

Lucino's brows narrowed, his gaze followed the disappearing blue. "We believe they are the keepers of this grotto, old spirits watching over the waters."

Wonder swelled in my chest. *This place is magical.*

"Thank you, Lucino. Everything you've shown me here, it's all breathtaking."

The blue in Lucino's eyes shined, and I dared to move closer until my dress brushed the side of his outstretched leg. The medallion he wore around his neck sparkled under the waning light. I reached out to touch it. "May I?"

He nodded.

I lifted the heavy necklace and rubbed my thumb across the snake emblem. "What is this? You're never without it."

"It is called the ouroboros. It means eternity." He lifted the chain around his neck and held up the symbol. "This is the spiral of life."

"It's a bit dark."

He smiled. "Would you rather I wear a butterfly around my neck, my lady?"

I laughed. "That would be very interesting. I can imagine all your guards wearing butterflies on their armor."

Lucino laughed, and for the first time, his face brightened. Since we'd met, Lucino had always acted proper and very formal. I'd never seen him relax or enjoy himself. Seeing this side of him opened a flurry of different emotions. In this place, he wasn't a lord, and I wasn't a peasant. We were simply two people lost in the magic.

"Thank you for bringing me here," I said, and reached for his hand.

His eyes searched mine. He grabbed my hand, sending my heart into a whirlwind. "You may come here anytime you like."

"I'd like that, very much."

CHAPTER THIRTY-FIVE

AVIKAR

The next day, Raven showed me around town, Bruno trailing behind us. His dumb, dopey smile made me smile. Derrick went with Jericho to follow a lead. Apparently, Jericho's good buddy had overheard another guard talk about Lucino's betrothed while visiting the "tunnels"—no idea what those were, but I knew Derrick would bug Jericho for a deeper explanation. I wanted to go, but Jericho couldn't take both of us. Too risky. Derrick argued with me for a good portion of the morning, and I finally gave in.

Back to the market we went. With Derrick, I hadn't paid attention to any of the vendors or wares. We were too busy scouting. Even with an escort, I felt a little uneasy. I kept thinking a local would notice me. They'd scream OUTSIDER and then I'd have to fight my way out. Luckily, nothing like that happened.

Raven talked about Daath. She was clueless to the rest of the world. She thought Daath more advanced than the primitive lands surrounding it. She described Lucino as god-like both in stature and appearance. I wondered if she knew he could shapeshift into a reptile.

143

"You ever wonder why people think Lucino is a god?" I watched her face, waiting to see if she knew anything more than she claimed.

"Well, there are stories, but they're old fables. None of them are true."

If she only knew. "Tell me one."

We passed by a vendor selling smoked meat. My stomach growled.

Her eyes darted to the right and left, just like the other day.

"Don't worry, you can trust me," I said, nudging her shoulder with mine. "They're not true anyway, right?"

"He's been ruling for longer than anyone can remember, and yet, hasn't aged a day. Some think he wields powerful magic, but I don't believe it. Daath has powerful herbs. I know because I collect them for coin. I've heard the herbalist in town talk about a mandrake that can renew the skin to younger years. I bet Lucino found it."

She stopped in front of a weapon merchant. A gleaming rapier caught my eye. *That is true beauty.*

"Excuse me," I said. I squeezed past her to pick up the blade.

Iron.

It made sense that Daath would have iron weapons. There had to be mines on this side of the mountains. The merchant had a table full of daggers, short swords, throwing knives, spiked maces and even a doubled headed axe. It was a shame Derrick wasn't here to see the collection.

Placing the blade back on the pile, I searched for Raven.

She'd walked over to a nearby fruit merchant who was talking to a man in an oversized hat. She strolled by, and when the two men began arguing, she flicked her wrist, grabbed an apple and shoved it into her pocket.

That little thief.

She walked by a few more carts before heading back to me. "Find anything you like?" she asked.

"He's got a nice collection." I gestured at the weapons merchant.

We started walking again. Once we bended the corner, she took the apple out of her pocket.

"Can I have some? I'm starving." I rubbed my belly and winced.

"Sure." She tossed the apple to me, and I put it into my cape.

Without giving her an explanation, I turned around and headed to the fruit merchant.

"Where are you going?" She asked while following me.

I grinned and kept walking.

She ran in front of me, pressing her palms against my chest. "Avikar, what are you doing? You're not going to tattle, are you?"

I winked and walked to the fruit merchant.

"Hello, good sir." The fruit merchant nodded, and I pointed to a bunch of apples. "I'll have two of those and one of those oranges in the back." When he turned around, I took out the apple. "And this one too."

He nodded, and since I didn't have a basket, he dumped them in my arms.

When I reached Raven, her cute face was bright red. I handed her back the apple. "Here you go, and if you're still hungry, there's plenty more."

"Grr." Her forehead scrunched, and she stomped down the street.

"What's the matter?" I called after her. "I thought you were hungry?"

"I was," she grumbled.

"Raven."

She whirled around, furious. "Why did you have to do that? Are you trying to make me feel like an idiot?"

I laughed and brushed the hair out of my face. "Who's the idiot who stole the apple?"

She scowled and stormed off again, this time walking a lot faster. I sped up, but the closer I got, the faster she walked. I didn't feel bad. Short of starvation, there was no excuse for stealing. And with Anna's cooking, nobody was starving.

After what seemed like forever, she slowed, and I draped my arm around her shoulders. "You still mad at me?"

"A little," she mumbled, crossing her arms.

I closed my arm around her neck, pulling her into me. "But you were being bad."

She gave me a tiny smile, grabbed my wrist and twisted.

"Feisty."

She sighed and laughed, tossing my wrist aside. I refused to let her know that move actually kind of hurt. I pointed to a nearby bench. "Can we sit for a minute? I'm tired of walking."

She nodded, and we sat. I chomped into the apple. It tasted nice and crisp. "What's your story? Why would you steal? You can get killed for that."

She smirked. "I never get caught."

Eyeing her, I asked, "I'm sure, but why do it?"

Raven leaned her head back, gazed up at the sky, took a deep breath, let it out and said, "It's a rush."

I coughed and punched my chest, dislodging the piece of fruit I almost chocked on. "You're going to risk your life for a rush? There are other things you can do than stealing."

"I know, but it's fun. The anticipation, the way your heart races ... there's nothing like it," she sighed.

I slid closer to her until our legs touched.

"If you want your heart to race," I said softly in her ear. "I think I can manage that." My arm slipped around her, and my fingers brushed the side of her neck. I could see her chest rise and fall under her white chemise.

"What are you doing," she whispered.

I licked the bottom of my lip and watched her eyes go wide. "Is your heart racing?"

It took her a moment to get my hint. When she did, she scooted away from me, giggling. "I bet you dazzle all the girls back home," she said.

"Me? Never. I was simply making a point."

"I'm sure, but that's not the kind of rush I'm looking for."

I shrugged my shoulders. "Only trying to help." My voice took on a serious tone. "Promise me you'll stop."

"Give me one good reason why."

I saw the challenge in her eyes.

"I'll give you five," I proclaimed.

She folded her arms, grinning. "They better be good ones."

"Oh, they are." I threw the apple core on the ground. "One, you're the most beautiful girl I ever set eyes on. Two, your smile warms my soul. It's invigorating. Three, you have these deep eyes that suck me into their dark depths and I can't pull away. Four, you could have the whole world if you wanted, all you have to do is ask. Five, stealing is a disgusting habit and the only thing it does is taint your beauty, making moot everything else I just said."

Her eyes glistened, and I thought she'd kiss me right there. We stared at one another, her looking starry eyed and me starting to feel foolish. I bet my father would never say anything romantic like that, but I was only doing it to sweeten her up. I needed more information about Lucino. Something useful.

"Were those adequate reasons?" I asked, hoping to diffuse this strange moment.

"I've … I mean … they were okay."

"Promise."

"I promise. No more stealing."

She gathered her hair into her hands and ran her fingers through it. I watched as her eyes desperately tried to avoid mine, but I wouldn't let them.

"How long will you be staying?" she asked, biting her lip.

"I'm not sure, a few days, maybe more."

She looked in the opposite direction. "Oh."

Her hair blocked her face, which I didn't like. Our knees barely touched, but it was enough to make my blood heat. Sitting next to a pretty girl, flirting, her flirting back—it was distracting. Everything in me said to stop, but it'd been long since I'd felt anything other than pain. This was a nice change.

Her leg moved, rubbing against mine. I needed to walk.

I stood. "You ready to show me the rest of this town?"

Her mouth opened, but then she shut it. "Sure, let's go."

We walked down a back street and an old woman crept out of a shabby house. "Have your fortune read, sweetie?" the hag asked while trying to coax us inside.

"No," I said, coldly.

Raven tugged on my arm. "Come on, it'll be fun."

I shook my head. "I'm not going in there."

"Pleeease." Raven cupped her hands to her chest. "We won't be long. I promise."

She made it hard to say no. "Fine, let's go."

The hag brought us inside and to a small wooden table surrounded with white candles. The candles had melted onto the table, creating a pile of messy wax. The place stunk of sage, dried bundles of it hanging throughout the house. Strange knick-knacks cluttered the room on crooked shelves, making the place seem even smaller and stuffier. A small cracked window was partly open.

We sat, and I motioned for Raven to go first. Raven held out her hand for the hag to examine.

The hag rubbed her knobby fingers over Raven's palm. "You're quite the adventurer, aren't you, my dear?" the hag cooed.

Raven bobbed her head in excitement. Anyone could guess Raven wasn't your typical girl. What girl doesn't wear a dress and knows how to fight?

"But you've been hurt," the hag continued, "I see a lot of pain in your past and betrayal … someone very dear to you hurt you."

Raven's smile faded, and her hand clenched into a fist.

"Don't worry, my child. There is love in your future," she said, and her glance drifted towards me.

Why is she looking at me? I pretended I hadn't heard her, or seen Raven sneaking a glance my way.

The hag laughed, softly, and dropped Raven's hand. "Your turn dear." She held out her hands, waiting for my palm.

I have a bad feeling about this. Raven nudged my arm, and I grunted.

The hag's brow furrowed in concentration. Her glassy white eyes widened, and she muttered. I leaned in closer, trying to hear what she said.

Then her deathlike eyes glared at me. "You are a special one. Come to see the visitor. Fate has something special for you, boy, but you should not be here. You don't belong in Daath ... outsider."

My heart beast so fast I thought I'd puke. I pulled my hand back, but she tightened her grip, keeping me in her icy grasp.

"Death awaits you if you stay. You must leave now."

I jerked my hand away from her. "I don't believe in fate." I stood and stormed out, almost knocking over the table.

"Wait!" Raven yelled, "don't listen to her. None of that stuff means anything."

I ignored her.

Death, whose death? How could that old hag know about me?

"Avikar, slow down!"

I waited for her then continued running.

"Where are you going?" She asked. "Why are you so upset?"

I stopped, turning to face her. "Death, Raven. She said death was close by."

Raven rolled her eyes. "She also told me true love was in my future. Should I believe her?"

"... That's different ..."

"How so?"

"It is. I'd rather have love in my future than death." Before she got misty eyed, I started walking.

CHAPTER THIRTY-SIX

AVIKAR

Why, why were we back at the lake? Raven wanted to race, and once I realized where she was running, she was too far ahead. How could I tell her that her favorite place made me sick, and every time she brought me here, I wanted to scream.

She stood at the bank, gazing in. "Turn around," she said.

"Why?"

"Because I'm hot and want to go swimming, and I don't want you to see me undress."

Immediately, images of her naked torso popped into my mind. I put my back to her. I could hear the brush of her clothes as she took them off. *One peek, that's all I need. What's the worst she'll do?* My head turned slightly, but the only thing I saw were her toes sticking out of the water.

"Okay, I'm in!"

The lake still tormented me, but with her in the water, smiling, happy, it didn't seem so bad.

I still wasn't going in.

Sitting on the grass, I thought about how stupid this was. Even though Raven wasn't completely nude—thanks to her undergarments—I should have been in there with her. Laughing, tickling her, maybe even kissing her. But I couldn't.

"Won't you come in?" she hollered, her pretty eyes begging me to say yes.

I can't.

"Can't you swim?"

I frowned. "Of course I can swim. I just don't feel like it."

Her smile faded. "It's the lake, isn't it?"

For the first time since I met her, I didn't want to look at her. Panic consumed my chest, squeezing it until I couldn't breathe. I rested my arms across my knees and dipped my head, taking in deep, slow breaths. *1... 2... 3... 4... 5... 6... 7...*

Something touched my back and I jolted.

"I didn't feel like swimming, either," she said.

She leaned her back against mine. For a minute, I thought she was undressed, but I noticed the pile of clothing gone. I knew she was going to prod. Every girl prods.

I'm not telling her a thing, I thought. And it wasn't just the lake. It was everything. My sister, my brother, my fear. Fear that I'd fail. Fear that I'd get someone else killed. I wanted to brush it all aside, disconnect from the emotion. Back on the farm I could do that, but not here.

But to my surprise, she said nothing. Instead, she hummed. My stomach twisted with nerves, waiting for her to ask me about the lake, but she never did. She rested her head on my shoulder, humming; until that turned to soft breathing.

Staring at the lake, hearing her sleep, made me feel all sorts of crazy. I wanted to break down, cry my eyes out, and I wanted to reach around, grab her and thank her for doing nothing. People had treated me different after Jimri's death. They were careful and always had a sympathetic look that made me feel like dirt. Raven didn't do any of that. She didn't know about my past and she didn't force me to talk about it—which I found refreshing. She was content to just sit.

In the distance, I could see Bruno chasing after a rabbit. I closed my eyes, hoping sleep would take me far away.

A scratchy, wet object licked my cheek. I opened my eyes to see a white shaggy face drooling over me.

Bruno panted, and I pushed his furry body away. It was dark already. I stood and stretched. Raven lay on the grass, still sleeping.

I knelt by her face. Her hair was draped over her side and small breaths came out of her mouth. "Raven," I whispered.

"Hmm."

Gently, I shook her shoulder. "Time to wake up."

She grunted and frowned.

"Raven."

Her eyelids cracked open. "Nighttime? Perfect." She yawned and rolled into a ball.

"Raven, get up."

She groaned and waved me way.

"You're worse than my baby sister." I shook my head, scooped her into my arms and started walking.

"Hey!" she said, finally waking.

I cradled her like a baby and whistled for Bruno. "Come on, boy."

"I can walk, you know. Put me down!"

She wiggled out my grip and placed her feet on the ground.

"It was either carry you or leave you there."

The wind lifted her hair, blowing it around. Her mouth open then shut. "Sorry," she mumbled.

I shrugged. "You're nothing compared to my little sister. You wake her and it's instant tears and screams."

Raven pulled her hair into a bun, smiling. "I was probably like that when I was young. How old is she?"

"Five." I slipped my hands into my pocket and rolled one of the marbles. I remembered the first time I showed Calli how to shoot marbles. She beat me on her first try.

"What really happened between you and Jericho?"

The question jarred me. "What do you mean?"

"You didn't think I bought that story last night, did you? All three of you were acting weird, and if Anna wasn't so busy making sure everyone had enough to eat, she would've noticed it too."

"It's not my business to say."

She eyed me, a little fire burning in those dark eyes. "He's my cousin. It's my business to know. I heard what the guards said. I know you guys aren't telling the truth. Please, Avikar."

I sighed. "You won't believe me, even if I tell you."

"Try me." Her hand touched my arm, and I swear she gave me goose bumps.

"Well, Derrick and I, as you know, were headed here, that part was true. We caught Jericho trespassing on our land." Her eyes widened and sweat pooled at the base of my neck.

"Trespassing?" Her hand stayed in place, linking my arm with hers as we walked.

"He was spying."

"For what?"

I scratched my head, thinking of any useless fact I could spin. Then it came to me. "We have certain plants with high medicinal purposes. He was trying to steal them."

"Why? We have herbs here?"

I leaned to the side and lowered my voice. "These are special herbs, said to keep you young."

Her eyes lit up. "The mandrake," she whispered.

I stifled a chuckle. "Jericho begged us to let him go, so we made a deal."

"But what about his comrades, didn't they search for him?"

I shook my head. "No, they must have assumed he failed his

mission." I kept my expression stoic and continued. "He was lucky it was Derrick and I who found him, anyone else and he would have been slaughtered."

Her eyes watered, concern rippling across her face. I started feeling a little bad. "He bragged about the landscape and beautiful women. In exchange for his rescue, he offered to be our guide and to give us a place to rest."

Raven glared at me. "You saved my cousin to see girls?"

"Pretty girls," I corrected.

She groaned, and I wrapped my arm around her shoulders. "I can't help it," I said, "I'm weak when it comes to a pretty face." Then, into her hair I whispered, "If I'd known about you, I wouldn't have hesitated."

She lifted her chin, her eyes smiling. "Flattery will get you nowhere."

I could see the sparkle in her eye, and the slightest hue of red in her cheeks. She believed me, and that was all that mattered, even if I did feel bad for lying. Telling Raven the truth was too dangerous, for all of us.

"But don't say anything," I said. "Jericho is embarrassed about the whole thing. I can trust you, right?"

She pretended to zip her lips.

"Good. I know you're fast, but how fast are you really?"

She smiled. "Faster than you."

CHAPTER THIRTY-SEVEN

AVIKAR

A fire burned in the stone fireplace, filling the room with warmth. Anna had cooked another amazing meal. She and Raven were cleaning while the rest of us hung by the fire. Jericho smoked from a wooden pipe. The smoke smelled of sage and strawberries. I'd never seen anyone smoke save for the old merchant in our village. Up North, there were fields filled with a smoking herb called red warrior. Large plants with red flowers and sharp bristles. They were calming plants said to relax the body, but mostly they were given to warriors with grave injuries, or to the sick.

Jericho offered his pipe to us. Derrick shook his head, but I was too curious. The pipe was smooth. A carved claw held the bowl portion. I had no idea how to smoke. Was there a special technique? Guess I'll give it a go. I put the pipe to my mouth and inhaled. Before I could taste anything, my lungs heaved the smoke back out.

Jericho laughed heartily while I punched my chest. "It takes time getting used to," he said.

My coughing fit continued until Derrick whacked my back. "Should we burp you?"

There was no point in trying to give him a witty retort—I couldn't talk.

Jericho leaned back in his chair. "How was your day with Raven?"

"Fine. Did you find anything out?" I said, the smoke remnants finally gone.

"Lucino has your sister at his estate," said Jericho.

"What? Why?"

"Because that monster plans to marry her," Derrick said, his face twisted in agony.

"What will happen to my sister?"

"I don't know."

The way Jericho said it made my stomach clench. That hopeless feeling swept over me and I wanted to puke.

"What can we do?" I asked.

"We go in and get her," Derrick said.

My head turned to both of them. "What do you mean? How?"

Derrick glared into the fire, rubbing his hands.

"We'll try sneaking into his estate and getting her out the night of the ball," Jericho said. "If anyone sees you, claim you're a lost patron. It's our best chance."

"What's the plan?" Derrick said.

Jericho puffed on his pipe and blew a ring into the air. "You won't be able to go to the ball without an invitation and I haven't been able to locate one, but we'll keep looking until the ball. Otherwise, Raven will help you get into Lucino's through a secret entrance. You can go in at night."

"Raven?" I couldn't believe he would suggest dragging her into this.

"That girl is one of the best thieves I know," Jericho said. "She can break into anything, including Lucino's home."

This can't be happening. I rubbed my forehead, silently screaming into my hand. "When are you going to ask her?" Maybe I would have time to talk to her, explain everything.

"Now," he said. "Raven!"

She walked in, our eyes met and she smiled, a warm, inviting smile that made me feel lower than a snake.

"Yes?" Raven said.

"Sit." Jericho motioned to the chair and she sat.

Jericho told her everything. I mean everything. Not once did she glance my way or say a word. Once Jericho finished, she asked when we wanted to go in.

"The night of the ball," Jericho replied.

"I'll see you then. If you'll excuse me." She shoved past me as if I wasn't even there.

The front door swung open and slammed shut. Anna called after her.

"I don't know what you did, but you better go fix it," Derrick said.

I grunted and ran after her.

CHAPTER THIRTY-EIGHT

AVIKAR

Cold raindrops poured out of grey clouds. I shielded my eyes, searching for her. The wind howled, ripping right through my clothes and freezing my skin. Where did she go? And where did this storm come from? I ran. I only knew a few things about Raven, but I had a good guess of where she might have gone.

By the time I reached the lake, the storm thundered and poured sheets of rain. Beneath the dark sky, the open water looked even more desolate. An angry bolt of lightning touched down on the lake, lighting the sky on fire.

"Raven!" I held my cape as it flapped with the wind.

"Go away, Avikar!

She sounded close. "Please, Raven, hear me out!"

"No!"

Barely visible, I spotted her sitting on one of the willow tree branches. "Let me explain!" I pushed through the storm, getting closer to her.

"There's nothing to explain."

"Come back to the house with me and we can talk," I pleaded. Through the thunder, I thought I heard her crying. "I'm sorry I lied, but I had no choice. I did it for your benefit."

"My benefit? Are you serious? Why did you tell me that ridiculous story? I believed you, everything you said today … I believed and it was all a lie!"

"I had to tell you something. Jericho told us to say we were from the Shores. It was the only way for us to be safe."

"I wouldn't have told anyone. He's my family."

The rain soaked through my clothes, and I shivered. "I'm sorry. Will you come down from there?"

"It's not that simple. You can't just apologize and expect everything to be okay."

"Why not? I said I was sorry. What more is there?"

The wind became so strong I had to keep one hand on my head to anchor my cape. "I'm the one whose sister is being held hostage. I had every right to do what I did. Who's to say you wouldn't have done the same thing to me!"

"You're right. I would've done the same. After all, we just met. How could we possibly trust each other? We're practically strangers."

"Raven …"

"I don't even know who you are; except that you're a great liar."

I shook my head. This was pointless. We could stay out here all night going back and forth. "I'm sorry. I hope one day you'll understand and forgive me, but if you're not coming, I'm leaving. I'm not standing out here in the rain all night, watching you throw a temper tantrum."

"Ugh!"

A twig hit me in the face. "You're crazy! I don't even know why I followed you out here. I'm leaving!" I turned around and she didn't argue, or call after me. *Let her stay out here then. What do I care? I'm not here for her.*

Saying I didn't care didn't make it true. Sloshing my way back to Jericho's, I tried not to think of her sitting in the tree, soaking wet, crying … but I couldn't. I don't know why, but seeing her upset twisted my emotions into a tumult of chaos.

I should go get her. I stopped. Lighting and thunder screamed at me, forcing me to keep moving. No. I apologized more than once.

If she wants to come home, she will.

CHAPTER THIRTY-NINE

JESLYN

Of all my dreams, I never thought being a real lady would ever come true. I never believed my parents would wish me away, yet they had. Was I just another mouth to feed? Did they expect to gain wealth out of this? Or did they simply not care?

A storm raged outside, attacking the windows viciously. Thunder cracked in the night sky, and I hugged my pillow tighter.

They didn't even want to come. Mother, who always spoke of Daath with a smile on her face, had no desire to see it. I knew this time of season Poppa was busy, but still, they could have made the journey.

Tears slipped from eyes, and I sobbed into the bed.

Did this mean I had to marry Lucino? If they had wanted me home, Mother would have said it.

I couldn't escape the sorrow flooding my heart. Thoughts of my family, thoughts of Avikar and Derrick, and question after question.

Could I leave? See my family, speak with them in person. This couldn't be what they wanted—to never see their little girl again.

This had to be a mistake, but what choice did I have? And would it be so terrible to marry Lucino?

And what did I have waiting at home for me, besides my family?

The candlelight flickered with the storm. Shadows bounced off the walls, and I pulled the blanket around me.

I had never been this conflicted.

I had never been this alone.

Lucino promised to take me home after the ball, or the wedding, if I accepted his proposal. He hadn't asked me again, and I wondered if he assumed I had agreed.

Or maybe he was staying true to his word.

Either way, I only had days to decide. I prayed I would choose wisely.

CHAPTER FORTY

AVIKAR

All three of them stared at me wide eyed. **I threw off** my cape.

"What?" I said.

Anna handed her daughter off to Jericho and scampered after me. "Oh, dear, you're drenched. Let me get you some dry clothes," she said, bustling upstairs.

"Guess it didn't go well," Derrick said.

I grabbed a nearby towel and patted my head. Anna came back down and handed me a shirt and trousers.

"Where's Raven?" she asked.

"Sitting in a tree," I stated, coldly.

"Jericho, it's too dangerous for her to be out in this weather," Anna said, her face creased with worry.

Jericho stood. His daughter cooed in his arms and he stroked her mop of blonde hair. "If anyone can take care of themselves," he said. "It's Raven. She'll be fine. Avikar, go change and meet us by the fire. Anna, warm some milk for us."

I stepped into the small washroom. The tiny room had a bench,

163

a seat with a chamber pot and a table with a bowl of water. I stripped off the wet clothes and tossed them on the bench, shaking my head the whole time. Wondering how a girl could aggravate me so much.

Jericho had a fire roaring when I came in. His daughter slept in his arms and the sight reminded me of the decision I'd made. When I wanted to kill him, I didn't wonder if he had any family. I just wanted him dead. Now, I knew I'd made the right choice.

Anna walked in with a tray of steaming mugs. I took one and held the hot mug in my cold hands, warming them. I sipped the milk, and sighed. It soothed my dry throat.

"What did you say to make her so mad?" Derrick asked. His big arms stretched out behind his head. I guessed he was finally getting used to Jericho not being the bad guy.

"She wanted to know the truth about how we met Jericho and I kind of lied."

Derrick smirked. "I can only imagine what you said."

"I didn't think we'd be recruiting her."

Jericho held his hand up as if he wasn't to blame. "Don't look at me. I didn't tell you to get cozy with my cousin and get her liking you."

"Me?" I pointed to my chest, and Jericho nodded. I thought about it. We were both flirting, and I definitely liked her, but … "I told her I was sorry, and she was still mad. She even threw a branch at my head!" Derrick and Jericho chuckled which irritated me even more. "Women. Doesn't she understand the danger we're all in?"

Jericho sighed. "Unfortunately, when it comes to a woman's heart, nothing is more important, especially Raven's."

"What does that mean?"

Jericho stayed silent, and I pushed the subject. "Tell me. What happened to make her so darn sensitive?"

"He'll just annoy you until you tell him," Derrick said.

"It's not my story to tell, but I will say she had her heart broken, and she's never been the same since."

Who could do that to her? She's nothing but sweet.

164

Derrick asked Jericho question after question about Lucino. I should have been paying attention, but Raven kept entering my mind. Her broken voice, and the hurt in it when she called me a liar. To her, I was another trickster. Someone who couldn't be trusted. I didn't want to be known as the guy no one could count on, but no matter what I did, that's who I was, and it made me sick. I had to change.

The clay broke in my hand and I threw it at the wall. Great, now I'm out. Derrick had fallen asleep a while ago, and I'd been sitting here scribbling away my frustration, hoping I'd get tired. It didn't work.

The rain beat against the window. I searched outside for any sign of her, but the storm made it impossible to see. My stomach churned with worry; if anything happened to her it'd be my fault.

Not wanting to wake Derrick, I tiptoed out of the room and down the stairs. Loud thunder shook the whole house. When I reached downstairs, I grabbed a cape and slowly creaked the door open. I walked only a few steps when I spotted a shadow in the rain. My heart fell into my gut. Raven.

I sprinted to her. Her arms huddled her body, and she was drenched.

"Raven, are you okay?" I draped the cape around her shivering shoulders.

"Fine," she stammered.

I put my arm around her and rushed her into the house. I led her to the fireplace. "Here, sit down. I'm going to find you dry clothes and start a fire."

Raven pulled the cape tighter. "I ... don't ... need ... your help."

I ignored her and went upstairs. There were only three rooms, and I was sure Jericho's was the furthest from the stairs. *Here we go.* I opened the door across from our room and walked into a small room. Raven had a bed, with a little nightstand and a rack with clothes hanging on it. You never would've known I was in a girl's room. Not one dress or girly decoration. I grabbed an outfit and hurried back downstairs.

"Here, put these on," I said, handing her the pile

She gawked at the clothes. "How *dare* … you … go through my things!"

"I have two sisters. Stop being stubborn and change before you get sick."

Her hair plastered to her face and her normally bronze skin had gone pale. "I can't … change with you here."

I turned my back to her and put two logs in the fire. "I won't look. I promise." I grabbed the fire making tin and took out the steel striker, flint and amadou tinder. I placed the dried fungus on top of the flint and struck it.

She didn't reply, but I could hear her changing. I rapidly struck the flint, focused on creating a spark and not turning around. The fire lit, and I fanned the flame until the fire swarmed over the logs.

"I'm done."

I turned around and stood. Her body still shivered, and she hugged herself. I grabbed a blanket, lying across the sofa, and draped it around her.

"Thank … you."

"Come here." I guided her to the couch and sat next to her. Slowly, I pulled her into my chest and wrapped my arms around her.

"What are you doing?" she fussed.

"I'm going to make sure you're warm, and then I'll leave you alone." Her dark eyes questioned me. "Be calm," I said softly.

She pouted, but gave in. I rubbed her arms and we sat in silence. The fire cracked and popped and the flames jumped with each sound. She leaned against my chest, letting me fully embrace her. Her breathing returned to a normal pace.

For what seemed like hours, I held her in my arms. The fire had died to barely a flicker. She'd fallen asleep, and I was content to hold her until morning, but I told her I'd leave and I needed her to trust me.

Sliding out from underneath her, I moved the blanket to create a pillow, and then tucked the rest around her. Her damp hair hung around her face. I bent down and swept it back behind her ear.

You are so beautiful. I grazed her cheek with my finger. *I wish you could understand how sorry I am. I never meant to hurt you.*

I kissed the top of her forehead and left.

CHAPTER FORTY-ONE

·LUCINO

Welcome, tonight is a night of fun and pleasure," I said, clapping my hands. "Eat, drink and enjoy all that there is to offer. "And now to start off the festivities, let's bring in our entertainment!"

At my introduction, into the ballroom stepped a group of female dancers, adorned in elaborate feathered masks and matching headdresses. On their fingers were small gold cymbals that clicked with each flick of their wrist and twist of their hip. In the corner of the hall, the string quartet quickened their tempo. All of the costumed guests cleared out a space in the center of the room, allowing the dancers to perform their number without interference.

I leaned back on my throne. The ball was off to a splendid start. The nobles I'd invited seemed to be enjoying the revelry. I expected no less from the eager humans. Their entire blindfolded journey created a sense of mystery, which they all thought riveting, but I could not let them know how we navigated the eastern shores.

For the first time in centuries, Daath had been revealed, and to think the fools actual believed I meant to trade. It was a shame most wouldn't live through the night.

The dancers finished their number and mingled into the crowd, enticing guests to join them. A trumpet sounded by the ballroom doors.

Willis stood, trumpet by his side, looking stiff as usual. "May I introduce to you," he shouted, "the fair maiden, Jeslyn!"

CHAPTER FORTY-TWO

JESLYN

The doors swung open. People dressed in the most elaborate gowns and costumes stared at me. For a moment, I froze, paralyzed by the splendor. Willis cleared his throat, nudging me to enter the large room.

In my silver shoes, I stepped on the sparkling marble and walked through the parted guests. At the end of the line, I saw Lucino. My heart fluttered. His pants and shirt were the color of midnight, and a long scarlet cape draped his back. He wore an ivory mask that covered almost every part of his face, except his mouth, eyes and left cheek. His sapphire eyes blazed from the two holes. No man could ever look as regal, as daring.

I could hear the low whispers of women and men inquiring about me. I kept my hands clasped in front of me, and every step or two I would glance down at my sky-blue ball gown. The soft material sparkled, like a large shimmering gem.

When I reached Lucino, he took my gloved hand and twirled me around until we were both facing the guests.

"Ladies and gentleman," he said. "Please welcome, my darling betrothed!"

A round of applause ensued, and I curtsied. Lucino snapped his fingers and the ball continued. We walked up two small steps to the thrones. I sat down in the one next to him.

In my dreams, I imagined a moment like this, and yet it didn't feel right. Lucino had promised we would go home, after the wedding. Yes, I had agreed to marry him, out of nothing more than selfishness.

My family wanted me here, and I couldn't go home knowing both my brothers were gone. Lucino could take care of me, and as soon as we were wed, I would convince my family to live here. Away from the pain and loss of Lakewood. Here my family could start over. A new life with new memories.

And Lucino was a good man who treated me with kindness, looked upon me with passion. Each day I'd spent in his presence had only increased my affection for him. I was falling for him and Daath.

Derrick passed through my mind often, but he was gone, and I couldn't think of him or the feelings we shared. I had to move on and forget.

Lucino touched my hand, and I flinched.

"Everything all right, my lady?"

"Yes," I said, my shaky voice betraying me.

"Come." He stood, holding my hand in his, and guided me to the ballroom floor.

The guests cleared a circle for us. He placed one hand on my lower back and held mine with the other, staring at me as if he'd never seen a girl before. I didn't know how to dance like a noble. I prayed it was similar to the more common routines I knew.

He led me around the room, one graceful step after another. His posture perfect and his feet never missed a step, though mine did.

"Relax, my darling," he whispered, his blue orbs beaming at me from the slits in his mask. "You can dance. Let the music take you."

Nodding, I listened to the different instruments all in harmony. A grey mist swirled in Lucino's eyes. I lost myself in them, feeling nothing but the way we moved. His hand pressed hard against my back, drawing me nearer and causing my heart to leap higher than the ceiling. The sound of a cello mixed with a harp created a passionate duet. The deep bass and airy melody made me think of magical nights when the mist hovered over the lake and nothing shone but the stars. As the tempo increased, Lucino swung me around his body. His eyes bore through me, making me feel giddy, and the closer I came to his face the more I hoped he'd kiss me.

After the dance, we sat back down and the guests began approaching Lucino, offering their thanks and hinting at a future gathering. Lucino politely spoke with each one, but from his straying gaze, I could tell he was growing bored.

Lucy entered the ballroom. Seeing her outfit made me feel childlike in mine; my breasts could never fill out a corset like hers. She walked through the crowd, grinning and laughing with guests as she passed. Her golden corset contained little sparkles of ruby, and black silk trailed behind her every step. Her bright eyes hid behind a black lace mask, still brightly aglow.

She sauntered to Lucino's throne, grabbing a wine goblet from a passing servant. "Our other guests have arrived," she said, and emptied her goblet in three long sips.

Lucino grinned. "Very good, bring them to the parlor. I shall meet them there."

Lucy bowed and disappeared into the crowd.

Lucino leaned over to me. "My dear, I have some guests I must attend to. After the next dance, retire to your room. I'll come see you later."

When Lucino first told me of the ball, I never imagined it would be this grand. I didn't want to leave. "Can't I stay?"

"It's not proper for you to be alone among the guests."

"Very well."

He kissed my hand and glided away.

The guests danced a new number. Excitement filled me. I knew I couldn't leave just yet.

CHAPTER FORTY-THREE

LUCINO

Inside the parlor stood a small group of men, black capes hung low over their heads, covering their faces.

"Ah, welcome, my brethren," I said. "I trust the journey was enjoyable?"

One of the figures stepped forward and, in a raspy tone, replied, "As enjoyable as can be expected."

"Falcur, it is good to see you. It's been far too long." I placed a fist across my chest in greeting.

Falcur mimicked the gesture. "Yes, it has."

"I don't see why we should waste any time." I asked. "Are you all prepared?"

Murmurs and nods swept through the room. "Good, as of now our guests are being served the drink I've concocted. It should take only a short while before the hallucinations begin. I added more serum to the wine that will make them more agreeable. It should be no problem grabbing the targets." I clapped my hands and a secret panel opened. "These are your husks."

Three of my personal guard brought in a group of gagged men. "I cannot have you scaring away all the nobles with your current forms."

Falcur moved to one of the males cowed on the floor. "Let us begin."

I watched as each of my kind placed a hand on one human and chanted. Black mists swirled in front of the humans creating a vortex. Their pathetic eyes screamed with terror as their aura left their bodies, draining them to the point of death.

Not only did a human's aura heighten our powers, but when completely drained, we could copy their form. The drain would kill them, but it made our mission much easier. Pretending to play human had become a game between my kind and only the most powerful Reptilian males had the desirable roles.

Falcur's face morphed from the familiar sharp-angled creature to the pale skinned human laying before him. When the transfer completed, I told the guards to bring the remains to Romulus. The old wizard always found use for dead humans.

"We are very close to the end brothers," I said. "After tonight, we will have control of six more lands. Leaving only four left."

"Very good," Falcur replied. "We have done our research as well and have brought with us some distractions. It will be easier to capture the males if they are persuaded off on their own."

He spoke a few arcane words. In the parlor appeared women wearing outfits that covered only the most private of areas. One glanced at me and I caught a glimpse of her eyes changing red.

"A succubus … very well indeed."

Falcur petted the succubus next to him. "We will take care of your female guests and these mischievous ladies will take the nobles to the designated areas."

"Are they bound tightly?" I remembered the last time a brethren summoned one of these demons in Mirth. The creature had charmed him into walking into a pool of acid.

Falcur laughed. "Do not fret over these minor demons. They are all under my control until their task is complete and I dismiss them. Show us this grand ball of yours."

CHAPTER FORTY-FOUR

JESLYN

I observed the party in wonderment, admiring the decorated masks and winged garments and forgetting my sorrow. Women dressed in flowing gowns and extravagant headpieces, each one more unique than the other. I frowned when nature called me away to the washroom.

One of the servants pointed to a door at the far end of the ballroom. I thanked him and lifted the front of my gown as I walked past, careful not to step on the delicate fabric. I pushed open the solid wood door and walked into the candlelit room.

Two women stood giggling and drinking from golden goblets. One wore the outfit of a barmaid with a white wig. The shorter of the two wore a frilly black dress and matching cat mask.

The woman dressed in black bounced over to me and smiled, her lips stained deep red. "Oh, look at how pretty!" she said.

I gave her a courteous smile. "Thank you."

The barmaid came around to my side and pointed a finger at me. "You are so lucky. I wish I was marrying Lucino. He is so dreamy." The woman fluttered her eyes and took a large gulp from the goblet she was carrying. She smirked. "I bet you're perfect too. Quaint, polite, well-mannered and probably still a virgin."

Her friend gasped. "Susie!"

Susie smirked again. "Well, it's probably true, just look at her. I bet you've never even had a sip of wine."

I ignored her hateful disdain and stepped around her.

"Why don't you have some wine?" Susie barred my way with the goblet.

"No, thank you." I didn't know what was wrong with this woman but she seemed unwell.

"One sip won't kill you."

"I'd rather not." Fear was in my voice and Susie walked closer, forcing me into the corner.

"You should have some; it's what all the nobles do. You don't want to stick out, do you?"

I dashed for the door and flung it open, but Susie moved quicker and slammed it shut.

"Susie!"

"Be quiet, Martha."

"But you're going to get us in trouble," Martha whined.

Susie waved Martha away. "You worry too much. We're just having a friendly conversation." She forcefully handed me the goblet. "Have a drink with us. Let's toast to our new friendship."

My eyes watered and my heart hammered, but I wouldn't be bullied. I stood straighter, holding my head high. "Thank you, but I really must get back. Lucino will be worried if I'm gone for too long." And I shoved past her.

Susie's eyes widened and she grabbed my arm. "You're not going anywhere, whore."

I slapped her across the face with my free hand. "I am *not* a whore, you common wench!"

She grabbed my hair, and I screamed.

"I hate girls like you. You think you can do whatever you please because of the way you look, it sickens me." Susie tugged my hair until it paralyzed me, then squeezed open my mouth, pouring the wine all over.

Tears escaped my eyes as the wine burned my throat.

"Men love proper girls like you, so innocent, but you're just as wicked and evil as the rest of us, you just don't look it."

"Susie, stop," Martha whined. "Leave her alone, she hasn't done anything."

Susie let go of my face and backed away. "I hope you enjoy the rest of the night, my lady. Martha, let's leave. I'm bored of this place."

Martha gave me an apologetic look and scampered after Susie.

I fell against the wall trembling. I looked at the beautiful blue gown stained in red and my heart broke. I hugged my knees into my chest and cried into them. *I don't want to be here anymore. I want to go home.* Sobs burst through my chest, filling me with irrepressible pain.

My mouth was sticky and I began to feel hot and lightheaded. There was a small table a few feet away with a wash bin on it. After several long minutes, I found the strength to move to it.

I cupped my hands and splashed my face. The cool water in the bowl refreshed me. Warmth spread through my body and I wet my face again, but it did nothing to cool the flame burning inside. Every breath was heavy and strained and parts of my body tingled. The room shrunk around me.

"I have to get out of here." I pushed the door open and walked back into the ball. With small steps, I carefully made my way through the mob of guests. Everyone laughed and danced around me, but I couldn't relate. My body felt strange. Fear enshrouded my mind. I needed to get to my room, quickly.

More dancers entered the ballroom. One glanced my way and the woman's eyes were blood red. Dismissing the image as a side effect, I kept moving. *Where are the ballroom doors?* Every step I took ended in the same cluster of people.

Another woman with the same frightful eyes glanced at me. I

turned in the opposite direction and ran, hoping I could locate one of Lucino's servants. *There!* I could see the doors.

"Why the rush?" A shirtless man with dark beady eyes gripped my arm, stopping my escape.

"I ..."

"Why don't you stay with me, enjoy the party?"

I tried to twist out of his grasp. "I really must go."

The stranger smiled coldly, and for a brief moment, his face distorted into a monster.

"Please, let go!"

He continued to glare, flooding me with fear.

"Excuse me, sir, but this fair lady is with me," Lucino said, firmly removing the man's hand.

The man bowed. "My apologies." He dismissed himself.

My breaths came in short spasms, and I held my head, trying to steady myself.

"Jeslyn, what happened to your dress?" Lucino grabbed my shaking hands.

The room spun with a hundred different colors. I swayed, trying to focus. Then his hands were under me, lifting me off the ground and into his arms.

CHAPTER FORTY-FIVE

LUCINO

I took Jeslyn into a private sitting room, summoning Lucy before I reached it. I placed her on the sofa. I grazed her vivid red cheek with my hand. "Jeslyn, did you drink any wine?"

Her head slowly nodded.

Rage boiled inside me. "Who gave it to you?"

Her head swayed a little, and she didn't respond. I cupped her chin, gazing into her half-open eyes. She was too weak to respond fully, but my spell would pull the information out from her.

"Jeslyn, tell me everything that happened since I left your side."

Her voice was groggy, but she managed to speak about the girls in the washroom. After, her eyes shut.

"Seems our little lady had too much to drink," Lucy said as she entered the room.

"Watch your tongue," I growled.

Lucy sighed and walked over. "My apologies."

Red stained Jeslyn's dress, her hair had been pulled out of one of the pinned sections, and her eyes were puffy.

I open my borders and these insects dare attack what's mine. I shall show

179

these frivolous women what happens when they disrespect me.

"Have her brought to her room and set guards outside the door. No one but me is allowed in there."

Lucy bowed her head. "As you wish. What do you plan to do?"

"Go hunting." Before my sister could protest, I vanished out the window.

"I thought we weren't allowed to leave the grounds?"

"Martha, stop being such a prude. Don't you want to see Daath? No one will even notice."

I watched the two humans scampering through the gardens, attempting to hide their little escapade. Fools. I stalked them, listening, waiting until they were far enough away that no one would hear their screams.

"Susie, I think we should go back."

The short one clung to a tree, nervously looking about. I crept around her, waiting for Susie to turn away. When Susie did, I grabbed her friend, clamping my hand over her mouth and dragging her into the dark.

"Shh," I said. The human's eyes widened and then I broke her neck. I left her body in the grass and glided to the tree where she had been standing.

"Martha, nothing is—" Susie turned around, her mouth hung open at my sudden appearance. "Lord Lucino." She immediately bowed. "I didn't realize you were out here."

"I like to stroll the gardens this time of night."

She lifted her head, daring to look at me. Her eyes wandered. I assumed she was searching for her friend.

"I told your companion to return to the party. We've had a bit of trouble with wolves out here. I didn't want anything to happen to one my guests."

"Oh, I had no idea." Her lip quivered, and I noticed her hands fidgeting.

"I'll escort you back."

She hesitated at first, and then when I stepped into the moonlight, her eyes widened.

"I know the way back. I wouldn't want to trouble you," she said, frantically looking behind her.

I grinned, enjoying her fear. "It is no trouble at all." I sensed her desire to flee. I did enjoy a good chase. "If you're thinking of running, I'd start now."

Chapter Forty-Six

Jeslyn

I opened my eyes and jumped. My chest heaved, the nightmare fresh in my mind. I realized I was in my room. It was night and the soft glow of candlelight came from the lantern beside my bed.

I need water.

I drew back the curtain and gasped. "Lucino! What are you doing here?"

He sat in a chair, staring at me. His mask off and his shirt ripped.

I pulled my robe on. His jaw clenched and his eyes were dark.

The lantern sent shivers of light around his frame, dancing wildly. He had never come to me at night. I knelt on the floor beside the chair and touched his leg. "Lucino?"

"How dare they touch you, attack you so menacingly. I couldn't allow them to get away with such insolence."

"It's all right, Lucino."

His face scrunched in disgust. "How can you not be angry at them?"

I took his hand. "Because they are fools, and I am not."

He half smiled. "I think that may be the wisest thing a human has ever said to me."

"A what?"

His expression changed and he leaned down, clasping his other hand over mine. "I'm sorry, my lady. I meant woman. My mind is crazed with anger. Forgive my strange words."

Wind blew in from an open window, whipping my robe. It occurred to me, this was the first time a man had seen me in my night chemise. Separated by only a thin fabric, desire stirred in me.

Lucino lifted a hand to my cheek, caressing it. The candlelight flickered. I noticed his blue eyes were solid black.

"Lucino, your eyes!"

He slid back in the chair, breaking the connection. "It's nothing, just the wine."

I didn't believe him. No man's eyes turned black from drinking. I moved closer to him. "What's happened to you? Are you sick? Hurt?"

"No, everything is fine." He withdrew from me and stood. "I think I should leave."

"Wait." I didn't want him to go. The night had been full of strangeness and for the third time since my arrival, Lucino had come to my rescue. The least I could do was calm his nerves. He seemed extremely agitated.

"Will you stay and talk with me? I'm still a bit shaken from earlier."

I thought for a moment he would leave, but he didn't. He turned to me, stepping closer, his blond hair covering his face.

"If that is what you wish." His hand stroked the back of my head, sending shivers through me. His eyes, which seemed dark and empty before, began changing back into beautiful blue.

I took a chance and wrapped my arms around his waist, hoping the gesture didn't spook him away. "I don't know what you did, but I know whatever happened was because you care." He stiffened in my arms, but I pressed against him and continued. "Thank you."

A small sigh escaped his lips. His arms enveloped me.

When I arrived in Daath, I thought all was lost. Then when I heard about Avikar and Derrick, I thought I'd never breach the sorrow, but now, wrapped in Lucino's arms, hope swelled. I would be safe and everything would be fine.

CHAPTER FORTY-SEVEN

AVIKAR

It was late at night and no one had seen Raven. I knew she wasn't coming because of me. I ruined everything. How could I be such an idiot? I should have never spent the day with her. I tried looking for her yesterday, but she'd vanished and now, when we needed her the most, she was gone.

None of this would be happening if I hadn't lied.

Derrick gripped the sides of the chair in front him, then went back to pacing. I couldn't look him in the eye.

Where are you Raven?

The door opened and in she walked. I sighed in relief. She looked tired, but calm.

"Avikar, can we talk outside?"

Even in the dark, I could see the slight puffiness around her eyes. Was she crying, again?

"About the other night … I'm sorry. I overreacted. It's not a big deal."

"It's not?"

She smiled that wide warm smile. "Well, maybe a little. I don't like being lied too. I need to know I can trust you if we're going to do this."

"I swear. I'll never lie to you again." And I meant it.

She stuck out her hand. "Friends?"

I shook it, inwardly cringing at the word. "Friends."

"Good, now let's save your sister."

We went back inside. Raven explained she'd spent the day scouting different routes in. She'd decided on entering through the sewers.

"What are sewers?" I had never heard the term before.

She bit her bottom lip. "They're … no, no time to explain. Just know they're smelly and full of rats."

"Rats?" Derrick shivered. "I hate rats. How do we even know this is going to work? What if we get caught? This doesn't sound like a plan."

Raven put a hand on his shoulder. "Don't worry. I know my way around Lucino's. All the guest rooms are on the second floor. She'll be in one of them."

"How do you know that?" Derrick eyed her.

"I got bored one afternoon and pretended to be one of his servants."

Jericho slapped his knee. "Ha! That's my girl. Now you understand why I asked for her help."

Raven smirked, and I grinned. "Seems I underestimated you," I said.

"Don't let it happen again." She winked.

"Good, we should leave now." Jericho said and picked up a lantern.

Raven grabbed the lantern from him. "Sorry cousin, you're too clumsy for this mission." Jericho argued, but she ignored him, repeatedly telling him we would be fine.

"I feel better without him around," Derrick muttered to me once we were far enough away. "How do you think Jeslyn would react if she saw us with him?"

I didn't think of that. We walked faster, heading farther away from Jericho's dimly lit house and deeper into the dark woods.

"Here is where we go in," Raven said, pointing to a small hill with a carved-out entrance, resembling a cave.

Derrick entered first. The shaft led us deeper until our only option was to climb down a ladder. We descended into a larger stone tunnel through which ran a small river of unknown liquids. The walkways along the water were wide enough to walk on, but scurrying rats made it difficult.

"This place stinks," I gagged. "Why would you ever come here?"

Raven crept past me. "The herbalist in town pays me good coin to gather herbs for him. I stumbled across this while searching for devil's claw, and even though this place does smell terrible, it's intriguing. These tunnels run all around town and through the surrounding area and they go on forever, ending in tons of different places. Some will take you to the temple, others outside of town and one will even take you straight to Lucino's place. I've wanted to see if one would leave Daath, but at some points the way is blocked."

I found it fascinating that the rodents didn't bother her. Derrick seemed to be the only one flinching. Anytime a rat came too close, he'd yelp and kick it away.

"Won't there be guards at Lucino's?" I asked.

Raven jumped over a piece of wood. "Very few people come here, and the tunnel leading to Lucino's is difficult to follow, lots of turns, and if you take the wrong way, you'll end up going in circles."

The walkway narrowed. We had to lean our backs against the wall in order to walk. I watched Raven carefully, making sure she didn't fall forward. We walked like that for a while until the path widened.

"Now where?" Derrick said, holding the lantern high.

"I'll lead from here," Raven said.

She took front and we followed her through one giant maze. Making turns and sliding through smaller tunnels, and in my eyes, getting lost. I'd never be able to find my way out.

"How do you know where you're going?" I asked as we made another right.

She pointed to her head.

"No one is that good," I said.

She shrugged. "It's just this thing I can do. I remember things, even if it's only once. I got lost down here and ended at Lucino's."

"How many times have you gone this way?" Part of me didn't want her to answer that.

"Just once."

You have got to be kidding me.

"I'm sorry, did you just say you've only done this once?" Derrick stepped in front of her.

"Yes, but—"

"I can't believe this!" Derrick threw his arms up.

"She'll get us there," I said, trying to diffuse his anger.

"We don't even know her and you're trusting her with Jeslyn's life?"

"Yes, I am. She said she could do it, and I believe her." I could see the anger boiling in him.

"If I can interrupt?"

We both looked at her.

"We're here," she said.

At the end of the tunnel, a stone stairway curved all the way around and up until you couldn't see the top.

I whistled. "That's pretty high."

Raven led first. "Watch your step."

The stairs had no railing and parts of the stone had crumbled off. I stayed close behind her, nervous she'd fall, but every step she took was calculated.

One slow step at a time, we walked up and up. I could see a wooden platform ahead with a large wooden door in the wall.

Raven quickened her steps. "That leads to the wine cellar."

I turned my head to the right and looked down. We had to be more than fifty feet high. A wave of vertigo hit me, and I steadied myself with a deep breath. Heights and I didn't get along.

Raven made it to the landing and turned to smile at me. A huge rat jumped down from above the door, hitting her in the face.

"Raven!"

"Eek!" She swatted the rat off, but moved too far to the left.

"You're too close to the edge!" I moved as fast as I could to reach her.

She glanced to the side and slowly began backing away, but her foot slipped and she fell.

"No!" I dove and grabbed her arm just as she went over. I would have gone over with her, but Derrick grabbed my feet.

I gripped her arm with both hands. She clutched a foothold in the wall with her free hand.

"Avikar, help!"

My grip slipped, and I growled. "Give me your other hand and I'll pull you up."

"I can't," her voice quivered.

"Derrick."

"I got you," he said.

"Raven, you have to trust me. I'm not going to let you fall."

Tears formed in her eyes. "I don't know if I can do it," she whimpered. "I'll fall."

"No, you won't. I'll pull you up. I promise. Raven, please."

She nodded.

"On three, okay … one … two … three."

She let go of the wall and reached to me. I caught her hand and pulled her onto the platform. Derrick let go of my legs and leaned against the wall, catching his breath. I grabbed Raven and hugged her. Her chest heaved against mine.

This is bad. I don't care how skilled she is. She shouldn't be here. It's too dangerous.

I held her in my lap, squeezing her.

"Are you okay?" I asked.

She wiped her eyes. "I think so." She glanced back at the drop. "If you hadn't caught me." She looked at me with big wet eyes, and I fell apart inside.

"We should keep moving," Derrick said and stood.

I helped Raven to her feet, but even when we were standing, I couldn't let go. I lost Jimri, Jeslyn is missing.

I can't lose anyone else.

"Avikar?" Raven's soft voice pulled at my heart, making me afraid to look her in the eye. Her hand touched my arm. "I'm all right."

I scratched the back of my head. "I told you I had you."

"Well, now that that's over with. We can move on." She readjusted her shirt and smoothed out her hair. She passed Derrick and mouthed a thank you. He nodded.

The wooden door had one lock, old and intricate. Raven slipped out a metal tool from her pocket. She knelt in front of the door, inserted it into the lock, and twisted. The lock clicked, and she opened the door.

We slowly walked into a small alcove. Raven pressed against the brick wall in front of us and entered a wine cellar. I followed her to the bottom of the cellar stairs and waited. When we didn't hear any footsteps, we tiptoed up.

The cellar opened into an enormous room with pots and pans of all sizes, hanging from large metal racks. I knew the servants must have cooked in here because of the two black stoves between the tables pressed against the far wall. My home seemed poor and feeble compared to this. We didn't have a separate room for cooking, and definitely not this big. The candles were doused, which meant the servants wouldn't be returning until morning.

Footsteps sounded from the stairwell to our left.

"Hide!" I hissed and grabbed Raven's arm, dragging her under one of the tables while Derrick hid by the cellar doors.

No, no. I unsheathed my sword. Raven crouched next to me, a dagger drawn in each hand. I didn't want her fighting. I had to make the first strike.

The footsteps came closer and the glow of candlelight bounced across the walls. I thanked The Creator it was night and we were somewhat hidden.

"Jeslyn?"

I heard Derrick say it, but I couldn't move. Raven's eyes went wide and she stepped out from under the table.

"Derrick?"

It is *her!* Jeslyn stood by the stairwell, holding a candle.

Derrick dropped his sword and rushed to her. "I can't believe it's you." He hugged and kissed her.

Her eyes met mine and I saw in them an emptiness. "Jeslyn." I walked over, staring at her. "Are you all right?"

Her eyes watered. She pulled away from Derrick and ran to me. "Avikar!" She wrapped her arms around me, crushing my chest. "I can't believe you're here." Her hands rubbed my face and she shook her head. "You're alive."

She looked at Derrick then. "This must be a dream. Lucino told me you were both dead."

"Dead?" Derrick said.

"He must have thought we died during the attack on Crain Village," I said, letting Jeslyn go.

"Just a misunderstanding," she said. "He'll be so happy you're both alive."

Derrick and I looked at each other, then back at Jeslyn who seemed creepily happy.

Derrick moved towards her. "He tried to kill us."

"No, he sent his men to look for you, but he was too late."

"He's fooled you then," I said, staring into her wide eyes and watching them tear.

She shook her head. "I don't understand. Why would he lie?"

Another set of footsteps sounded from the stairs.

Derrick reached for his sword and took Jeslyn's arm. "We need to get you out of here," Derrick said as we started moving toward the cellar.

"No."

All three of us looked at her like she'd gone mad. "Jeslyn, we need to go, *now*," Derrick said.

"I must speak with Lucino. If you're telling me the truth, then you're still in danger and if I leave with you, you'll be hunted."

"Jeslyn, we'll be fine," I said. "We have friends here."

"I can come meet you tomorrow in the gardens," she explained in a rush. "I'll find a way to sneak out. I won't risk your lives again."

The heavy footsteps were getting closer. "Lady Jeslyn?" A man's voice said.

Her eyes darted to the stairs. "That's the guard. Go, before you're caught." She whispered and rushed to the bottom of the stairs. "I'm here." She called to the guard.

"I'm not leaving you!" Derrick hissed.

"I'm not either," I said, pulling out my sword and readying it.

"Go," she said and before we could move, she ran up the stairwell.

"What do we do?" Raven whispered.

I kept my hand on my sword. "We're getting her out tonight. Who knows what Lucino will do to her? I'm not taking any chances." I moved past Derrick to the stairwell and listened. "Do you know what's up these stairs?"

"Follow me," Raven said, and with her daggers still drawn, crept upstairs.

At the top of the stairs, Raven held up her hand, stopping us then peered around the wall with a mirror. She held out one finger.

One guard. We couldn't afford a fight, not with Jeslyn so close. I pointed to the mirror and she handed it over. I positioned it and saw a guard standing at the middle of a long hallway. Besides a few fancy decorated tables with sculptures, the area was empty—no doors, except the one he guarded. I returned her mirror

"We need a distraction," Raven mouthed.

I reached into my pocket and grabbed a marble.

This better work.

I looked around the corner. On one of those tables, past the guard, sat a porcelain bird. If I could get it to break, he'd run to check it out. If I missed, he'd look this way.

One … two … three! I launched the marble, and the bird cracked in two. The guard turned his head and walked towards it. Raven stepped into the hallway and blew into a long thin tube. A second later, the guard toppled to the floor.

Derrick ran into the hallway first.

Raven followed and pulled the dart out of the man's neck. "He'll be out for a few hours, but we need to hide his body."

I grabbed the guard's legs and Derrick lifted the torso. Then we carried him back down the stairs, tied him in case he woke, and hid him in the pantry.

The door he guarded led to the guest wing. Raven began using her tool to unlock any doors we passed. I hoped Jeslyn was in one of them.

Raven unlocked the next door and peeked in. "Just a study," she whispered, and closed it.

"Wait." I stopped her. I don't know why, but I wanted to go in there. I needed to know more about Lucino, and the answer might be inside that room.

I walked in and they followed, shutting the door after they entered. Nothing seemed out of the ordinary: large bookcases, a massive desk, usual stuff.

"Look around," I told them, and headed to the desk. My stomach twisted with nerves. A part of me wanted to ignore the sinking feeling in my gut, but I couldn't.

"Why are we wasting time in here?" Derrick hissed. "We should be searching for Jeslyn."

"Just do it," I said and Raven hushed Derrick before he could argue with me.

The desk had a few rolled parchments. I gently unfurled one. Sprawling the page were words written in an unknown script. I put it down and opened one of the drawers. Nice knife. The dagger had a jagged edge. I picked it up, examining the unique curve of the blade.

Derrick glared at me. "We don't have time for this,"

I needed to find something and quick. A large landscape painting hung crooked on the wall behind the desk. I touched the side, fixing it back into place.

Click.

The painting moved down, revealing a map.

Is that ... ?

It was. It was a map of Tarrtainya and right in the center, a diagram of a red star. Belfur, Thebas, Jehoia, Esdrastas, Thummin, all five lands connected. I pointed to the middle of the star. Reading the name there made me want to puke. Tyre. Whatever he was planning, my home was smack in the middle of it.

"He's invading."

I heard Derrick say it, but I refused to believe it. "How can you be sure?"

Derrick's eyes glazed over the map. "They're strategic points. If he has control over these lands ..." he pointed while he spoke. "... he has control over the trade routes."

I rubbed my forehead, trying to take it all in. "Why? Why would he care about the rest of the world? He lives in Daath."

Raven tugged on my arm. "We can discuss this later, we need to keep moving."

I looked at the map once more, fear and anger colliding in my chest.

I don't know what you're planning, I thought, *but I'm going to stop it, no matter what.*

194

CHAPTER FORTY-EIGHT

JESLYN

They're alive. I can't believe they're alive.

Derrick and Avikar. My heart raced wildly. I sat on the chaise, running the brush through my hair and staring at the door. Tears rolled down my cheeks. I never thought I'd see either of them again. I had accepted this new life. Now, everything has changed, and I didn't know what to do. I didn't think Lucino would let me just leave and if he really did try to kill them, he was not the lord I thought he was.

Knock. Knock.

"Yes?" I said, continuing to brush my hair.

"I've come to see if you're feeling well. Reginald said you weren't."

I wiped my face and prayed to The Creator Lucino didn't notice. If he caught Avikar and Derrick in his home …

He opened the door and stepped inside. "What's wrong? Shall I fetch a doctor?"

In my haste, I'd told Reginald I felt queasy and needed to lie down in order to get him away from the kitchen. "No, I'm feeling better now."

Wearing just a plain black shirt and breeches, Lucino glided to me. He placed his hand on my forehead. "You feel very warm."

"Oh?"

His hand slipped to my chest.

"What are you doing?" I gasped. No man had ever touched me there.

He ignored my embarrassment. "Your heart beat is out of rhythm."

"My what? How do—"

He ignored me, again, and went to one of the bureaus. "I'm bringing you to Abigail. She'll see that you're given the right tonic to fix whatever ails you." He removed a lilac robe from the bureau and handed it to me. "Put this on, and I'll take you there."

I slipped the robe over my night chemise and fastened it closed.

"What were you doing tonight?"

I focused on the remaining buttons.

"Jeslyn." His tone changed, deeper and I was afraid to look at him. Afraid my eyes would give away the truth. "When I left earlier, you had fallen asleep."

"I woke and needed water and something to eat. I didn't want to bother the servants. They deserved a rest after the ball."

He stared at me and my chest tightened.

I placed my hand on my head. "I think you're right, Lucino … I don't feel …" I wobbled and leaned on the top of the chaise, pretending to be ill.

His hands steadied me, and I rested my hand on his arm. "I don't think I'll be able to walk. Maybe I should lie down."

"No, I'll carry you." He gently lifted me into his arms, holding me as if I weighed no more than a flower.

I put my arm around his neck and leaned into his chest. "Whatever you think is best, my lord."

I closed my eyes, praying he didn't ask any more questions.

CHAPTER FORTY-NINE

AVIKAR

We stayed in the shadows, stalking through the house, searching for Jeslyn's room. Jericho wasn't kidding about Raven's thieving abilities. She moved silent and fast. No locked door could stop her. Every moment I watched her work made me want her more.

She grabbed the handle on the next door and opened it just as we heard footsteps. Having no time to check the room, we bolted inside. It was a massive bedroom with wood paneling and a large canopy bed. A single lantern sat on a nightstand. The low light illuminated the deep red curtains around the empty bed.

Voices accompanied the footsteps. A man said, "This is the room."

My eyes darted around the room, looking for a place to hide. I grabbed Raven's hand and pulled her into an enormous wardrobe, while Derrick slid underneath the bed as the doorknob turned. Dresses stuffed the wardrobe, forcing Raven and I together. I strained to listen to the voices outside.

Images of us being slaughtered or tortured raced through my mind. Why had I let Jeslyn go? I should've grabbed her, forced her to come with us. What if we got caught? If anything happened to Derrick or Raven …

Raven's arms slid around my waist. She leaned into me. I could feel her heart pounding, just like mine. Two near death experiences in one night could make you mad. I enclosed her in a tight hug. I wanted her to know I'd keep her safe.

My head rested right above hers, perfectly. I smelled her hair. Honey and oatmeal. *How does she always smell so good?* It felt right to hold her. Having her close made me calm. I didn't understand why, but she had this soothing effect on my soul.

I wanted to see her face. To look into those dark eyes and disappear. I listened to her breathing. Why is she breathing heavily? Suddenly, I felt like an idiot. My stupid hands were intertwined with her long hair, twirling them. *My sister twirls her hair.* My stomach constricted. Being this close to Raven and not able to do anything but stand here was torture. Between the anticipation of death and the raw emotion Raven sent through me, I thought I would explode. I shifted my weight from one foot to the next. Then I rubbed my palms on the back of her shirt.

Stupid.

Wiping my fear-sweat off on her wasn't the greatest idea I'd had.

Her hands rubbed my back.

It could have been a friendly gesture, or something more. I put my hand on the back of her neck, cupping it. She gasped and I threw my free hand over her mouth. Any noise and we'd be a sitting target. Her hot breath beat against my palm. She breathed heavy. I listened for the voices. The room was silent … too silent.

I lowered my head, removed my hand from her mouth, and whispered in her ear. "I'm going to see if the room's clear."

"Don't go," she whispered.

I tilted her face in my direction. "I have to, unless you want to stay in here all night."

Her warm breath blew against my cheek.

I had to do it.

I pressed my mouth against hers. Her soft, sweet lips parted and every emotion you could feel concentrated in that one spot. She even *tasted* like honey. Her arms snaked around my neck. I slid my hands down her sides, until they were below her tiny waist, and lifted her, bringing her closer. I needed to feel her, all of her.

"What are you two doing?!" Derrick hissed as he swung open the wardrobe doors.

"Uh …" I had no excuse. I stepped out of the wardrobe, Raven followed.

"Did you even hear anything?" Derrick glared at me. I expected a wallop in the face.

"No. I tried, but it was all muffled."

"Raven, take us out of here. We're leaving," Derrick spun around.

"Wait," I grabbed his arm. "What about Jeslyn?"

Derrick shook me off. "She's gone."

What?

"Raven," Derrick said, and she stepped forward, taking the lead.

What does he mean by 'gone'?

CHAPTER FIFTY

AVIKAR

Raven took us home a different route. I think she got lost in the tunnels and didn't want to admit it. I understood. Derrick refused to talk to us, and he glared at me the entire trip. We ended at a tunnel near the market. At this time of night, the streets were clear. We walked past a tavern and four men stumbled out.

"Well, well, look who we have here. Our little friend from the alley."

Raven's brows narrowed at the man who tried to rob her the first day we met. He stood with three drunken fellows, smirking.

As a sign of peace, Derrick held up his hands. "We don't want any trouble, just passing through."

The four men circled us.

"Is this the girl who bested you? She's awfully pretty," one man said, licking his lips.

I stepped in front of Raven, meeting his harden stare. *I'd kill all four of them before I let anyone touch her.* Judging by their staggered steps, they wouldn't be hard to beat, either.

"It's been a long night and we would greatly appreciate it if we could pass by quietly." Derrick dug in his pocket and pulled out a coin. "This is for your troubles." He tossed the coin at one of the drunks who surprisingly caught it.

"One gold piece, huh? You think that will buy your freedom?"

"No," Derrick replied, "but it can at least buy a round of ale."

The four looked at each other. The man who caught the coin spoke. "Very well, but next time we see your pretty friend there we might not be so accommodating. My friend has taken a liking to her. Better keep her away from those alleys."

The man's friend gawked at Raven. "I can't wait," he sneered.

Raven spit at him, and I shoved her behind me before she launched a dagger into his throat.

"You put one hand on her and I'll cut if off," I said.

"Are you threatening me?"

"Yes, I am."

We glared each other. I itched for a fight, but it never escalated. Derrick steered us away while the drunks shuffled into the tavern.

When we reached Jericho's, Derrick veered off to the right.

"Where are you going?" I called after him.

He ignored me and kept walking.

"Go on back to Jericho's. I'll go see what's bothering him."

"Okay, be careful," Raven said.

I ran after Derrick. Luckily, he was a slow walker. I stepped in pace with him, debating if I should start the conversation.

Pushing the hair off my face, I took a breath and said, "What happened in there? Where's Jeslyn?"

Derrick spun around to face me, his face a cross between anger and hurt. "What's the matter with you?"

"Me? What did I do?"

"How can you even ask that question? Are you that dumb?" Derrick paced back and forth. "It's always the same with you, over and over. You never think of anyone else but yourself! Especially when it comes to women."

I thought back to all the times he referred to, but this was different. "You're the one who told me to use my charms on her."

"To get information, and I don't think you can discuss much when kissing."

I rubbed my forehead. "You misunderstood."

"No? What were you doing in that wardrobe before I interrupted?"

"She started it."

Derrick scoffed. "I doubt that. I don't care what you do with Raven, but do it after we save Jeslyn." Derrick stood in my face, his nostrils flaring. "Get your act together. If you were paying attention, we could've done something. Attacked those men and forced them to tell us where Jeslyn was going."

"I'm sorry. You're right."

Derrick walked over to a nearby tree and punched it.

"You're going to need that hand if you plan on fighting with it."

"She was in my arms. Why didn't she come with us?"

I'd been thinking that same thing. "I don't know."

Derrick tapped the tree with his head. "I should've grabbed her. When she said no ... I ... it happened so fast. What's she thinking?" His voice drifted into silence.

"We'll find her. At least we know she's alive."

"What if she doesn't want to leave?"

I put a hand on his shoulder. "Of course she wants to come home. Derrick, she was kidnapped."

His hands gripped the tree, and he shook his head. "I can't compete with wealth."

Hearing the defeat in his voice vexed me. "Are you forgetting the fact Lucino isn't HUMAN?"

Derrick pushed off the tree and rubbed his bloody knuckles. "You're right, and I doubt he revealed his true self to her."

"Do you know where they took her?"

He stood straighter. "Yes."

CHAPTER FIFTY-ONE

AVIKAR

At Jericho's, Derrick explained what he'd overheard at Lucino's. Jeslyn was taken to a woman named Abigail. In three days, she would be brought to the temple for the wedding. Jericho smoked his pipe, listening. We told him what happened at Lucino's, but left out the part of Raven almost falling to her death.

"I don't know who Abigail is. She could be the head mistress at the dollhouse," Jericho said.

"What's the dollhouse?" Derrick and I asked at the same time.

Raven said, "It's where Lucino houses his women."

"When do we go?" Derrick asked, pacing around the room.

Jericho shook his head. "Oh, no, you two might go in there and never return. Raven, think you can handle it?"

"Of course, no one will even notice me."

"This is a scout mission only. Any trouble and I want you out. I'll expect you back by nightfall," Jericho said.

"Understood," Raven replied, her glance shifting to me.

I didn't like the idea of Raven putting herself in danger, especially when I wouldn't be there to protect her. Derrick and Jericho seemed fine, but I had a bad feeling.

Without my journal, I couldn't relax. As Derrick snored, I sat staring out the window, watching the stars. I kept replaying Jeslyn's reaction. The far-off look on her face and the stiffness of her body when Derrick held her. Was Derrick right? I always knew Jeslyn hated our family's status and it wasn't her fault. Mother's father was a wealthy sea merchant. Since Jeslyn was a babe, he'd spoiled her with gifts, each one more extravagant than before. Jeslyn never understood why Mother left all that money to live on a farm, and she didn't understand why we couldn't live with our grandfather. Then Jeslyn had spent that summer at Luna Harbor, living her fantasy life—Mother should have never let her go.

Can I force her home if this is what she really wants? Did we come all this way for nothing? I shook my head, brushing off the anger. People had died on this journey, good men. I'd killed to come here, maybe even innocent men, and for what? Nothing.

Through the window, I saw Raven walk into the barn. I glanced at Derrick, still snoring, and snuck out.

Inside the barn, Raven was petting Onyx. She saw me and waved.

I waved back. "What are you doing in here?"

"Can't sleep, and when I can't sleep, I come here. I say hi to the horses and practice with my Bo staff."

"A Bo staff? That's an unusual weapon."

"I'm an unusual girl. How's Derrick?"

I kicked a rock on the ground, moving closer to her. "He'll be okay."

She walked over to the wall and took down two wooden staffs. She tossed one to me.

"You sure you want to fight me?" I slid my hands to the center of the staff and pointed it at her.

She rolled her eyes. "I don't think you're that tough."

"Oh, really?"

She came at me with a forward thrust. I blocked it, but almost dropped the staff. Staffs were not my favored weapon, too big and clunky.

She attacked again and after my clumsy block, she swept my legs, and I fell flat on my back. She stood over me, grinning.

Well, this is embarrassing.

I took a deep breath and vaulted onto my feet. She jabbed, twirled around and hit me with a low jab. I anticipated it and blocked. Using all my strength, I lifted my staff straight up and knocked hers out of her hands. She bounced back and tried to retrieve it, but I playfully slapped her hands away with my staff. I pointed at her and she threw her hands up in defeat. I dropped the weapon and bowed to her. She leapt past me and swiped the weapon.

"Cheater!" I yelled and sidestepped her incoming attack, grabbing her. She released the staff and we tumbled into a pile of hay. I landed on top of her. Before she could move, I pinned her hands to the ground.

"I knew you couldn't beat me."

"You're just lucky," she said in a breathy tone.

"What's my prize?"

Her brows narrowed. "Your prize?"

"The winner always gets a prize," I stated.

"I'll have to think about it, but how about you get off me, first."

I lowered my face, closer to hers. "What's the rush?"

"Because you're crushing me."

"Fair enough."

I backed off and stood, offering her my hand. She took it and I pulled her out of the hay. Once on her feet, she pulled her hand, but I held on to it. I reached to her face and she flinched. "Stay still," I said, and picked out a long piece of straw stuck in her hair.

"Thanks," she mumbled.

I nodded and let go of her.

"Good night, then." She turned around and walked away from me.

"Raven, wait."

"What?" She looked everywhere but where I stood.

Did I do something wrong? I walked over and placed a hand on her shoulder. "Raven?" When she didn't answer, I gently squeezed her. "Talk to me."

She sighed.

"Are you upset I beat you?"

She barely cracked a smile, but it was enough to ease the tension. "No, I'm not that much of a sore loser."

"Good, now come here." Without giving her a chance to refuse, I grabbed her in a big hug. "You should smile more."

She stiffened, but I could feel her heart race. "Raven?"

"Yes," she replied in a shaky voice.

"Look at me."

She lifted her head, and I brushed her cheek with my hand. This time she didn't flinch, but she closed her eyes, avoiding the connection we had.

"Avikar … "

Before she could finish, I kissed her. She felt perfect on my lips, soft and warm. I never knew I could feel anxious and blissful at the same time, but I did. Our lips parted and I whispered.

"I think I'm falling for you," I said.

I had never been in love before. I'd liked a few girls, but never this intensely and I couldn't ignore it anymore.

Raven nuzzled against my chest. "Don't say that, anything but that."

I pulled back. I wanted to see her face, but her head turned to the side, refusing to look at me. Her eyes watered and it nearly broke me.

"What's wrong?" I slid my hands to her face holding it between my fingers. "Raven, talk to me."

"I'm sorry. I have to go." Her voice cracked and she broke away.

Before she could run, I blocked her exit.

"Don't go," I begged. She tried to push me aside. I gripped her arm and pulled her into my chest. "Tell me you don't feel the same, and I'll let you leave."

She stared right at me, almost through me. Her dark eyes full of emotion. She didn't say no, so I kissed her again. Her arms molded around me, and I lifted her off the ground, kissing her with everything in me.

I held her in my arms, her feet back on the ground, kissing her forehead and stroking her hair. "I've never felt this way about anyone. You're all I think about, and when you're near me, all I want is to touch you, kiss you and inhale every scent of you."

Her lip quivered and I grabbed her hand. "What happens when this is all over?" she asked.

"What do you mean?"

Her hands fiddled with my shirt. "Will you stay in Daath?"

"No."

Her hands dropped.

I reached for her. "Let's not worry about the future. All that matters is the way we feel for each other. Who cares about the rest?"

Her mouth hung open and tears filled her eyes. She shook her head. "Who cares?" She shook her head.

"You're making this harder than it is." She pouted and I grabbed her shoulders. "Do you like me?"

"Avikar."

"It's a yes or no question."

She sighed. "Yes."

I smiled and cupped her chin. "That's all that matters."

I kissed her. This time she stiffened and backed away. I grunted. "You're driving me insane."

Her eyes popped at the accusation. "Me?"

"Yes, your mixed signals are making me crazy."

Her brow furrowed, and she folded her arms.

"I'm baring my soul and you're playing head games."

"You think this is a game to me?"

"I don't know, Raven. You obviously have issues."

Idiot.

"What I meant to say was … "

She cut me off. "What you meant to say doesn't matter, because I'm leaving." And she stomped past me.

I grabbed her arm. "Raven. I'm sorry. I didn't mean it."

Her glare was unnerving. She stood straighter and took a deep breath. "It doesn't matter. I should have known better." Then she gave me a half smile. "Hopefully, next time I won't be easily swooned by a pair of green eyes."

What?

"Can I go now?"

I shook my head in defiance. "No, not when I don't understand why you're leaving.

She pulled away from me. "I'm sorry, Avikar."

"You are the most complicated person I have ever met, and if it wasn't for the mere fact you've taken up all my waking thoughts, I would've been long gone."

Her face softened, but her eyes held an icy stare. We stood in an awkward silence. My head spiraled. Derrick was right. This was a mistake.

"I'm sorry I kissed you. It'll never happen again." I said it with venom, and I could see the crushing effect.

A single tear tread down her face.

"You shouldn't be upset," I said. "This is what you wanted, isn't it?"

That made her cry.

I walked past her, heading to the barn exit. I stopped right before leaving, her soft sobs tearing at my soul. Part of me wanted to hold her, tell her whatever she wanted to hear, but I wouldn't. She knew how I felt. I'd never said such things to a girl, only to be turned away.

I stole one more glance at her. She wiped her eyes. I could feel my heart tugging to where she stood. *No, this ends now,* I thought, and I walked out.

CHAPTER FIFTY-TWO

AVIKAR

The hot water soothed my skin, and the smell of jasmine relaxed my mind. Rose petals drifted on the water's surface. I touched one, admiring the delicate texture. I was alone, soaking in a tub full of perfumed oils. The woman, Abigail, had given me an herbal tea and put me in here before disappearing. I pretended to act ill, but I don't think she believed me. As long as Lucino didn't prod further, everything would be fine.

I needed time to think.

My head rested on the ring of the white porcelain tub. My toes tapped the opposite side, creating small splashes. Closing my eyes, I fell into a daydream, thinking of home and the life I was so ready to leave behind.

"My lady?"

A servant girl entered, carrying a tray of barrettes, brushes and ribbons. A bright red ribbon lay amidst the pastel pinks and blues.

"Are you finished bathing?" the servant asked.

I shook my head, my eyes frozen on the ribbon. "I need a few moments alone, please." She put the tray down on the vanity and left.

I stepped out of the bath, grabbing one of the robes hanging on a nearby rack and slipped in it. My hands trembled as I slowly grasped the ribbon. I rubbed it between my fingers, remembering...

...

"Close your eyes," Derrick had said, "and hold out your hands."

"Fine."

"And no peeking, either, Jeslyn."

A moment passed.

"There, now you can open them."

"It's beautiful, Derrick! Thank you."

"I love you. I always will, no matter what."

...

Tears sprinkled my cheeks. I was ashamed at my behavior. I cared for Derrick, but these past weeks with Lucino had changed everything.

Who do I choose?

I knew Avikar and Derrick wouldn't lie to me, but I also knew Lucino and I shared a connection, and I owed it to him to find out the truth. Sneaking off in the middle of the night would only cause more danger. And if someone tried to kill my brother, I needed to know who.

Who do I believe?

And I couldn't deny the way I felt for Lucino. He filled me with heat I didn't understand. I wiped my face and sniffled. Could a woman love two men? And if she did, how would the story end? If Lucino is innocent, then I should tell him what horrors his people do in his name.

"Jeslyn."

I spun at the whisper of my name, but saw no one. "Hello? Is someone there?" Cold filled the room. I shivered. "Hello?"

"Jeslyn."

The candlelight flickered, and a dark shape flew to my right. Too afraid to speak, I grabbed the closest object. I didn't think a brush would protect me, but I felt safer with it in my hands. A tingling sensation crawled under my skin, freezing me in place. My heart thumped.

Fingers touched my neck and I jumped.

"Stay back!" I swung the brush, hitting only air.

"Foolish girl. I'm here to help you."

A black shadow, with devilish eyes, appeared in front of me.

"Creator help me," I whispered.

CHAPTER FIFTY-THREE

AVIKAR

How are we going to get in?" Derrick asked.

"We are not going anywhere," I said, pointing to an open window on the third floor. "I'm going in through there."

We were outside the dollhouse. Since Jericho worked in the guard, he knew the house's location. Raven never came home and Jericho was worried something had gone wrong. I didn't think twice about going after her.

"Up there?" Derrick said as he handed me a length of rope.

I left the rope and patted him on the shoulder.

I darted across the lawn, making my way to the side of the wooden house where a large low-limbed oak tree sprouted from the ground. I jumped and grabbed one of the branches. Climbing a tree was easy. I did it all the time back home. Getting into that window would take a bit more skill.

I climbed the tree until I reached a branch near the window, shimming across it as close to the end as I could without breaking it. I dropped, holding onto the branch with both hands and swung my body forward and back. When I had enough momentum, I let go and swung myself towards the open window, grabbing the ledge.

That was close.

I pulled myself into the empty room. The room was dark and appeared to be a storage place, nothing but useless junk everywhere. I crept to the door, slowly cracked it open and peeked out into a dimly lit corridor. I had no clue where Raven was, and I definitely didn't have any nifty lock picking tools.

At the end of the hallway, I saw a large double door with light shining underneath. I carefully walked to it and put my ear against the wood. I could hear women laughing. I listened a little longer. *Only women inside.* I grinned as a plan formulated in my head.

Slipping out my dagger, I opened the door. Any plan I had vanished when I stepped into that room. Beautiful women filled the area, arrayed on pillows and couches like soft petals on the grass. I'd heard of harems, but never thought I'd see one. There were so many girls!

"What are you doing here?" A curvy brunette with bulging breasts examined me. "A little lost, honey?"

I slipped the dagger back in its sheath. "I'm a new guard. I came to inspect the room."

Someone pinched my side, and I turned to a gorgeous blonde smirking at me. "Guards aren't allowed in here," she whispered.

"We have a situation," I said.

Gasps erupted, and a bunch of women began rattling over one another.

"Are we in danger?"

I turned right, and a freckled red head with stunning blue eyes stared at me.

"We may have a thief in the house," I said. "Someone was seen running across the lawn."

The girl seemed satisfied with the answer and smiled. "Lucky for us we have you."

"Oh, he's cute!" squealed the blonde. "You should stay here."

Before I could refuse, they dragged me into the very inviting scenery. Crushed velvet covered the walls and spots of red and yellow oversized pillows surrounded everything. They pushed me onto a pile of sinking cushions. More of them crept near me, squealing and giggling.

I am in serious trouble.

Tiny beads of sweat dripped down my back. One woman crawled onto my lap and whispered provocatively in my ear. The suggestion ignited every boyish fantasy I had.

It can't hurt to stay just a bit. I can use them to find Raven.

No, don't be stupid, Avikar. Get up.

"Ladies … please." I tried to think of an excuse to leave, but my mind concocted every reason to stay.

"Avikar?"

I jumped at the sound of Raven's voice. The girl on my lap thumped to the floor. Raven wore a long silver dress with navy trim that hugged her body in all the right places. *Holy heifer.* Even though she was scowling, she looked utterly amazing.

The brunette who spoke with me before eyed Raven suspiciously. "How do you know him?"

Raven bit her lip.

"We're old friends," I said and gave Raven a big hug. "It's good to see you."

"You too," she replied.

The brunette crossed her arms. "Isn't this a tearful reunion."

I took Raven's hand. "If you ladies will excuse me. There's a pressing matter I need to speak with my friend about in private." I dragged Raven outside and closed the double door behind us.

"What are you doing here?" she hissed. "Trying to get us both killed?"

"I'm here to rescue you."

"I don't need to be rescued," she huffed.

I pointed a finger at her. "You were supposed to come back before nightfall. What happened?"

She looked down the empty hallway, and it was then the realization of what she wore hit me. Since the first day I'd met her, she'd always worn pants, or tights, never, ever a dress and her hair was usually down and straight, but now … the silver sleeveless gown accentuated every perfect aspect of her body, tight around her middle and flowing down from there, trailing a few inches behind her. All her hair was curled, part of it pinned up. Big loose curls hung around her cheeks. But her painted red lips were what really heated my blood. They were full, begging to be kissed.

"Why are you gawking at me like that?" She crossed her arms, attempting to hide her body. "I had to blend in. All the women dress like this."

"Do you know how gorgeous you are?"

She blushed. "Thank you, but I'm never wearing one of these dreadful things again."

I gasped. "Blasphemy."

That made her smile.

We stood in silence, staring at each other. I wanted to apologize for last night, but now wasn't the time. "Did you find my sister?"

She shook her head. "I'm sorry. I asked around. I'm the only new girl in a while."

I grunted and rubbed my forehead. "What's the layout of this place?"

"There are three floors. This floor has the main sitting room, a music room and storage. The second is mainly bedrooms and two washrooms. The bottom are eating and servants quarters."

"Where are the guards and how many?"

Raven fidgeted with her lip. "The guards stay on the first floor. Lucino doesn't allow anyone up here but the maids. How did you get in?"

"I'll explain later. Right now, I need to get you out of here. Jericho and Derrick are waiting outside."

"If I wanted to leave, I could."

I arched my brow at her.

"I can get out on my own. I don't need any help. You should go before someone tells one of the real guards."

I thought about the window. It'd be tough to jump to the tree and in that dress, Raven wasn't going to be able to climb. "That's not an option. Do you know of an exit? My route is kind of a one way trip."

"Lucino has a private entrance inside. If we can find it, it'll lead us out."

"And how do you suppose we snoop around without getting caught?"

Raven grinned. "You'll be our distraction."

"What? You actually want me to flirt with them?"

She smirked, opened the door and pushed me back inside.

CHAPTER FIFTY-FOUR

AVIKAR

He's back!"

I watched Raven slip away unnoticed.

"Sit with us," said the blonde locks woman, motioning for me.

"I could get in trouble if I'm gone for too long," I said. My newfound audience didn't agree with me. They laughed and dragged me back into their midst.

Keeping the ladies distracted was entertaining. They laughed at all of my jokes—something I greatly appreciated—and cooed when I talked about being in hundreds of vicious battles. They rubbed my arms, commenting on how strong I was.

Raven reappeared and glided toward the red plush couch on which I sat. Our gazes locked onto one another. A woman whispered in my ear, but I blocked her out. Another rested her busty chest on my side. The only thing I could see was Raven, her small hips swaying beneath that dress, her full lips mouthing 'I found it'. She moved gracefully through the women surrounding me and grabbed my hand, pulling me to her. It took every ounce of self-control not to grab her and kiss her right there.

"Where do you think you're going?" the brunette asked Raven as she intercepted us.

Raven eyed her. "You can have him when I'm through."

"Don't let her take him, Jezy!"

Jezy smiled at Raven. "You see dear. I am the lady of this house and I have to make sure my girls are happy. Right now, they're not, and that's a problem."

Raven stood straighter, but Jezy towered over her. "I understand," Raven said, "but your girls will have to wait their turn."

Raven shoved past her.

Jezy grabbed Raven's arm. "I don't think so love. I run this house, not you."

This isn't good. We can't afford a fight here.

"If I were you, I'd let go of my arm."

"Or what?" Jezy sneered.

Raven dropped my hand. "Or I'll force you to."

The two locked stares. "Ladies, why don't we settle this calmly?" I said, attempting to step between them. They both ignored me.

Raven yanked her arm free and Jezy's eyes went wide. She went to push Raven, but Raven shoved her first. Then they were on the floor brawling and yelling. I'd never seen two women fight. I kept waiting for a dress to tear. Raven had Jezy pinned and Jezy grabbed a handful of Raven's hair, pulling her head back.

"Ahh!" Raven yelled and punched Jezy in the side. Jezy screamed and let go.

This is getting ugly.

I grabbed Raven around the waist and tried pulling her off Jezy, but Jezy had Raven's hair again. Girls fight dirty. I pried Jezy's fingers loose and she kicked me hard in the stomach, sending me into a nearby table. The lantern on the table crashed to the floor and flames erupted from the broken glass, crawling up the fabric walls.

The room spiraled into panic. Women screamed and toppled over one another in an attempt to reach the only door.

"Get out now!" I yelled.

Jezy snarled at Raven and released her.

"We need to get out of here before the whole place burns," I yelled while dragging Raven out.

When the rest of the women were down the stairs, Raven and I followed. The fire spread fast and by the time we made it to the second floor, the third floor ignited.

The frenzied mob of women in front of us continued to run.

"Move!" I yelled, pulling Raven along.

One woman fell to the floor. No one noticed her, and she cried out when another girl scrambled across her back. I left Raven, rushed to the fallen women and helped her to her feet. She thanked me and hurried down the next flight of stairs.

A loud crash sounded behind me. Raven screamed.

Oh, no. I turned to see Raven lying on her stomach, leg pinned by a wooden beam.

I ran over. "Are you okay? Can you move?"

She grunted. "I think it's broken."

"Hold on. I'll get you out." I grabbed the beam, but it wouldn't budge. It was heavier than I expected. "Come on!" I tried again.

"Go, Avikar. It's too heavy. Leave me."

I squatted by her face. "I'm not leaving you. Either we both go or we both stay."

Her eyes glistened. She grabbed my shirt and kissed me. "Go," she ordered

"Not without you."

I held the solid wood in between both hands. Using my legs, I lifted, but it barely moved. *No, no, don't do this to me again, don't! I can't lose her!*

Heat from the fire singed the back of my neck. Smoke clouded the air, stinging my eyes and throat. I tried again. It was too heavy. *It's my fault she's here. It's always my fault.* I didn't know what to do. I'd never felt so desperate in my life. I needed a miracle.

I don't know if you're there, but please, if you need to take someone, take me, not her. Creator give me the strength to save her. I'll do anything, anything you ask, I'll do it.

I can't let her die.

I breathed in deep, exhaled.

I can do this. I can do this. I can do this!

I focused all my strength, all my anger, all my frustration into one single action—moving that beam. I gripped the wood, moved my legs to a better position and with every muscle strained, lifted.

"Ahh!" I screamed as the beam inched higher.

When she could, Raven slid her leg out. I dropped the beam, panting. Raven looked at me, her eyes sparkling. I leaned down, scooped her into my arms, tossed her over my shoulder and ran.

CHAPTER FIFTY-FIVE

AVIKAR

I guzzled a mug of water and slammed it on the table.

Derrick poured himself a drink. "What happened in there?"

We were sitting at the table. Jericho had brought Raven into her room, where he was inspecting her leg.

"Raven got into a fight," I said, "with one of the women. When I tried to break it up, we knocked over a table and set the whole place on fire."

"Are you serious?"

I leaned back in the seat, wiping my sweaty head. "Thank The Creator we made it out alive."

"Since when did you start believing in The Creator?"

I shrugged. I didn't want to explain my groveling. He would go on to say how happy he was that I'd returned to the faith. I didn't have the energy for that conversation.

Jericho walked in and we both stood.

"How is she?" I said.

"I gave her some tonic for the pain. She'll need to be off her feet for a while, but she'll live." Jericho crossed his arms and his tone changed. "I can't blame you completely. I shouldn't have let her go in at all and I certainly shouldn't have let you sneak in after her."

"Jericho, I—"

He raised his hand, cutting me off. "Both of you could have died. Even though I know you're both skilled, you're still children."

I opened my mouth to protest.

"I swore I would help and I intend to keep that promise. You're not the only one who wants Lucino gone. I have men I can trust and it's time we took a stand."

"We should go see this temple and plan an attack," Derrick said. "We know she'll be there in two days."

"Agreed," Jericho replied. Then he looked at me. "You can see her if you want."

Derrick followed me upstairs.

We bumped into Anna who was walking out of Raven's room. "She's getting sleepy, hurry and say hello."

Raven lay in bed, propped against a few pillows. She smiled when we entered.

"Hi," she said softly.

"How are you feeling?" Derrick asked.

"It hurts, but I've had worse."

"Good." Derrick glanced back at me.

I couldn't seem to move from the doorway.

"Get well soon," Derrick said and left the room, patting my shoulder as he past.

I stared at her, and she waved me closer. I knelt beside the bed and stared at the floor.

"What's wrong? You're a hero. Because of you, I'm alive."

"Because of me, you almost died," I replied.

She reached for my hand and I gave it to her. She squeezed it. "It wasn't your fault. What are the chances we'd cause a fire?"

"My chances are always high when it comes to disasters."

"If it were anyone else in there tonight, I'd be dead. What you did was amazing and I will always be grateful you saved me."

Her words crushed any barrier I tried to hold. Tears filled my eyes and I clasped both my hands around hers, holding them to my face. "I don't know how I did it. I thought we were both dead." My voice cracked and a tear slipped down my face. "I wouldn't have been able to leave you." I buried my face in her hand.

"I wouldn't have allowed you to stay."

I glanced at her. "Allowed? I don't think you were in a position to do anything."

Her lip quivered and she bit it. "About last night."

"Shh, forget about it."

She shook her head.

"It doesn't matter," I said.

"I'm sorry for the way I acted," she sobbed.

I kissed her hand. "I'm the one who should be sorry."

"Avikar."

I smiled, loving the way she said my name. "Let's start over."

"I'd like that. Will you stay with me until I fall asleep?"

"Of course." I moved closer, touching her arm.

She smiled and rested her head back on the pillow, closing her eyes. I stroked her hand and gently placed it on her chest. Standing, I pulled the blanket around her, tucking her in. Her chest rose and sunk as she drifted into sleep.

The night breeze blew in from the open window. I walked over, went to close the shutters, and stopped, staring at the moon instead.

So much has happened since I left the farm. I feel different.

I blamed The Creator and myself for Jimri's death. I thought The Creator had abandoned me and, back then, maybe he had, but not tonight.

"I won't forget about my promise," I whispered to the air.

I closed the shutters and locked them. As I left the room, I took one last glance at Raven, burning into memory the image of her peaceful slumber. If I never saw her again, I wanted to remember the sweet serenity on her face.

CHAPTER FIFTY-SIX

LUCINO

I sat in the study, examining Tarrtainya's literature. This world had strange writings, most of them useless. These humans wrote stories of imaginary places and people who did not exist. We had no such books in Mirth. They served no purpose. Our race wrote about subjects that mattered: history, formulas, spells, research, philosophies and math. What use is a fictional book?

I flipped through a book of poetry. I found these writings were different from the rest. They were pleasing to read. Words were carefully chosen and I deciphered messages within them. It seemed poets were more intelligent than the others. I'd have to see if Romulus had any dead poets lying around. It would be interesting to see if their mind was molded different.

A knock at the door.

Never a moment's rest.

"Enter." I continued flipping through the pages. "I'm sure you have a very good reason for disturbing me at this hour."

"Yes, my lord. There was a fire at the dollhouse," my second lieutenant said.

"And?"

"The entire house burnt, my lord."

I sighed and closed the book. "Any survivors?"

"Yes. They are in the guest wing. We're awaiting your orders."

I rubbed my chin. "Do we know what caused the fire?"

"Not yet, my lord. We're looking into it."

"I want a new place built for them. In the meantime, find somewhere in Daath to house them."

Lucy appeared in the doorway wearing a wicked grin.

"You are dismissed." I waved the lieutenant away.

He gave a salute before leaving.

"And why are you so amused, my dear sister?"

Lucy glided into the study and sat on one of the leather chairs. "You should know how disaster excites me. A good woman loves chaos."

"Then we should have fires more often."

Lucy grinned. "Ahh, but then where would we house your precious dolls?"

"Indeed."

Lucy folded her hands on her lap. I sensed she had news I would not be pleased with. "What is it?"

"I've received word that The Council is deciding on who will be your steward in Daath when you return home."

"I assumed it would be you."

"It is not. Dago."

I jumped from my seat and slammed the desk with my fist, cracking the wood. Dago, my enemy since birth. His family wanted the ruling power and would stop at nothing to achieve it. "The Council thinks to replace me with him! This is an outrage!"

"He will take your wife in your absence."

"He will *not* have her."

Lucy met my hard gaze. "You will have little choice. You cannot bring her to Mirth."

"Argh!" I flipped the desk over. Lucy jumped out of the way before it hit her.

"Calm yourself. She is nothing but a human."

A human unlike any I've ever met.

I stood and straightened my coat. "Go see Romulus. Tell him to poison the ceremonial wine."

"Why not just drain her aura completely?"

"Because then she would die during the ceremony and The Council might find it odd that I killed her. You know how they feel about keeping these human pretenses. The nobles will think Jeslyn is ruling while I'm away and Dago will be her trusted advisor."

Dago was the crudest of our race. Even though Jeslyn was a human, I wouldn't abandon her to Dago and his treacherous ways.

"Make sure the poison doesn't cause too much pain," I said. "A low dose that will slow her heart. Let her die in her sleep. That is the best I can do for her."

"Very well, brother. I'll see it's done."

CHAPTER FIFTY-SEVEN

AVIKAR

The next day, Jericho took us deep into the forest. A few of Lucino's guards—Jericho's childhood friends—came with us, swearing their loyalty and sword. With the newly combined men, we were thirteen. I prayed it was enough.

Jericho explained little about our destination. When he did speak, it was in grave whispers. The townspeople feared the temple, saying it was cursed. Old tales spoke of a pit with no bottom, located in the center of the main hall: a secret gateway to another world. An old man in town swore he'd witnessed strange creatures crawling out of it when he was a boy. No one believed him, but the stories were enough for everyone to keep their distance.

The closer we came to the temple, the more the vegetation around us changed. Old trees, covered in mossy green, bent in awkward directions. Branches that should have been reaching for the sky instead touched the ground. I tilted my head to the side, staring at those strange shapes.

It's as if the whole forest is broken.

I walked past a spider web strung between two trees. If I hadn't been paying attention, I would have walked right into it. I hated spiders. The large web was taller than I and at least seven feet wide. A sparrow flew by, and unlike me, it didn't see the web. The animal landed right at the top. Its feathers stuck to the stringy substance. It batted its wings in a futile attempt to escape. I watched in horror as a brown tarantula, bigger than both my combined fists, skittered down from one of the nearby trees. Every hair on my body stood in fear. Before the bird had any chance of survival, the spider spit out webbing and began to roll the bird between its long spiny legs. I slowly stepped back, my eyes never leaving the deadly creature. When there was a good distance between that bug and me, I ran to Derrick.

The air became hot and humid. I took off my shirt and tied it around my head, keeping my hair off my face. I grabbed the canteen hanging from my belt and in two long swigs drained half of its contents.

"This isn't natural," Derrick said, wrapping his shirt around his waist.

I put the empty canteen back in its place. "I agree. Now I know why the townsfolk stay away."

The surroundings filled me with dread. My hand instinctively went to my sword hilt. The atmosphere tingled with a foreign sensation that seemed otherworldly. In school, I'd learned about different climates. This jungle did not belong in Daath.

Jericho whistled and held up his hand. He pointed to a friend who went to scout ahead. A few minutes later, we heard another whistle and began moving again. I could see the white dome of the temple looming above the trees. No birds chirped and no animals crept through the brush. Even the wildlife knew to keep their distance.

The trees broke and there, standing in the middle of the forest, was our destination. The ancient structure had two large statues guarding the entryway. Each figure sat atop a large throne with strange carvings running along the sides.

"What are these?" Derrick stood next to one of the lizard men statues, perplexed.

The expression on Jericho's face changed. He looked afraid. "We believe that is the statue of the god Lucino worships."

"No, you're wrong."

We all looked at the scrawny man who spoke.

"What do you mean, Rufus?" Jericho eyed his friend.

"That's him."

I didn't want to know how this man knew that and I didn't want to ask any more questions. This thing planned to marry my sister.

Derrick growled and kicked the statue.

My head spun. *All the sculptures we've seen … they're all him?*

I breathed in.

As we entered the temple, Jericho explained the plan for tomorrow night. His comrades were able to find out information about the ceremony and Jeslyn. She would be unreachable until arriving at the temple from a secret location. They weren't sure what type of ritual would take place with the wedding, but it sounded ominous, and only Lucino's personal guard would be on duty that night.

I worried for my sister. Every time I heard Lucino's name it filled me with rage. I knew my sister was proper; at least I didn't have to worry about that. Who knew what that creature would do to her once they married?

Creator, if you're listening, please watch over my sister. Protect her from danger.

The entrance opened into a large hallway that broke to the left and right. Every six feet was an archway that led into the main part of the temple. The temple was one gigantic dome, the sky its ceiling.

The hairs on my body stood. I could feel a presence in the temple, an evil force. I focused on the black center and walked towards it. Rows of steps led down into the pit in a circular formation. An unseen force drew me closer and closer until I found myself standing over the hole peering into its depths. A low humming noise emanated from inside. My sword and dagger vibrated. I tried to see the bottom but there was no end. Only a column of darkness. I took out a marble, kissed it and flicked it into the pit. I waited, expecting to hear the *thunk* of it hitting the floor.

Nothing.

Impossible. I leaned forward to get a better look and wobbled.

"I wouldn't get that close if I were you," Derrick said as he grabbed my arm.

"What do you think is down there?"

"I don't know, and I don't care." Derrick rubbed the ribbon around his wrist.

I patted his shoulder and continued exploring the temple. If this was going to work, we needed to memorize the layout.

Strange runes were etched into the floor and columns. Next to the runes were lines connecting them together, creating an intricate matrix of shapes. The images reminded me of constellations. I bent down, examining them more closely. I traced the outline of one. The edges were perfectly smooth and round. To cut stone like that would have taken years. The runes looked vaguely familiar.

It can't be.

I slid out my dagger. On the hilt next to the rubies was a tiny rune, an exact replica of the one on the floor.

This can't be.

My father had never mentioned anything about Daath. I flipped the jeweled hilt over and placed it on the floor. There was no mistaking it. The runes were identical.

Derrick was by my side, staring at the floor. "I've never seen anything like this."

"Me either." I put the dagger away. Once this was over, I planned to have a long talk with my father. For now, I had to concentrate on scouting the rest of the temple.

"What are all those lines?" Derrick said, pointing to the floor.

I jumped onto one of the white pillars in the room and shimmied up. I followed the lines around the room, blocking out the runes that intercepted at various points. The pattern screamed at me.

"A labyrinth," I muttered.

"A what?"

I rubbed my head in disbelief. "Never thought I'd see one."

I hopped down.

"It's a labyrinth. I've seen drawings of them in one of my father's books. They're used in magic rituals."

"Used for what?"

I looked at him wide eyed. "I don't know, but they are extremely powerful. We need to find Jericho."

Jericho was at the entrance discussing battle tactics. I asked him about the labyrinth but he didn't know what that was. There were no books in Daath, except the few religious texts Lucino provided. If Lucino dabbled in the dark arts, Jeslyn was in graver danger than I could have imagined.

Chapter Fifty-Eight

Lucino

The torchlight bounced off the stone walls as I headed to the preparation house. The walk was not something I enjoyed. The tunnels were damp and had a foul, wet smell to them, nothing like the burning sands of Mirth, but they were necessary. They allowed us to travel unnoticed throughout Tarrtainya.

When I arrived at the steel door, the two guards saluted and let me pass. The door opened into an empty basement. I walked up the stairs to the first floor where Abigail was waiting.

"Hello, Abigail. I'll be in the parlor. Please bring Jeslyn in."

The plump woman curtseyed before leaving.

The parlor was decorated with gold paneling and ivory white wallpaper. An oversized oil painting of a sunset hung on the wall above the white sofa. The art in this world was intriguing. The humans had a creative side that varied from my people. I admired the small smooth brushstrokes creating the vibrant scene. It reminded me of home and when our sky used to be filled with pink and orange hues.

Jeslyn stepped into the parlor and Abigail closed the doors behind her. I walked to her with open arms. Her eyes lit and she fell into my embrace. She smelled of flowers, her skin like satin. She leaned against my chest.

"I'm glad you came," she said. "I had a horrible nightmare last night and haven't been the same since."

I stroked her silky hair that hung past her shoulders. "Tell me about your nightmare."

She shook her head. "No, it's too terrible. I just want to forget it. Can we talk of something else?"

"Anything you would like. How was your day?"

"Strange …" her voice drifted and I didn't care for the sound of it.

"How?" I stroked her again.

She pulled back, gazing into my face. Her eyes had a dullness to them. Possibly from the prior night's affliction.

"The other night when you brought me here, I fell asleep in the bath and when I woke … I was in a different room. Abigail said I walked there, but I don't remember. It's as if my head is full of clouds."

There was still much about the humans we did not know. Was this a reaction to something or a side effect of nerves? I needed to learn more. Reptilians did not dream and I found the process intriguing in humans.

"I know what will set you at ease," I said. "Maybe then you can tell me of this nightmare."

She followed me to the piano and sat next to me on the bench. The piano was an instrument I admired, many different chords and only seven notes. Fascinating. I tapped at the keys, playing a symphony I'd created in my first years in this world. Hypnotic notes filled the room. Not even Lucy's song spell could compare to the melody of the piano. I closed my eyes, focusing on the notes and nothing else.

Jeslyn sang. Her voice, like a soft bird, harmonized with me.

"In the night/when the world comes alive/All that breathes/Will sing with me/A song of fate/ To spread love's joy/ Till the morrow comes."

My hands feverishly brushed the keys. I lost myself in her song. I had never had a human sing like that for me, and never while I played. The combination affected a part of my mind I was not familiar with. Strange warmth flowed through every one of my fibers.

When I finished playing, Jeslyn clapped her hands. "That was magnificent! You're a wonderful pianist."

"Thank you. The piano is a fine instrument." I turned on the bench, facing her. "And who knew my betrothed was such a song bird."

She smiled. Suddenly it bothered me that she would soon be dead. *If she dies, she will die in bliss.*

I gazed at her, activating the spell held within my eyes. Holding her hands, I spoke. "Our wedding will be a joyous day and nothing will upset you. Do not be troubled this night—"

"There's something I wish to discuss with you," she interrupted.

"What is it?"

She breathed in deeply before speaking. "What do you know about the attack on my brother? How do you know he's dead?"

"Why do you think of such dark things, tonight?"

"I need to know," she said softly.

I wondered where her curiosity came from. "My Council sent me word about the attack on Crain Village. They had mentioned two young boys were slaughtered."

She stared at me with wide eyes. "How do you know for certain it was my brother?"

Holding her hand, I met her gaze. "One of the men was still alive. When my people had asked of Avikar, he pointed to one of the slain boys."

She shook her head.

"What is it? What do you know?" Her questions stirred questions of my own. Did the Council truly succeed in their actions or had they been fooled? With the ball, the invasion and Jeslyn, I had never thought to inquire further. Even if her brother was still alive, he'd never make it to Daath.

"Jeslyn?"

Her head shifted slightly to the left, as if she couldn't face me. "I know he's alive. I already lost one brother. If Avikar's dead, I would feel it."

Feel it? Humans and their feelings.

"If there's any chance The Council is mistaken, I will find out. This I swear."

She nodded, satisfied with my answer. "I know you are a good man, Lucino, but I do not trust this Council of yours. I do not think they have your best interests at heart."

How right you are my dear. "I will be careful."

I lifted her hands to my mouth and kissed them. "Sleep, well, my lady."

"There's one more thing," she said, her cheeks flushing with color.

I lowered her hands. "Yes, my lady?"

She leaned forward.

What is she doing?

She moved closer and then pressed her lips against mine.

No!

This was forbidden. The law stated no intimacy with a human until after the ceremony. The ceremonial wine contained a sterilization element that would affect the human, making our human brides unfertile. A Reptilian/human offspring was considered an abomination. If The Council found out, I'd be stripped of my position.

Yet her lips were inviting and I found I could not pull away. The touch set off different sensations, very overpowering sensations. A red haze clouded my mind.

I scooped her into my arms, forgetting the law, forgetting the consequence.

I wanted her in a way I didn't understand. Desire to touch her and kiss her skin. It was unexplainable. As we landed on the sofa, she broke the connection. When her lips left mine, I regained composure.

This must end, quickly.

Strange feelings blocked out the logical side of my brain. Her hands reached for me, pulling me closer to her face. I activated my spell, before things turned worse.

"Jeslyn, we must stop this."

She ignored the order.

What? My spell. I jumped away from her. "What have you done to me?"

Her eyes were glassy. "I'm sorry." Her hand went to her mouth. "I don't know what came over me. You've never kissed me before, and I ... I'm sorry."

I placed a hand on her shoulder. "Don't be sorry. After we are married you may do as you please."

"Forgive me," she whispered. "That's not like me at all. I've wondered what it would be like to kiss you ... then this strange urge came over me ..."

"Of course. I must say goodnight." I should have removed myself from the sofa, but I was drawn to her. Inexplicably. Her eyes met mine and I kissed her. I could feel the beast inside breaking free, the animalistic part of our nature. The part I had buried. Giving into desires was considered a weakness.

I stood, pulling her to her feet and wrapped my arms around her, kissing her with a severity that worried me. Our lips parted. I could see the hesitation in her eyes, but also the desire.

My control broke.

CHAPTER FIFTY-NINE

LUCINO

No!" **Lucy ripped Jeslyn out of my grip.**

I growled as she passed her off to Abigail.

"Take her upstairs, now!" Lucy ordered and locked the parlor doors behind them. She met my hard stare and screamed a mental order: *Pull yourself together!*

Roaring, I leapt at her, wanting to rip her apart. How dare she take what's mine. Slamming her against the door, I grabbed her neck and squeezed.

Lucino, snap out if it!

I squeezed and squeezed.

You leave me no choice, brother.

Bursting pain shot through my groin and into my stomach. I grabbed myself and fell to the floor. I couldn't find the strength to do anything more than breathe. When the pain passed, I stood.

"Was that really necessary?" I grunted.

Lucy swiftly moved out of reach. She rubbed her neck, adorned with red hand imprints. "Considering you almost killed me, yes, I think so."

"My apologies. You know I would never willingly harm you. I don't know how I allowed things to get out of control."

"I do," Lucy glared.

"Explain."

"Abigail contacted me about Jeslyn acting strange since her bath last night. I went to the washroom and found this." She held out a finger with a yellow substance on it.

"Is that sulfur?"

"Yes."

"Demons. Take her back to her room and put a ward over it. No one except you or I will enter that room. I must see Romulus."

When I entered the laboratory, Romulus was working on another one of his lavish experiments. He had moved on from lizards to actual humans, dead ones. Normally his work didn't bother me, but seeing the human's chest ripped open with metal prongs, its organs arranged on a table, was a bit revolting. The putrid smell was enough to gag me.

"Hmm, the prince pays me a visit."

I walked around the large metal table and stood further from the stench. "I've been busy, but now I seek your counsel. Lucy found the trail of a demon near Jeslyn."

"That is interesting. Only the elders possess the power to call demons. Perhaps your brethren have turned on you, hmm?"

"No, Falcur is loyal."

"Hmm." Romulus bobbed his head and dug into the human's chest with a scalpel. "These specimens are very interesting. Did you know humans are the only animals to have emotional tears? This one cried obsessively before it died. Fascinating creatures."

"There is another issue I wish to discuss."

Romulus scrunched his fat bulbous nose as he removed another organ.

I averted my eyes. Experimentation was critical, but I preferred not to see it.

"My captivation spell had no effect on Jeslyn," I said.

That piqued his interest.

"That is very interesting." Romulus wobbled to the door and called outside for one of the guards. "Bring me Specimen D from the cage." When he entered the room, again, he ushered me to the side. "Sit and we will test your powers."

The guard brought in a woman, battered and skinny. Romulus pointed to a chair adjacent to mine. "Place her here."

The woman must have been drugged; she neither fought nor tried to run.

"Do a simple order, hmm," Romulus said, moving out of my way.

Staring into the woman's eyes, I activated the spell. "Touch your nose."

She did.

"Again," Romulus said.

"Close and open your eyes three times," I ordered.

She obliged.

I sighed. "The spell works fine."

Romulus told the guard to take the specimen away. Then he turned to me, tapping his chin. "Tell me about this human girl."

"What is there to say? She is human."

"Hmm, yes, but you've spent some time with her, alone?"

I stood, towering over him. "Yes, but that means nothing. I've been alone with humans before. My spell has always worked."

"When was the last time you captivated her?"

I thought back to earlier. After I played the piano, though there was no way of knowing if it had worked. "I'm not sure."

"If you are not honest with me, I cannot help you." He turned and went back to his corpse.

Telling Romulus what happened would be dangerous. Even though he was loyal to the royal family, it was too risky. But if my powers were ineffective, I would need his counsel. I checked the room, making sure we were alone. I went to Romulus and whispered, "She kissed me."

Romulus' eyes bulged. "And your powers, they stopped working on her after?"

"I can't be certain, but possibly."

Romulus mumbled to himself and tapped his head.

"What does a kiss have to do with my powers?"

He muttered and paced around the room. "I must think on this. Very disturbing."

Telling by his frantic mumbling and pacing, he would not speak much more with me this night. "I'll be in my chambers. See me with your findings."

And I left him to his madness.

Later that evening, I sat in my private chamber by the fireplace, contemplating the day's events. How could a human cause me to react in such a lucid manner? Jeslyn had more of an effect on me than any female I had come across. It was distressing.

There was a knock at the door.

"Enter."

Lucy walked in and sat in the chair across from me. "I discovered the spirit used was a demon of coercion."

I was not expecting that. "But the way she acted? By the sulfur you found, I assumed it was a possession spirit."

Lucy shook her head. "Jeslyn would have had traces on her skin. She was clean."

"Do not fret my child. This is one of many attacks coming against our house."

"Father!" Lucy and I looked at each other in shock. It had been months since our last contact.

"Yes, it is I, my children," he said, his voice echoing in our minds. *"This attack came from The Council."*

"The Council? What would they gain? Lucino returns to Mirth in less than two days."

"Before I explain, I must tell you something that has been kept from you both for all your lives. Do you know why you two are unique among our race?"

Twins were rare; almost non-existent—I assumed it was because of that. When neither of us answered, Father continued.

"Your mother is not your real mother. Your birth mother ... was human."

"This cannot be!" Lucy's expression mirrored my own.

"It is the truth. A small group of us discovered the gate to Daath when we were searching for a new world. That was over three hundred years ago. There I met a young woman; they were not forbidden then. We did not know much about the humans. It was all new to us. Your mother was astounding. She showed me what the humans refer to as love—a powerful emotion they possess, capable of great deeds. She gave birth to you two—half-human, half-Reptilian."

Lucy buried her head in her hands. "No."

She hated the humans more than I did.

"Eldesar and I were both on The Council. When he found out about your mother, he killed her. He only spared you two because of me. The Council is afraid of what you two possess—the best from each race. It was then they created the law about humans and the incident was never spoken of again. You two have been raised thinking you are simply an anomaly, but you are so much more."

I had many questions to ask him, but only one pressing matter. *"Why am I a threat now? My loyalties have always lain with our people."*

"The abilities you and your sister have are enhanced by your human traits. The Council is afraid your human side will be more dominant after you ascend and your current objectives may change, but there's no more time to discuss this. I must go."

"Father, wait!"

"Not now, Lucino. I will see you soon. In the meantime, watch yourselves."

Our father broke the mental connection, leaving us in disarray. Lucy stood and headed for the door. "Where are you going?" I asked.

"I need to be alone."

"Lucy, we need to discuss this."

"It changes nothing," she said. "I am full Reptilian, regardless of what Father says."

She stormed out of the room.

Human? All these years I've been planning their extinction and treated them as the lower species. I had discovered I am part of that which I despise.

CHAPTER SIXTY

LUCINO

The night hours passed by, long and arduous. My father's words haunted me until the moment the suns rose. Too many unanswered questions rattled my mind. I decided to pay Jeslyn a visit.

When I entered her room, she was still asleep. Her hair feathered across the pillows. I stood at the door, watching her. When she woke, she bolted upright in bed. Her chest heaved and she frantically looked around the room.

I was by her side in an instant.

"I had such a horrible nightmare," she moaned.

I rubbed her back gently. "You've been having a lot of those lately. They are only dreams. You are safe."

She sighed.

I stared at her rosy cheeks and the freckles splashed across them. Her chestnut hair was messy, diminishing nothing of her beauty. That foreign warmth spread through me and I slid away from her.

"Are you upset about last night?" she said. "I shouldn't have been so bold. That's not like me."

"Not at all, but I should leave. You have a big day ahead of you. I'm sure you need to get prepared."

"Today's the wedding," she said quietly, her hands pulling the blanket closer to her.

"It is. I will see you shortly." I bowed and left the room.

On my way out, I summoned Lucy. She was in my chambers when I arrived.

"I have changed my mind about killing Jeslyn."

Lucy crossed her arms, glaring at me. "I'm sure you have a valid reason, especially since the girl diminishes your powers."

That loud fool told her. "Yes, I do have a valid reason, sister."

Lucy grabbed a canter from the table and poured herself a glass of red wine. "This should be interesting."

I ignored her sarcasm. "I need to study her. Did you not find it odd that The Council did not use a spirit of possession?"

Lucy raised an eyebrow. "Yes, coercion demons can only influence not control. They made a poor choice."

I rubbed my chin, shaking my head. "No. I don't think they were able to." Now I had her full attention. "I have read about this creature the humans refer to as The Creator. Jeslyn mentioned this deity on occasion and I observed her performing an act they call praying. I believe this deity protects her. We need to find out if this deity, spirit, whatever denizen it may be, can be controlled. That may be why my powers were losing effect on her."

"You think she's being protected?"

"Yes, and I believe she actually loves me, or thinks she does. That's the only reason the coercion spirit worked."

Lucy emptied the goblet. "What do you propose, brother?"

"I need you to switch out the wines before the ceremony. Once Jeslyn's aura is fused with mine, she won't go against me. Take Jeslyn to Dune Island where I will meet you after I make an appearance in Mirth. We'll say Jeslyn tried to escape after the wedding and we had to dispose of her."

"And after you study her, what then? She must not live, not after what Romulus told me. If you do not kill her, I will."

"You dare to order me?"

Lucy glared at me with an intense malice. "I will not have a human weaken the prince of our race. You are too important. Kill her, or I will. Do not make me inform father."

"Very well, sister. She will die by my hand."

"Good." She placed a hand on my shoulder. "If you'll excuse me. It seems I have some work to do."

The hours drew near to my ascension and the wedding. Anxiousness bubbled under my skin. I visited Jeslyn one last time, to see if my powers truly did not work.

I entered the room quietly, observing her. She faced a full-length mirror, wearing a flowing white gown encrusted with crystalline beads, creating an iridescent design. The dress draped off her delicate shoulders. Shoulders I suddenly wanted to touch.

"It's bad luck to see the bride before the ceremony," she said softly, staring at me through the reflection in the mirror.

"I have a gift for you," I said, walking to her.

In my hands, I held a silver pendant with a heart-shaped emerald in the center. I dangled the necklace in front of her. "I hope you would honor me by wearing it."

She touched the locket. "It's breathtaking. Thank you." With one hand, she lifted her hair and I clasped the necklace around her neck. She stared at us in the mirror, her fingers grazing the sparkling gem. "I've never seen its equal."

I slid my arms around her waist, staring at our reflection. "You are absolutely stunning."

She smiled and her cheeks tinged pink. "You flatter me too much. And you are quite handsome yourself. It's strange a man like you had trouble finding a bride."

You came in here to test your spell, now do it.

Staring at her through the mirror, I thought of what I wanted her to do. When she was locked in my gaze, I activated the spell. "Close your eyes."

She smiled ruefully. "Why?"

I hid my disappointment and anger. "Because I have another surprise for you."

"All right." She shut her eyes.

Placing my hands on her shoulders, I turned her around. I lifted her chin with my hand. The pink of her cheeks reddened. Slowly, I placed my mouth on hers. Her hand reached for me, sliding across my chest, and in that moment, I understood why my spell had no effect.

CHAPTER SIXTY-ONE

JESLYN

Avikar and Derrick were both alive and somewhere in Daath. Once Lucino and I wed, I would find a way to send word to Avikar, and bring both him and Derrick to the mansion where we could sort out this mess. I didn't believe Lucino was as evil as they portrayed him to be. I sensed goodness in him. Any other man may have taken advantage of me, but not him. A true gentleman through and through.

I was going to be the Lady of Daath. That title gave me an exciting shiver. My family would never go hungry, and we could all live here in Daath.

The only issue tugging at my mind was Derrick.

How could I explain my marriage to Lucino after Derrick came all this way, for me? I didn't want to hurt him, but I knew he would be.

Every choice will leave someone in misery. But didn't I deserve my own happiness?

Lucy arrived at my room in another tight-fitted gown. Her sense of fashion had always made me feel as if I dressed in children's clothes, but not today. Today I was a woman, and I was beautiful.

My hands slid down the fine smooth cloth, a mix between satin and the softest cotton. I stared in the mirror and at the gem around my neck. Magnificent green sparkled from the necklace. My heart raced faster. When I envisioned my wedding day, I never thought I would look this beautiful.

If only Mother could see me.

"Are you ready?"

I turned and nodded to Lucy.

Her eyes looked over my dress then my face. "Hmm, something is missing," she said and searched the nearby vanity. "Perfect." She came back over with a jeweled comb and placed it in my curled hair.

"Look," she said, guiding me to face the mirror.

The comb had a vibrant blue butterfly in the center. Tiny studded diamonds crusted the wings.

"It's beautiful. Thank you."

"We're ready," she said.

I followed Lucy out of the room and down the stairs. Reginald followed, like always. Outside the mansion stood the same carriage in which I'd arrived. The horses had been adorned with flowered wreaths. A man, I didn't recognize stood next to them. We walked past, and I wanted to inquire about the stranger, but we were in the carriage before I could.

Since my arrival in Daath, I'd only seen Lucino's grounds, the beach and the grotto. I assumed we would be wed in a beautiful temple with hundreds of residents standing by, a true royal wedding.

"What is happening?" I grabbed hold of the wall, watching the ground fall beneath us as we rose into the sky.

"Where we are going, the horses can't travel," Lucy said, relaxing back into the seat.

"But how is this possible?" I didn't know whether to be frightened or awed.

"Magic."

My head spun with questions. Everyone knew The Order

controlled magic in Tarrtainya. Any magic users found were immediately captured and recruited. But Daath lived outside of The Order, far from the king's eye. I had never met a magic user or seen magic. What wonders it could do.

We flew past trees, higher into the clouds, and I slid closer to the window, absorbing in the sensation of flight. I could see the trees change, the faster we went. Giant moss-covered oaks, bending in different directions and beautiful green everywhere. From up here, the forest shone like the emerald in my necklace. Breathtakingly beautiful.

I lost myself in the scenery and jumped when the carriage landed. *We're here.*

The suns were high in the sky, shining on the large white temple.

Reginald held my arm, escorting me from the carriage and to the entrance.

The closer we came to the temple, the more my heart beat against my chest. There were no residents, no cheering village folk, just the silence of the forest and my quaky footsteps.

"I'll take her from here," Lucy said to Reginald, placing a hand on my back.

I looked to Reginald for support. I didn't want to be left alone, but he stepped aside.

Tears stung my eyes and I lost my courage. Walking to the marriage altar with Lucy, a girl who plainly showed her disdain for me, was disheartening. My family wasn't here, and I needed someone who cared for me to be by my side. I craved the support of a loved one. Someone to look me in the eye and pat my hand, reassuring me.

Lucy led me inside the massive temple and down a stone corridor which opened up into an enormous chamber. The inside of the temple had been decorated with candelabras, bustles of white roses and plum colored flowers. But what drew me in and held my attention the longest was Lucino.

He wore a leather doublet with green embroidery, matching breeches and black boots that had the most intricate golden buttons. His hair had been tied back and his golden sword hung at his side. All of that was lovely, but it was his gaze that set me on fire.

His eyes smiled at me under the sunlight. I thought I should walk to him, but he moved towards me first. With our eyes locked on one another, he stepped closer and closer. The fear and doubt melted away as I saw true passion rise in his cheeks. When we met, he grasped my hands, his eyes still on mine.

"I never thought I could feel the way I did when you first walked in," he said.

His voice was hushed, as if he only wanted me to hear. "This may not be the ceremony you were expecting, and for that, I am grieved. A woman who looks as stunning as you should have a gala where the suns sing, but my people have their traditions."

He glanced away from me and towards Lucy, who stood off to the side watching. Her forehead creased.

Lucino moved beside me, whispering in my ear. "Don't be frightened about anything you see, I swear, everything will be fine. Do you trust me?"

I knew nothing of what he meant or the strange traditions of his people, but I believed him. His eyes had lightened as if a fog had been obstructing them. They shone bright and clear, and I knew, no matter what had transpired or lies had been told, right now, he meant what he said.

"I do."

He smiled, lifted my hand to his lips and kissed it. "Then let us be wed."

CHAPTER SIXTY-TWO

AVIKAR

We were near the temple. Drums beat in the distance. The sound made my heart pound and I glanced at Derrick who was already in position. Our job was simple—take out the perimeter guards and do it quickly. The large moon almost covered both suns; time was running out.

An owl hooted—our sign from Jericho.

One … two … three

I shot an arrow at the nearest guard. The missile cut through the air and landed in the center of the man's throat. Before the guard collapsed, I ran full speed, stringing my bow with another arrow.

We moved at lightning pace. Guards dropped before they could scream a warning. Rushing wind flew through the trees and whipped around me, matching the increasing tempo of the drums. Four guards blocked the temple entrance. We had one chance. I stepped around a tree and pulled back on my bow. I lined the shot on the guard to the far right and waited. Another hoot. I counted to three and released.

Three of the guards fell clutching their throats while the fourth stood looking at them in horror. *I missed! I can't believe I missed.*

The lone guard screamed and ran in my direction. I watched him as he drew closer and closer. When he came in range, I aimed the bow at him, another arrow notched.

He waved his hands rapidly. "Please don't kill me. I have a family!"

Derrick kicked the guy and sent him running into the forest. "Get out of here and tell no one or we will kill you!"

Jericho and the rest of our group were waiting at the entrance. He handed each of us a black cloak. "Keep your hoods up and stay behind the pillars like we planned. When the eclipse happens, move in."

I slid the cloak on. "Don't forget, Lucino is ours."

Hesitation filled Jericho's eyes. Yesterday we had argued over this for half the afternoon. "Jericho, you promised," I said, reminding him.

"Yes, I know. You'll have your shot. We'll take care of the rest."

We slipped into the temple and broke out into three separate groups, each entering the main hall from different sides. Derrick stayed by me, cautiously walking to the first set of pillars.

Before us stood twenty or more black robed figures chanting and making strange gestures with their hands. Their bodies lurched back and forth in weird spasms. The runes around the temple glowed an eerie blue. In front of the dark pit knelt Jeslyn, in a white gown, next to a man dressed in all black.

Lucino.

The priest performing the ceremony chanted in a strange language. The same language Lucy sang in. All three of them were before a black altar with a creature tied to it. It was too far away to discern.

I heard a low growl next to me. Derrick, staring at Lucino, clenched his fists. The hooded figures chanted louder and began lighting torches on large candelabras around the room. Each lamp changed the rune next to it to blood red.

Clouds passed over the moon as the moon turned the sky black.

Arrows descended onto the dark figures who immediately screamed and scattered. I dashed down the steps and towards Jeslyn.

"Avikar, to your left!" Derrick yelled, slashing one of the robed men with his claymore.

Lucy. I strung my bow, aiming for her head. Not this time. I shot the arrow, but she moved out of the way. "Jericho!" I pointed at Lucy. "Don't let her sing!"

Jericho chased after Lucy, who started running out of the main room. Lucino had his arm around Jeslyn. They stood in the center watching the chaos.

"Jeslyn!" I shouted, running to her, readying my sword.

Derrick reached her first. He pointed his claymore at Lucino. "Get your hands off her."

"Derrick? What's going on?" Jeslyn stepped out of Lucino's embrace. "Why are you attacking?" She looked back at Lucino with a confused expression.

"You are a fool if you think you're going to escape here with your lives," Lucino said, pulling out his long sword. "How dare you interrupt us."

"Wait!" Jeslyn put her hand against Lucino's chest. "There's no reason to fight. This is a misunderstanding."

With Lucino busy watching Derrick, I crept to the side and grabbed Jeslyn.

"Avikar, what are you doing?"

I held her arm. "Getting you out of here."

She shook her head. "This is ridiculous. Someone will get hurt. I'm only getting married. I would've sent word, but after I saw you, Lucino had me sent to a preparation house. I planned on finding you after the wedding."

"Jeslyn, he's not *human*!"

Her eyes widened. "What?"

I didn't know what had happened to her in the past few weeks, but seeing that shocked expression said enough.

"Jeslyn, please," I said, "go with Derrick."

She shook her head. "No. You lie. Why would you say that?"

"What?" I couldn't believe she was acting like this.

Derrick moved before I could react. He swung his claymore at Lucino who blocked the attack.

"What have you done to her?" Derrick sidestepped and attacked Lucino again.

"I have done nothing," Lucino grunted, easily fending off Derrick's vicious swings.

"Stop it!" Jeslyn screamed, but both of them ignored her.

"We need to leave, now," I said.

She looked at me with sad eyes. "Make them stop, please, Avi."

It had been a long time since my sister had asked me for anything. She ordered me around a lot, but nothing like this. It reminded me of days past, when she didn't blame me so much. I wanted to give in to her, to be the brother that made her smile.

"I can't." It killed me to see her cry. "Jeslyn, you don't understand. He's not what you think."

Her expression hardened. "I don't care. I will not watch the two men I care for kill each other."

What did she say?

I should have grabbed her, done whatever I could to stop her from walking away, but her words paralyzed me. I watched her scream at Derrick and Lucino, begging them to stop as they ignored her and continued to fight. The scene unfolded in slow motion. Her cries, Derrick's loud warrior yell and the fury on Lucino's face. Jeslyn stepped too close to the fight. I think I screamed her name, horrified at what I knew was about to happen.

Derrick threw his whole body into the next attack; his sword slashing at Lucino's left side, right where Jeslyn stood. He realized his mistake, but not soon enough.

"No!" I sprinted and caught her before she hit the ground.

"Oh, no, what have I done. Jeslyn ..." Derrick dropped to his knees.

Blood spilled from her side. She gasped and I held her in my shaking arms.

"Don't die on me." I held her close. "You'll be fine. I'll get you out of here."

"You fools!" Lucino yelled.

I glanced up and saw a red haze outlining Lucino's body. He glared at Derrick, who sat on the ground shaking his head in disbelief. Lucino gripped his sword and snarled.

He's going to kill him. I ripped the dagger out of its holder and threw it at Lucino. My aim was dead on. He screamed and went to pull out the dagger.

"Derrick, you have to get her out of here. Find Jericho," I said.

Derrick's face paled.

"Derrick!"

He snapped out of his daze and moved.

The red aura around Lucino vanished. I kissed Jeslyn on the forehead. "Stay alive."

She whispered my name, blood trickling out of her mouth. I couldn't watch the life leave her eyes. I turned away and prayed she would live.

Derrick gently picked her up and held her in his arms.

I stood to face Lucino. "Go. I'll take care of him," I told Derrick. My body shook with fear, adrenaline and rage. I focused on the anger, letting its power fuel me. This creature was the reason my sister was dying. Everything happened because of him.

CHAPTER SIXTY-THREE

AVIKAR

Lucino charged first with a powerful swing that threw me off balance when I blocked. He was stronger than I. This was going to be a tough fight. I adjusted my grip on the sword and stabbed forward. Lucino blocked the attack as if swatting a fly. I raised the sword, trying a different technique, and slashed down, stepping to the side at the last second, sending the weapon in an arc to Lucino's stomach. Lucino blocked.

Blocking Lucino's attacks were taking all of my energy and I couldn't get any swings close to hurting him. I focused on breathing, and tried again, rushing forward. Lucino's blade pushed the thrust aside.

Lucino sneered. "Do you honestly think you are going to win?"

I spit at him. "Whatever it takes, you die today."

Lucino grunted and twirled his sword around at me with such power it knocked my own blade right out of my hands.

"It seems I was correct." Lucino stepped forward, pointing his sword tip at my chest.

I can do this. I know I can do this. I just need time to think.

I stepped back attempting to put distance between us. Lucino lunged forward, driving his sword into my shoulder. I cried out in pain.

"You humans are so weak." Lucino looked at his own wound. "Your little dagger barely scratched my skin, but it did seem to stop my transformation." He glanced at the dagger lying on the floor. "You're from The Order. I've always wanted to fight one of you."

The Order? Why would he think I'm from The Order?

"Do you even have skin?" I panted, holding my shoulder. "Shapeshifter."

His brows narrowed. "So you know the truth."

Keep him talking. "Yes, I know what you are and what you plan to do." I dug my free hand into my pocket, pulling open the bag of marbles.

"Did you also know there are hundreds of my kind walking among you?"

Hundreds?

Lucino laughed. "Ahh, no, you did not. Of course you wouldn't know the extent of our reach."

My hand grabbed a handful of marbles. A few more seconds. "Why are you here?"

"Does it matter? Soon, we will rule."

"You will never take over," I said and ran, forcing Lucino to chase me. I threw the marbles at his feet. I checked to see if it had worked and ran straight to my sword, picking it off the ground. I whirled around and saw Lucino smirking as he drove his sword into my stomach.

He laughed. "You really are a fool."

The sword fell from my hands, clanging as it hit the ground. Pain shot through my body and I pressed my hands against my stomach. *No, this isn't how this ends. I won't give up. I won't.*

Lucino turned his back to me. I looked around for anything I could use to stop him. One of the candelabras stood next to me. With the last of my strength, I hauled the stick at Lucino. The candles ignited his clothes, and he screamed. His arms flailed as he tried to put out the fire.

Since Lucino wasn't human, I didn't know if fire would kill him, or even hurt him. I knew I was dying. The life was already draining from my body, but I wouldn't rest until I knew Lucino was dead.

Lucino was close enough to the pit, if I could summon the strength, I could push him over.

Creator, please, just a bit longer. Help me rid of this filth.

Grabbing the candelabra, I staggered towards Lucino.

"Go back to whatever cursed land you came from," I growled, thrusting the stick into Lucino's chest, driving him over the edge.

He fell, his screams fading on the descent. Then the whole temple exploded with a bright light.

I closed my eyes and waited for death.

CHAPTER SIXTY-FOUR

JESLYN

I'm so sorry," Derrick said, his tears falling on my cheeks. "This wasn't how this was supposed to end. We were supposed to save you."

I held his hand. "It was an accident." I winced at the pain; even talking took all my strength.

Derrick shook his head. "There has to be something I can do."

It wouldn't be long now. The pain had taken on a numbing effect. Tears filled my eyes. I would never see Calli grow into the woman I knew she'd be and I'd never see Mother and Poppa again. And Avikar … There was so much that needed to be said. I don't know when we grew apart, maybe after Jimri died, but now there was no more time. No time to talk about the past, or relive the memories we shared. All I had was a moment; a moment that slipped further and further away.

My eyes fluttered. It was getting harder to keep them open. Above Derrick's head, I saw a blue light. The butterflies.

"Derrick, look." It took all my strength to raise a finger to the blue creature hovering over us.

His voice dripped with sorrow. "It's just a butterfly."

The butterfly flew down, landed on my chest and then fluttered away. "Follow the butterfly," I said to him.

"What? No, Jericho is getting help. I'm not chasing an insect."

"Derrick … please, there is a place … a place … it can heal me." I was losing consciousness. "Please, hurry."

Derrick watched the butterfly. He lifted me. "Are you sure? You're certain?"

I nodded, even though I wasn't certain, but I hoped.

Time slipped to and fro. Had hours or minutes only passed?

I heard my name, a soft whisper on the wind, calling me back from this place of emptiness. I opened my eyes.

"I think we're here," Derrick said, his eyes wide. "What is this place?"

In the dark, flowers glowed vibrant greens and blues, dotting the enchanted pool.

"The water …"

He stepped into the pool. The water rose around me until I floated just below the surface, wading in his arms.

"Jeslyn." There was so much anguish in his voice.

I stared into his eyes, wanting to say all the things I should have.

"What are those?" he asked.

The butterflies.

The blue swarm flew gracefully from the grotto, flying to us. They landed on me, in various spots. Their wings moved slowly as they sat, still and magnificent. A warm tingling spread through my body.

"It worked," I whispered, closing my eyes.

"Jeslyn?"

"Jeslyn … don't, don't close your eyes. I can't lose you!"

"You won't," I said, falling into sleep.

CHAPTER SIXTY-FIVE

AVIKAR

When I woke, I was lying on the grass. My hands went to my chest where Lucino had stabbed me, and to my surprise, the wound was gone. I looked around. I was alone, except for a tall man in brown robes. I got to my feet and cautiously walked over to the stranger. The ground sunk in with each step. A dense fog clouded everything but the few feet surrounding the stranger and me.

"What's going on?" I asked.

"Peace, Avikar." The man motioned to a nearby stump. "Please, sit."

"I don't have time for this. Where is everyone? Is Jeslyn alive?"

The man smiled. "Yes, your sister lives. Sit and I'll explain."

I paused before finally agreeing. The man's scruffy appearance reminded me of my father.

"Avikar, you are dying. Right now you lie in a bed with a severe fever and you've lost a lot of blood."

"Lucino is dead. Jeslyn is safe. I've done my duty."

The man frowned. "That's all? You did your duty and now your life is forfeit?"

Nothing mattered now. I fulfilled my oath.

The stranger grabbed my arm.

"Hey! What are you—" A bright light flashed and we were in a room. There I was, lying on a bed, Jeslyn sitting on a bed next to me. Derrick, Raven and Jericho sat in the room watching an old man apply compresses to my face.

Jeslyn sat, crying, Derrick holding her. Seeing her upset, seeing them all upset over me, was crushing. I reached out to Jeslyn, but my hand passed through her. I turned around at the stranger. "Why are you showing me this?"

"Because you think you are worthless and here are people who love you, grieving for you. Your death will affect them in a way you cannot fathom."

I fought back the tears. "What does it matter now? Aren't I dying?"

The stranger placed a hand on my shoulder. "Not yet."

There was a burst of brilliant light. I shielded my eyes, and when I removed my hand, I was back home at the lake. "What are we doing here?"

The stranger disappeared, leaving me alone in the one place I hated the most. I stood by the shore, looking at the calm waters of the lake.

From far away someone laughed. I turned in the direction of the voice. There running towards me, was Jimri. *It can't be.* My knees buckled and I dropped to the ground.

"Avi, Avi!" Jimri crashed into my arms wearing a dimpled smile. I wrapped my arms around him.

"Jimri, I'm so sorry," I cried against his shoulder, hugging him as if he'd disappear.

"Aww, it's all right. It wasn't your fault. I slipped on a rock."

"I shouldn't have ignored you. I should've been a better brother. I should've never let you out of my sight." I hugged him harder. "I couldn't save you. I tried, but it was too late."

His small hands patted my back. "I know, Avi. You're my big

brother. You always watched out for me." He wiggled out of my grip and grabbed my hand. "You gotta get up." He tugged on my arm forcing me to my feet. "Time's running out Avi. You have to go back."

I wiped my eyes. "Can't I stay with you?"

He pulled me away from the lake. "No, Avi, you have to go back!"

"Why? What for? I'd rather be with you."

"There's lots of great things. Plus, you're a hero now. They'll write stories about you. And that girl Raven, I like her."

I managed a smile. "Yeah, I kind of like her too."

"It's time to go, Avi."

"Will we see each other again?"

Jimri's big dimples smiled at me. "Yup."

I knew what it had felt like when Jimri had died. I wouldn't let Jeslyn go through that. I wouldn't let her lose another brother, not when I could help it.

"He's awake!" Jeslyn leaned over and covered my face with kisses.

"No need for the smothering," I said in a groggy voice.

She grabbed my hand. "I'm glad you're okay."

"Now, now, you can all visit later. The patient needs his rest." An old man ushered them away. "Give the boy some space."

"Wait," I said, looking at my teary eyed sister. "I want a few moments alone with Jeslyn." The old man nodded and everyone left the room.

Jeslyn's eyes watered.

We sat in silence, both staring. Where to start? Using my hands, I pushed myself into a sitting position. I groaned and Jeslyn re-arranged the pillows.

"You need to be careful, Avi," she said.

"I thought you were dead." I was too weak to fight the tears and for the first time, I didn't care.

She grabbed my hand, squeezing it. "Well, I'm not." She smiled.

"How? What happened? And Lucino, is he dead?"

She leaned over me, her other hand clamping over mine. "There's a lot we need to talk about."

I nodded.

"But first, you need to rest."

My body ached, but I couldn't sleep, not yet.

"Jeslyn, I know things have been different with us ever since …"

"Don't, Avi." She shook her head, a tear running down her face. "What happened in the past is the past. I haven't exactly been the sister I should have been. I'm just as much to blame. I miss how it used to be."

An image of Jeslyn and me, before Jimri and Calli were born, entered my mind. We were hiding in the stables, laughing as Jumper tried to find us. Back then, we played pranks together.

"Me too," I said.

Exhaustion forced me asleep, but before I closed my eyes, I saw Jeslyn smiling. The same smile as when we'd sneak into Mother's pantry and steal pieces of leftover cinnamon cake.

In that moment, I knew everything would be all right.

CHAPTER SIXTY-SIX

AVIKAR

I spent the next few weeks lounging around Jericho's, waiting for my wound to heal enough to travel home. Raven kept me company and Anna tended to me like a mother hen. Derrick and Jeslyn had been off on their own, visiting the town and learning more about Daath. I worried about her. She seemed distant.

We'd asked her a dozen questions about Lucino, but she gave us very little information except that he was very kind. I didn't want to say anything to Derrick, but I sensed my sister was hiding something.

Word had spread through Daath that Lucino had died during a tragic fire at the dollhouse. Lucy had been spotted near Lucino's mansion, but had yet to make her agenda known. For now, Lucino's personal guard still had control, but not for long.

Jericho had created a secret committee to free Daath from Lucino's guard. The first step was to find alternate routes in and out of Daath then find Lucino's hidden ships.

The night in the temple was still fuzzy. I spent a lot of time trying to remember the whole fight. Derrick had found me lying in a pool of blood and Lucino nowhere in sight. By the pit were several scraps of burnt clothing. Watching Lucino burn was the only image that had stuck in my mind. Something about the fight bothered me, but I couldn't remember. The doctor said my memory would return in pieces as I healed.

We accomplished our goal and soon we would be leaving.

Home—it's been so long.

I stared out the window, watching Raven throw a ball to Bruno. She glanced at me and waved. I smiled and waved back. Things between us were good. That intense chemistry was still there, but I ignored it, or tried to. Any time she was near me, I couldn't help myself. I'd flirt, apologize, pretended I wasn't interested, then flirt again.

"Why do I have to leave?" I said, pressing my head against the window pane. When the words left my lips, everything made sense, and I shuffled outside.

Bruno charged at me. I slowly bent and rubbed behind his ears. Bruno's leg rapidly kicked the ground.

"Hi, boy."

Bruno licked my hand happily and I moved to scratch his side.

Raven walked over. "How are you feeling today?" she asked.

I touched my chest. "I think it's almost healed. I'll be able to go soon."

"That's good. I'm sure you're anxious to get home." Raven bit her bottom lip, staring at the ground.

"Not really," I said. "I'll just have to go back to working on the farm, no more adventuring for me. I would've loved to explore more of Daath." I let the thought linger, trying to read her reaction.

Her eyes sparkled. "If you wanted to stay, I'm sure Jericho wouldn't mind and I could show you more. There's so much to see. You'd love it."

I grinned.

She'd been reserved around me. Pretending she didn't like me in that way. Although, whenever I made a flirty comment, she blushed.

I walked to a hammock slung between two tall trees. I grabbed the netted material and attempted to sit on it, but the hammock swayed away.

Raven giggled. "Want a hand old man?"

"Ha-ha, no, I'm fine, thank you," I grumbled. I gripped the hammock tighter and jumped into it, only half of me actually making it in. I held on trying to regain my balance which wasn't working.

Raven placed her hands on the hammock.

"I said I was fine," I protested.

She laughed. "Yes, I saw how well you were doing. Stop being a baby and let me help you."

She held the hammock in place while I pulled myself in. Once I was lying in it comfortably, she let go.

The hammock swung back fast causing Raven to lose her balance and stumble on top of me. I groaned.

"I'm sorry!" She tried to scramble out, making the whole thing swing even more.

I groaned again.

Raven tried lifting herself off, but it was an awkward position and she couldn't hold it long. I started laughing, which made my chest hurt more, which made me groan more.

"Avikar, are you okay?"

Seeing it was pointless for her to get out, I wrapped my arms around her waist and pulled her next to me. "It's much safer if you stay in it with me."

She sighed. "All right."

I let go of her waist and moved over slightly until we were side by side. Putting an arm behind my head, I stared at the clear blue sky. The smell of Anna's newest cake drifted through the air. Fig. Raven peered up at the sky, the sunlight beamed down, making those dark orbs of hers sparkle like topaz.

How can I leave Daath knowing I'm leaving her?

"Raven, I think I want to take you up on that offer to stay."

She turned and we were eye to eye. "What about Jeslyn?"

"Derrick can take her home and Jericho planned on sending an escort with us. They'll be safe."

"What changed your mind?" she asked.

"You."

"Me?"

"I don't want to leave you."

She looked away. "Do you really mean that?"

"I told you I would never to lie to you again." I grabbed her hand. "I need to know how you feel about me?"

"Do I need to answer that?" she huffed. "You know how I feel."

"Do I? Sometimes I think you like me and other times I'm not so sure."

Raven pouted. "I've been trying to hide my feelings because I knew you were leaving."

I inched closer. "I'm not now," I whispered. She chewed her bottom lip and I squeezed her hand in reassurance. "I love you and I'd never leave Daath, unless you were coming with me."

She closed her eyes and smiled. "I've been waiting for you to say that since the first day we met." She opened her eyes.

Before she could say another word, I kissed her. My hands slipped down her back, caressing her. Life stayed still while we kissed. Nothing mattered but the way she felt in my arms. Each kiss more intense than the one before. My hand slid under the bottom of her shirt, tickling her belly. She giggled and pulled away.

"Sorry," I whispered between breaths, gently kissing her cheek, then trailing my lips down her neck.

"Avikar," she giggled, twisting as my fingers playfully pinched her sides.

I rolled to the side, wrapping my arms around her waist. "I guess I have my answer."

Closing my eyes, I rested my head in the hollow of her neck. She hummed to herself and brushed my hair with her slender fingers. The wind swayed us back and forth. My body relaxed, a smile formed on my lips, and, for the first time in years, I was at peace.

CHAPTER SIXTY-SEVEN

JESLYN

Even in Daath the suns looked the same. Bright and magnificent. Derrick sat on the cloth we had laid on the grass, examining the food in the basket Anna had packed for us. In Lakewood, Derrick and I often had picnics by the lake. The familiar setting made me long for home. I couldn't wait to return. Daath had too many strange memories.

Derrick told me about Lucino's heritage, and even though I knew it was a blessing we were rid of him, I ached. The necklace he'd given me lay hidden beneath my chemise. I thought about throwing it away, but that seemed silly. I could sell it and the money could be used to buy supplies or food. It made sense to keep it; although, I did hide it from Derrick. I didn't think he'd be pleased if I wore it.

"Here," Derrick said, handing me an apple. "I think there's some cheese in here too."

"Thank you." I took the apple and held it in my hands.

"Everything okay?"

Derrick smiled. His face reminded me of wonderful days. "Yes."

His stare became more intense and he moved closer, reaching for my hand. "I love you."

"I love you too." The words flowed out, but the meaning had lessened over the past weeks. I was not the same girl he fell in love with.

He smiled and leaned over, his hands cupped my face and he kissed me. Part of me thought of Lucino. I hated myself for it, but I couldn't erase him from my mind. Every time Derrick touched me, I thought of Lucino.

"Marry me," Derrick whispered.

"What?" I pulled away, shocked at the question.

His hands grasped both of mine. "I already have your father's permission. I planned on proposing during the festival, but I don't want to wait any longer."

He waited for my response, but I couldn't breathe or speak. Marriage? It was too sudden. Too many things had happened.

"When you were taken, I was terrified. I never want to lose you again."

My chest pounded. "Derrick ..."

CHAPTER SIXTY-EIGHT

AVIKAR

We stood on the road, heading towards the valley, where Jericho and one of Lucino's disloyal guards waited to take us back home. I hadn't told them about my decision to stay. I didn't know how either of them would react.

I walked over to Jeslyn and hugged her.

Her face scrunched in confusion.

"Tell Mother and Father I'll be home soon."

"What do you mean? You're not coming with us?" Jeslyn stared at me with wet eyes. "I don't understand."

I glanced at Raven. "I'm going to stay here for a while."

Jeslyn hugged me again, and then stepped aside, letting Derrick step forward. I slapped a hand on his shoulder.

"Take care of my sister. Get her home safe."

"I will," he said and we locked arms. "I've asked Jeslyn to marry me. If she accepts, we'll be wed by the winter festival."

I hugged him. "Then we'll be sure to visit before then."

We finished our goodbyes. I watched them get into the carriage and waved. I knew I'd see them again soon.

I draped an arm around Raven. "What do we do next, pretty lady?"

Raven's stomach growled before she could answer. "Excuse me," she said, covering her belly with her hand.

"Guess that answers that. Let's eat, but first one back has to cook." I removed my arm and shifted my left leg forward. "On three."

She smiled at me, determination in her eyes.

"One … two …" I gave her a quick smack on the butt. "Three!" And sprinted away.

She squealed. "Not fair!" She chased after me and within seconds, passed me. She really was fast.

"Hey, get back here! I can't lose. I'm a terrible cook!" I held my side as I ran, trying to catch her.

She glanced back over her shoulder and winked before heading onto the path that would lead us back to Jericho's.

Pumping my legs harder, I sped faster.

Somewhere between lies and truth is reality, and that is a dangerous place.

But now I was ready for it.

Epilogue
LATER

In the past one hundred years, I never thought I would be frustrated with spending my afternoons in the palace, but I no longer belonged in this world. It was only a matter of time before my wounds healed, and I could finish what I started. New jade skin covered my body. The burns almost gone. In Daath, I rarely stayed in my true form, but now that I knew about my human side, which form did I consider true: Reptilian or human?

The court physician stood by the door. Our physicians went beyond physical ailments. They were doctors of the mind. Very strong in psionics, and our court used them for more than just healing. "Prince Lucino, you have a visitor."

I nodded, allowing the physician to open the steel door.

"You are looking much better," Krischa said.

My old friend, here for another visit. With my hand, I motioned for the physician to leave. Krischa folded her hands neatly in front of her. Her long crimson hair fell around them. The overhead light danced across her pale green skin. Reptilian women were exquisite creatures and none were finer than Krischa.

She opened her cloak and revealed a thin black bottle. "I thought you might yearn for something other than groth."

"You know me too well." I took the bottle from her hand and ignored her lingering stare as our hands touched. "The doctors think this drink will slow the healing process. Fools."

Twisting the top off, I grinned, then drank the cool sour liquid. It warmed my throat as it went down, relaxing my body and sharpening my mind. The taste was potent compared to the healing brew I had been drinking.

I gestured towards two seats positioned in front of a large window that over looked the royal red city. Krischa willingly followed.

"Tell me, Krischa," I said, "you've come to see me quite often since my arrival. Surely, you have better things to do."

She glimpsed out the window, pushing her hair back behind her pointed ear. "You've been gone a long time. I feared you would never return home."

"There's much to learn there."

She turned to me, her gold eyes meeting mine, eyes I used to enjoy watching. "My father says hunters will be sent to kill the human who did this to you."

Her father—our royal emissary and a very powerful wizard—tended to overshare with his daughter, but not without reason. Krischa held the power of foresight and was keen to our dealings on Tarrtainya. It was her vision of the future that had led us to the danger faced by our planet. The rest of our people thought the mission was to bring new resources and knowledge back home. They did not know our sun is dying.

The view from the window overlooked the diamond towers of the palace and the flickering sands of our borders.

"And what did you see?" I asked.

"I see failure."

I laughed, then leaned towards her. "Impossible. You think a mere human can defeat them?"

"He bested you."

"Enough!" I stood, infuriated by her accusations. "Your visions are neither law nor absolute."

Krischa stood, facing me. Her posture straight and rigid. I had known her all my life and there was always more behind her words.

"What else did you see?"

"Enough," she said in a low voice.

"If you have not come to share your wisdom, leave."

A long breath left her mouth, and she lifted her head to look at me. "I saw that I am no longer the female you desire."

Her words paralyzed me. I had spent the past weeks thinking of Jeslyn and her death. I had not excepted it to affect me this much.

"I will not share my vision with anyone, but if I saw it, another seer could."

My chest rose with agitation, and I turned away. Even though Jeslyn was no longer a threat, The Council would see my *feelings* as treachery. I could not afford to lose anymore trust.

"Lucino."

Lightning flashed in the dark clouds moving closer to the city. The electrical storms came frequently now, burning any foliage they touched upon. We only had a few more cycles before this place would no longer be habitable.

"Lucino, I fear you are in great danger. If anyone finds out—"

"It does not matter. She is dead. What is past is past."

"Dead? Lucino, the female lives."

I had seen the blade strike her chest. "Are you certain?"

"Yes."

"And what did you see in this vision that has you so concerned with my wellbeing?"

Krischa gripped my arm. I winced and growled, ready to throw her off for her insolence, but her wide eyes stopped me. I saw fear in them.

"She will be the end of you … and all of us."

ACKNOWLEDGMENTS

I can do all things through Christ who strengthens me—this verse has not only helped me persevere through the doubt and struggle, but it's lifted me up on my darkest days.

Of course, I have a ton of people to thank, and no idea where to start, but here it goes.

First, one giant hug and thanks to my critique partners. You've all helped me in so many different ways and I love you all. To my backspace girls, Laura, Tonya and Lynn, you three are a cheerleading squad, full of creative thinking and spunk. I'm so thankful to have you in my back corner. Heather and Erin, we've created our own little clique, and I love skyping and hashing out stories with you. Annette, you are a genius at first person. I hope I make you proud. Jordan, the amount of stories you write is inspirational. I can't wait until the world gets to read them. Marlene, you've helped me improve my writing and you never shy from re-reading my work. I know when I'm having a rough day, I can always vent and you'll always listen. We've both come a long way and we're only getting started.

Taylor, you were the first teen to read my story. You're excitement and suggestions helped make this shine, thank you.

Thanks to Jessa Russo and Curiosity Quills Press for believing in my story. None of this would be happening if I didn't have the support of a great team. My editor, Mike Robinson, thank The Creator for you. You saw my weaknesses and helped me shine. Jade Hart, guru of production, thanks for keeping us all in line.

I thank my favorite authors, R.A. Salvatore, Elaine Cunningham, and many others who write magical stories that whisk me away and inspire me to write. Great books inspire great writing.

I'm blessed to have such an amazing family that's always supported me. Bus', I was terrified for you to read my story, but you did, and you loved it. Thank you for pushing me and correcting my grammar in every letter I've written since the third grade. Grandpa, I'm one hundred percent convinced I get my storytelling from you. No one gets stoned in this novel, but I promise to add in a stoning somewhere.

Mom, you never gave up on me. You've taught me the definition of strength, and everything I've become is because you raised me right. I know I don't say it enough, but I love and appreciate you, more than I can express.

To my son Noah, you're too young to read, but know you were the driving force behind all of this. I've always wanted to be published, but you made me go after it.

Lastly, to my husband, Cory. This story started off as a birthday gift to you and then it blossomed into a full length novel. You've always been a seed of creativity and source of motivation. I see how you paint the world and I want to paint it with you.

A Taste of...
WICKED PATH
DAATH CHRONICLES

ELIZA TILTON

PROLOGUE

Lucy stomped along the blood-red corridor leading to her father's private chambers. Five of her elite guards flanked her, adorned in black armor, chrome masks and razor katans; they were a vision of death. No one would dare to step near her with them by her side.

As Lucy reached for the iron handle that opened the side entrance, a familiar voice entered her head. *"No, child, the way is not safe; enter through the secret passageway to the north."*

Lucy veered right and headed down the opposite hallway, her entourage trailing like an elaborate cloak. She stopped at an intricate sculpture of a twisted rhino, grasped the large horn, and pressed in. The sculpture slid to the side to reveal a long hallway. Two of her guards walked in first, then she followed.

The guards stood outside the iron door while she entered into the room. With its slate walls, the library seemed empty, but Lucy knew every tome had a hidden spot within the wall.

She bowed her head forward, ignoring the incredulous black statue of her father that loomed beside her. "Hello, Father."

King Reagan pushed a silver circle on the wall and slipped a tome back into its place. He slowly turned his head to regard his daughter. White hair fell past his shoulders, contrasting against his forest green skin.

"You wear your human form often," he said. "Do you prefer it to your true self?"

Lucy straightened her shoulders. "Of course not, Father. This is more practical, considering my comings and goings."

King Reagan stepped toward Lucy. His raised-collar robe swished with his steps. "Let's not forget you are human."

Lucy's eyes narrowed. "Half."

He nodded and waved at the egg-shaped seat, inviting her to sit. "We have much to discuss, little one."

Lucy didn't have time for one of her father's drawn out conversations, but she couldn't be rude either. "Father, I am pressed for time. Dago will be arriving in Daath in a few days. I need to return and await his arrival. You know how demanding he can be."

"Understood, child, but remember, you do not serve him. He is a temporary regent until your brother is well. Have you visited Lucino?"

She winced at her brother's name. His burns had charred a good portion of his skin and the healing had been slower than normal. His foolish obsession had nearly cost him his life and hers. A mistake she had a hard time forgetting.

"Do not fret, he is well," King Reagan stated, misinterpreting Lucy's silence.

Lucy responded by clasping her hands together in her lap and eyeing her father. Her fingers clenched and unclenched as she waited for him to say more.

King Reagan grabbed a large metal case off the crystal desk in the corner and brought it to her. He unhooked the latches and revealed six metal bracelets. "These are nanobuilds. They will provide you with a cloak of invisibility. You can use this to spy on Dago, and for your guard to pass through Tarrtainya undetected."

The Elite Guard always remained in their Reptilian form, strong, tall, and savage, with yellow eyes and dark, leathery skin. They considered it a dishonor to shape change into lesser species. This gadget would expand Lucy's power as well as her guards', strengthening their forces in Tarrtainya, and allowing the Elite Guard to leave Mirth for the first time.

Exhilaration skittered through her veins.

She would be unstoppable.

Lucy's father closed the case and left it in her lap. "We only have three cycles left before the first sun collapses. Our people need to transfer to the new world before our atmosphere becomes unstable. The Council sees this change as an opportunity to rid our race of the weaklings. As the royal family, we have a duty to save all our people, not just ensure the strongest of our species survives."

King Reagan cared for their kind, but Lucy found most of them just as intolerable as the humans. She nodded, feigning agreement.

"If Dago is The Council's errand boy, we'll need to be rid of him quickly. No one but me will know of the guards going with you. Use them wisely. In the meantime, dispose of the human boy before he stirs more trouble."

"Gladly," she replied coldly.

King Reagan lifted her chin with his leathery hand. "Lucino is lost and confused, and The Council watches me too closely. Until your brother's mind clears, this task falls to you."

Lucy met her father's ancient gaze, seeing the approval in his eyes. A fire lit inside her, pulsing with determination. "I will see it done." A smirk spread across her face.

CHAPTER ONE

AVIKAR

I'd always wondered why people celebrate a harvest. With winter soon to blow its winds, it seemed there were more important tasks than drinking and dancing. Why not celebrate afterward, when the snow and cold had left, and everyone you loved had survived?

"Dance with me." Raven grabbed my hand and pulled me away from my thoughts. Firelight danced around her cheeks, making her face warm and alive.

"As if I have a choice." I grinned, spinning her body away from mine.

Musicians plucked chirpy melodies on fiddles, women twirled their long skirts, and men tramped alongside them. Raven brought her hands up, clapping by her left ear. I mimicked the gesture, eyeing her dress, which I still couldn't believe she'd worn. The dress, a dark blue, almost black, hugged her midsection, accentuating the curves of her small frame. When she twisted her hips and smiled, I wanted to sweep her away from the crowd and disappear into the night. She should wear dresses more often, but she called them an inconvenience—something I'd seen for myself during one of our earlier spars.

Watching her laugh and dance reminded me of what my mother always said: 'We celebrate because we are thankful'. I had a lot to be thankful for, especially Raven. She forced me to live and not just exist.

Jericho's wife, Anna, had braided Raven's hair, weaving it with different colored ribbons. The blue and red strands bounced around her sweet face as she danced.

I grabbed her waist and pulled her body closer, then pushed my lips against hers. Even after spending days together, each kiss felt like the first.

She looped her arms around my neck, and I swung her in a circle, making her laugh until she begged me to stop. When her feet touched the ground, she snuck another kiss, and then grabbed my hand, dragging me to the merchants, who cooked a medley of roasted lamb, sweet honey figs and black-peppered mushrooms with butter.

"I need one of those," I said as a man passed us, gnawing away on a stick of meat.

"There." Raven pointed to a fat-bellied vendor handing out long twigs with pieces of roasted meat skewered on them.

The pungent, sweet scent of lamb lingered in the air. By the time we reached the merchant, my mouth watered and my stomach screamed for food.

Raven chatted about the festival while I ignored her, focusing instead on the lamb's smoked taste and apple glaze... I'm sure whatever she said was important, but this food had my full attention.

"Raven... ? It *is* you!"

An older version of Raven stood in front of us. The similarities were striking: chocolate hair and brown eyes on a petite frame. Although, this girl's facial features weren't as perfectly shaped as Raven's.

"Hi, Rachel." Raven stood still while Rachel hugged her tight.

"How have you been? I've been meaning to visit, but Lucas and I have been busy."

"Hello, Raven."

Raven eyed the man beside Rachel. I waited for her to introduce me, but she didn't.

"I'm Avikar." I extended the hand not dripping with lamb juice.

"Lucas," the man said, shaking my hand in return.

"Did Jericho tell you the good news?" Rachel took Lucas' hand and smiled.

"No." Raven's gaze shifted toward Lucas, whose light eyes met hers.

I bit off another chunk of lamb while Raven fiddled with the front of her dress.

"Rachel's with child," Lucas said.

"Congratulations," Raven said as Rachel threw her arms around her neck. Raven hugged her back, her eyes watering.

Lucas placed his hand on Rachel's back. "My parents are waiting."

Rachel nodded, then quickly kissed Raven on the cheek. "I miss you," she said. "Will you come visit me soon?"

"I'll try. I need to finish gathering herbs before winter."

Rachel's smile faded, and I wondered what had happened between them. Raven rarely mentioned her sister, and when she did, a snarky comment or sigh usually followed. The way Raven portrayed Rachel, I would've thought her to be a big snob, but she seemed nice.

Raven never mentioned Lucas. She glared at the two of them walking away and I wondered why she was so angry.

"What's wrong? She seems nice."

"She isn't," Raven replied bluntly. "I'm going back to Jericho's. You can stay."

I'd wanted to go to the festival since Raven told me about it, but she was upset and I wasn't going to let her leave alone.

"I'll go with you."

"No."

"Raven."

"I want to be alone, Avikar. Please, I'm fine."

"Are you sure?"

She nodded.

I kissed her lightly on the lips. "Be careful."

"I always am." She left before I could change my mind.

Even though I had been in Daath for months, I never felt settled, even though no one had seen Lucy in weeks and there were rumors she'd left Daath. Tonight, I was going to enjoy myself.

The townsfolk had dressed in costume tonight, each one representing a different flower or animal. Villagers passed by, faces hidden behind twined masks, carrying mugs of golden liquid.

A girl wearing a white mask depicting a lily grabbed my shirt. She smiled and handed me a black crow mask.

"Put it on," she said.

I slid the disguise into place and tied it behind my head.

"Now you fit in."

Another girl wearing a red cat mask appeared by her side. "Don't forget this." She handed me a wooden cup filled with a purple liquid.

"What's this?"

The girls giggled at each other, then back at me.

"Have you never come to the festival?" Cat Girl asked.

"I've always had to leave before dark to help my mother return home. She isn't well."

The girl in white lifted her cup to mine. "Then you are in for a treat. May the journey bring wisdom and blessings to those who seek answers hidden beneath the veil."

She put the cup to her lips, drinking, and I followed.

Warmth coated my throat and stomach. It tasted like wine, vanilla, and something else, a sharpness I couldn't place. I took another sip. Colored lights hung from lanterns spread across the market, their bright colors swayed with the breeze. The clear sky held thousands of stars, all twinkling brighter than I'd ever seen before.

The wind carried music and the aroma of roasted meat, and everyone near me smiled and laughed.

With the mask on, I didn't have to be afraid of anyone noticing me. The feeling lightened my steps, and I moved through the festival, excitement heating my blood. Lanterns made into the shapes of flowers dangled from above, their glow heightening the ethereal mood. Fiddlers increased the speed of their notes and someone banged on drums. Feet tapped, legs kicked, and there wasn't one frown in the mass swaying around me.

A group of girls donning ivy wreaths and red rose masks danced in a ring. When I walked near them, they opened their hands and trapped me within their circle. Their smiles widened and their voices rose with laughter. Holding my drink tightly to avoid spilling, I nodded at them, and they raised their arms, skipping around me in one more circle, then broke apart, moving their dancing to the next patron.

This festival wasn't so different from the ones in Lakewood. Just like at home, this festival had plenty to drink, succulent food, music and energy filling the air. I drank the rest of the liquid in the mug, then placed it on one of the empty benches.

A small crowd had gathered around a fire performer. Face hidden beneath a fox mask, he swung a long cord with metal balls tied on the ends, pricked with tiny holes. The man swung the fire balls around his body, painting the air with flames. I squinted at the spinning light, losing myself in the whirling trails.

My muscles relaxed and my head swam as the music thumped through my chest, and every note echoed within my body. All the masks and costumes blended into a kaleidoscope of bright colors that moved too fast for my brain to follow. I rubbed my eyes and focused on standing upright.

People bumped into me, their sweaty bodies hitting my arms and chest. I elbowed my way through, sweat sliding down my neck. *Why is everyone standing so close?*

Someone smacked my shoulder.

I spun around, my breath catching. A giant lizard stood over me, its smile wide and crooked.

Just a mask, I told myself, stepping back from the forked tongue I knew couldn't possibly be there.

The man wearing the oversized mask ignored me and pushed his way forward.

My pulse sped. Squeezing through the crowd, I walked farther and farther away. Another villager, wearing a similar lizard disguise in yellow and red shades, laughed and held two goblets up in the air. A woman dressed as a dragonfly giggled by his side.

Nausea rolled through my stomach. I needed a drink of water.

Drums and cymbals clapped a wild melody, and people swayed around me, their identities hidden by costume. Pushing my way through the crowd, I found an opening and jogged out.

Barrels of varying sizes and girth dotted the sides of the buildings along the cobbled street. I grabbed a mug from the empty trough next to the barrels and dunked it into the water, drowning myself in the cool liquid until the heat and thirst left, then sat on a wooden bench.

A small group of festivalgoers strolled past me wearing various bird masks hiding their faces, splashed with bright reds and yellows. One of the girls, adorned in one of Daath's signature purple dresses, stopped and walked toward me. The bright fabric draped over one shoulder and cinched at her tiny waist. Her legs slipped through the high slits as she walked. When she moved forward, the dress broke apart around her in thin strands, showing flashes of creamy skin.

"No one should be alone tonight." She leaned over, placing one hand on the back of the bench. "Fire dancers scaring you away?"

"I needed a drink of water."

She hovered closer, examining my cup. "You're a strange one."

"What do you mean?" I stood, not liking the way she loomed over me.

A dangerous smile appeared on her face, and she trailed a hand across my shirt. "You're not from here are you?"

"Where else would I be from?"

She leaned closer. "The other side," she whispered.

Panic rose in my chest, but I acted normal. "I think you've been enjoying the wine too much."

She laughed, throwing her head back. "I like you. I'll keep your little secret, for now. Tonight is a celebration."

I grabbed her wrist and ripped her hand from my shirt. "I really don't know what you're talking about."

"I don't know what you call water where you live, but that isn't it."

"I thought it tasted minty."

"Better go home," she said, patting my hand and smiling. "Wouldn't want you drinking anything else."

Before I could ask her another question, she winked and walked away, returning to her group of friends who had almost disappeared into the crowd. I looked around to see if anyone was watching, then sniffed the liquid in the mug. Mint. When I tilted the mug, allowing the light from the festival to shine inside, a green hue flashed in the liquid.

Warmth swarmed over my skin in waves. I threw the mug on the ground, wondering what drink would taste of mint. The green liquid spilled out, and I swore it formed the shape of a lizard.

Ever since the fight with Lucino, my mind hadn't been right. The details of the fight faded in and out of my memories. The most important moment of my life, and I could barely remember it. But something else bothered me, no, haunted me, something I had forgotten.

Ugh. I ran a hand through my hair, pushing it off my forehead, and closed my eyes as the night breeze blew against my hot face. All the excitement of the night left, and suddenly I wanted to see Raven. I was done with Daath and its strange festivals.

THE STORY CONTINUES IN...

WICKED PATH

DAATH CHRONICLES

ELIZA TILTON

AVAILABLE WHEREVER BOOKS ARE SOLD

About the Author

Eliza Tilton graduated from Dowling College with a BS in Visual Communications. When she's not arguing with excel at her day job, or playing Dragon Age 2, again, she's writing.

Her YA stories hold a bit of the fantastical and there's always a hot romance.

She resides on Long Island with her husband, two kids and one very snuggly pit bull.

THANK YOU
FOR READING

Please visit http://curiosityquills.com/reader-survey
to share your reading experience with the author of
this book!

The Lure of Fools, by Jason King

"Adventure is the lure of fools" Jekaran's uncle has warned him, but that doesn't stop the bored farm boy from rescuing a beautiful fey woman and bonding a magical sword that transforms him into master swordsman. But his uncle's admonition proves all too true when Jek's actions plunge him into a quest to avert a war of extermination, and the magic sword he wields begins to exert a will of its own.

Catch Me When I Fall, by Vicki Leigh

Seventeen-year-old Daniel Graham has spent two-hundred years guarding humans from the Nightmares that feed off people's fears. Then he's given an assignment to watch over sixteen-year-old Kayla Bartlett, a patient in a psychiatric ward. When the Nightmares take an unprecedented interest in her, a vicious attack forces Daniel to whisk her away to Rome where others like him can keep her safe. But when the Protectors are betrayed and Kayla is kidnapped, Daniel will risk everything to save her—even his immortality.

Night of Pan, by Gail Strickland

Fifteen-year-old Thaleia is haunted by visions: roofs dripping blood, Athens burning. She tries to convince her best friend and all the villagers that she's not crazy. The gods do speak to her. And the gods have plans for this girl. When Xerxes' army of a million Persians marches straight to the mountain village Delphi to claim the Temple of Apollo's treasures and sacred power, Thaleia's gift may be her people's last line of defense. Her destiny may be to save Greece… but is one girl strong enough to stop an entire army?

Wilde's Fire, by Krystal Wade

When Katriona Wilde inadvertently leads her sister and best friend through a portal into a world she's dreamed of for six years, she finds herself faced with frightening creatures and a new truth: her entire life has been a lie.

CPSIA information can be obtained
at www.ICGtesting.com
Printed in the USA
LVOW12s0227150917

548806LV00001B/169/P